TEDDY LANCASTER
and the *Eye of Naroshi*

JOHNNY RAPP

Copyright © 2022 by John Rapp

All rights reserved. This book may not be reproduced in whole or in part without written permission from the author, except by a reviewer who may quote brief passages in a review; nor may any part of this book be reproduced, stored in a retrieval system, or transmitted in any form or by any means, electronic, mechanical, photocopying, recording, or other, without written permission from the author.

ISBN: 979-8-9855735-1-0

First Edition

For you,

Contents

I --- A World Within --- **7**

II --- Zarmore --- **23**

III --- The Outskirts --- **43**

IV --- Dean Spear --- **59**

V --- That Which is Unseen --- **77**

VI --- Orientation --- **87**

VII --- The Arena --- **109**

VIII --- Extracurricular --- **121**

IX --- Detention --- **145**

X --- Restricted --- **163**

XI --- Full Mun --- **173**

XII --- Déjà Vu --- **185**

XIII --- Vibrational World --- **221**

XIV --- Frosted Sweets --- **235**

XV --- Horsepower --- **251**

XVI --- Shadow Play --- **265**

XVII --- Lucky Charms --- **277**

XVIII --- Strangers in the Dark --- **293**

XIX --- The Zarmore Cup --- **317**

XX --- The Eye of Naroshi --- **327**

A World Within

One can taste the dirt in the air as a sea of red engulfs the sky, and the sun walks the line between dusk and dark. A crowd of several hundred brown and furry, white-bellied goblins from around the colony gathers at an entrance of an old barn and demands entry.

"What you see out there is just a reflection of what's in here!" one of the goblins running security tonight shouts back toward the pushing crowd. "If you all wanted tickets, you should have arrived earlier! We're at capacity!"

Three more goblins wearing black security jackets run up to the barn door to help pull it close.

"No, no, don't you dare shut that door!" A furry female goblin from the crowd screeches as she flashes her barbed teeth toward the males. "I've been in line for three hours!"

"Sorry, ma'am," one of the security grumbles as he continues to struggle pulling the door close. "We weren't expecting to have a traveler singing tonight. Come back and see us next week!"

The heavy barn door finally locks shut, and the crowd bangs away with their fists from the outside.

Inside, the hundreds of waist-high goblins that do have tickets to tonight's event screech and cheer as a tall and lanky human boy no older than thirteen pushes through the makeshift curtains and onto the flimsy wooden stage.

Dusty bulbs of lights dangle and clink from the creaky barn ceiling above, casting a yellowish glow down upon the dark and glassy plum-sized eyes of the miniature monster crowd below. The goblins smile up toward the boy on stage, drool dripping from their large and pointy canine tooth underbites.

Someone hits a switch, and darkness falls upon the barn. The goblins elbow each other for more space, and a horse neighs in the distance.

When the lights flicker back on, the tall boy is standing in the middle of the stage with a microphone in his hands. He fumbles a step backwards as the faces of the crowd come into view for the first time. Each one of them gazes back up at him with that same maniacal expression—something of a mix between hunger and adoration.

The boy throws his white hoodie over his shaggy and curly brown hair while cupping the mouthpiece of the microphone with his hand. Without thinking, a beat to the background of a song comes to his mind. He takes a deep breath in, then utters the sounds into the microphone at the tune of a deep and medium-paced rhythm:

"UhLooh-Laylooh UhLooh-Laylooh UhLooh-Laylooh UhLooh-Laylooh..."

Back by the curtain, a goblin in a three-piece suit with a greasy and slick comb-over haircut walks onto the stage and joins the boy, launching the crowd into another level of frenzy.

"We love you, Caesar!" someone shouts near the front of the stage.

With a wink and a smile, the goblin in the suit sends the young fan fainting. The boy continues providing the background beat into the microphone while the goblin grabs a mic of his own and takes lead to the vocals of the song with his high pitched yet slightly raspy voice:

"Ohhhhhh, WHHHYYY do you MAKE me SO blueeeee?
Baby, IIIIII don't WANT to HURT yooouuu.
Now, PLEEEASSSEEE don't MAKE me WARN yooouuu.
All I wanna DOOOOOO is EAAATTT your shoeeeeee."

As the boy continues providing the background beat, rhythmically bobbing his head, his vision sharpens, and the questions pour in:

"What am I doing? How did I get here? Why is that goblin so handsome?"

Deep in thought, he realizes something is off. The boy looks up, and hundreds of furrowed brows and offended eyes from the crowd of goblins below meet his gaze.

"Come on, Teddy. What are you, crazy?" Caesar whispers out the side of his mouth. "Bring the beat back up."

"Oh yeah, uh sorry," the boy replies to the suited goblin as he pulls the mic back up to his lips and recontinues with the beat in mind:

"DuhDoo-Daywomp Duhdoo-Daywomp Duhdoo-Daywomp Duhdoo-Daywomp..."

"WHAT on Slaybethor are you doing, man?! These guys will eat you, AND THEN they'll kill you!" Caesar whispers just a little louder before smiling and turning back to address the now growing restless crowd. "Everything is fine! Everybody can relax. It just looks like we're having some technical difficulties with Teddy's mic, folks. We'll be right back up in just oneee second."

"I, I can't. I don't remember the beat I was doing," Teddy begins. "I don't even remember how I got here or who you are or..."

"What are you talking about? This is our fifth gig this month. I'm your friend. My name is Caesar. Hi, nice to meet ya again. Now play the darn beat, Teddy!"

But he can't. He's not even able to move. Teddy feels his heart drop to the bottom of his stomach as he thinks to himself:

"Am I...? I think I'm... Is this a...?"

Although he's been keeping dream journals since he was six years old, Teddy Lancaster has yet to discover a surefire method to remind himself when he is, in fact dreaming. It's always just some random or odd act inside the dream that eventually snaps him out of the hypnotic spell and allows him to see everything as it truly is. Tonight, that act is himself.

PLAAP! Something lands on the right side of Teddy's face. He looks around for a second, then raises a hand toward his cheek and wipes away a gooey substance.

"Oh, would you look at that, Michael?" One young goblin says to another near the right of the stage and next to a small horse stable inside the barn. "Looks like *traveler boy* doesn't like your Sloppy Joes."

Teddy looks off stage toward the two young male goblins and watches as one of them reaches both paws down and into a brown pile of something which looks like mud.

"Maybe he'll enjoy mine!" The goblin grunts as he chucks another brown ball of goo toward Teddy's face.

Teddy ducks, and a whoosh of air blows past his head.

"Look, it's still in his hand!" Another goblin from the crowd shouts in laughter.

Teddy pauses for a moment, then looks down at his own right hand still covered in brown goo from moments earlier. He then looks back toward the creatures by the stable, then down at his hand again.

"Bon appétit!" One of the young goblins shouts.

Teddy raises his hand toward his nose, and the laughter and heckling from the crowd increases. It doesn't take long for him to guess what the gooey substance is, but he still proceeds with closing his eyes and taking a sniff. Immediately after that, he's gagging.

"This is about to get ugly, Teddy—you gotta go!" Caesar yells while the crowd screeches and bangs the stage with their tiny fists.

"About to?!" Teddy shouts from his bent-over knees position, trying to refrain from throwing up. "I just got blasted with horse crap from a couple of demonic hairballs! How much uglier can we go from here?!"

The weak wooden stage trembles as the crowd of short and furry beasts rail against it.

"Listen, kid!" Caesar shouts back toward Teddy from the front of the stage as he continues to try and calm the crowd down. "A Sloppy Joe will be the least of your worries if you don't leave here this very second! Now quit messing around and give me your shoes! I'll hold them off as long as I can!"

"My shoes?"

"Now, Teddy!"

Teddy mumbles something under his breath, then unties his sneakers and tosses the pair to Caesar, who wastes no time as he grabs hold of the laces and starts spinning his body like a shot-putter trying to gain momentum. After three turns, Caesar lets go, and the worn-out pair of shoes land near the entrance of the barn, bringing with them the majority of the crowd.

"Go!" Caesar screams at the boy. "Take the back exit!"

Teddy sighs, then turns around and jogs back through the raggedy curtains off stage. He's seen enough to be sure that he's in a dream now.

"This one's going to need some heavy review and reflection in the morning," he thinks to himself as the rear door exit to the barn comes into sight.

That's the thing with dreams; no matter how random or nonsensical they may appear, he knows that at the end of the day, they're entirely a creation of his own mind.

It's been nearly ten days since he had his last lucid dream, and he needs it more than he's prepared to admit. For Teddy, dreams are his escape. They're a place where he's in charge and calls the shots. He's not at the mercy of a mother who thought it would be a great idea to move them across the country his first day of junior high. Nor does he have to deal with any of the toxic emotions that sludge through him every time he thinks of how his father is no longer part of his life. No, this is his world, and even though he just got ran off stage by a bunch of angry-horse-manure-throwing-goblins, he calls the shots here.

Teddy digs a shoulder into the back door and stumbles through the exit. Flurries of dirt and debris whip across his face forcing him to shuffle backwards and the door to slam shut behind him. He coughs a few times, then works to regain his footing and looks out into the distance.

Within eyesight, although hardly visible, lies a silhouette of what appears to be a large man tending to a team of horses in a stable that looks like it might not hold up through the gusty night. Teddy puts his head down and covers his eyes as he maneuvers through the whirlwind of grit and toward the stranger. Just ten yards away now, the image becomes more apparent.

The man's better days are clearly behind him, with his wrinkled and weathered skin looking fragile and on the verge of tearing. His head is nearly bald, save the sides, and he has a gleaming white beard better suited for a Viking than a farmer. Brown grime coats the man from his facial hair to his overalls, and he wears a leather patch over his left eye.

"How much for the white one?" Teddy startles the old man. "I have to get out of town."

The farmer briefly looks up. "I can't see you, boy; it's far too dusty out tonight. Step a little closer, would ya."

Teddy takes a few more steps toward the man before he's ordered to stop. "Phew! Scratch that; I don't need to see you, child. I can already smell you and don't need you getting these horses here any dirtier than they already are with that crap in your hands."

"I'm sorry, what?" Teddy says.

"Is that not horse dung in your hand, boy?" The farmer replies.

"What? No! Well, I mean... yeah, but things are different now," Teddy starts while working to scrub the rest of the gooey manure off with the bottom of his white hoodie. "I'm back in command now."

The farmer shakes his head then continues to brush one of the horses. "Well, good for you then, child. Now, as per your request, that white horse over there is Naroshi, and you most assuredly *cannot* have her. You see, she's been with me for almost three thousand years now, and I'm not sure I could carry on a life without her. Any of the others, you're welcome to make an offer."

Something about the way the man talks makes Teddy feel unsettled.

"I'm just going to take her, alright?" Teddy says as he opens the stable gate to where the horse is standing. "Like I said, I'm back in charge of this dream."

The old man chuckles as he reaches for a wooden staff that's resting against the stable, then stands up and turns toward Teddy. "Do you not know where you're at, boy?"

There's a crack of wood, then a roar of shouting coming from back by the barn.

"Teddy!" Caesar screams from somewhere in the shadows behind him. "RUN!"

"Teddy?" The old man says with a puzzled look.

The horde of crazed goblins sprint out the back exit of the barn through the dirt and dust and straight toward the stable.

The old man grunts, then turns his attention away from Teddy and focuses it on the mob. He points his wooden staff directly at the goblins and waits until they arrive close enough to where they can see him through the dust. Once they are and see the man, there's nothing else he needs to do.

"NO, NO, NO, NO, NO!" A goblin from the front of the pack shouts as he screeches to a dusty halt, then spins around and yells back toward the mob. "RETREAT! RETREAT! RETREAT!"

The old man chuckles as he watches the goblins flee back to the barn. He then turns around and looks toward Teddy. "Now, I'm going to need you to..."

The boy is too quick amongst the chaos though and already gone before the man can finish his sentence.

"Thanks!" Teddy shouts, now atop the white horse's back and riding away from the scene. "I'll take good care of her!"

There's a gust of dust, and not before long, the barn and stable are entirely out of sight. Teddy returns his gaze forward and covers his mouth with the neck of his sweatshirt as Naroshi gallops faster and further into lands unknown.

. . .

Naroshi is as graceful as she is beautiful, trotting smoothly through the beaten dirt paths of the countryside toward an open pasture of lush greenery. Her snow-white body is strong and steady. The mane of her long hair feels soft and silk-like as it periodically brushes over the top of Teddy's hands as he grips her loose reins. He takes a deep breath in through his nostrils and smiles as he smells the wet grass that's now within view.

"Why can't life always be like this?" He thinks.

Teddy's mind then starts to drift, and for the first time in over three months since his father passed away, he actually feels something for that man—not that he didn't have any feelings toward him before or something. It's just that, his dad is dead, their relationship is over, and every time he thinks about that, it hurts. So, after the first few initial days of pain, he just chose to stop thinking about him entirely.

This moment is different though. Right now, it feels good to think about his father and reflect on how much he had given him. Teddy is thankful that his father taught him not to disregard dreams and simply forget them in the morning. He's thankful for how much he was pushed to learn from his dreams, to take charge, and "go with the light," his dad would always say. He's even thankful that he was forced to document all the dreams he had, including many around the time of four in the morning that he may or may not have recalled had *someone* not happened to walk into his bedroom and turn on the light.

His father always told him that life is more than the senses we possess and that there are realms and worlds that will become available to us when we're ready for them. Although Teddy understands that his father was looked upon as a bit strange by outsiders and personally refuses to believe some of the stories his father would tell, he appreciates that he had educated him on being aware of and learning to live inside the dream plane, because in this moment, right now, he has it all.

Teddy and Naroshi are now several miles away from the farm and close to entering an abandoned pasture through a small opening where part of an old wooden plank fence has deteriorated. Naroshi gallops faster, and Teddy can feel the joy in her bounce. A fresh and cool gust of autumn-like air then rushes past his face, sweeping much of his shaggy brown hair behind his ears. Teddy smiles as they cross the threshold to the pasture and waits for Naroshi to slow down before hopping off.

Once down from Naroshi's back, he takes a few steps into the tall wild grass then proceeds deeper into the pasture. Waves of wonder and happiness flow through his body, and he doesn't want to ever leave this moment. The birds are chirping, the weather is perfect, and then, without warning, it's all swiftly robbed away from him with one single thought.

"This is just a dream."

He walks over to an old oak and sits down in a collapse, resting his back against the tree's deeply ridged trunk.

"Nothing that happens in here changes anything at Cameron Creek or the real world," he says while staring down into the grass.

Cameron Creek is the new junior high school he just started less than twenty-four hours before. It's located in New York City, and his first day played out in such a way that made him never want to see a second.

Although he usually feels relatively strong and sure of himself inside his dreams, Teddy is nowhere close to matching that persona in the real world. His overall shy and awkward demeanor makes him an easy target to be picked on by the older kids, who always seem to travel in packs like wild hyenas.

He leans his head back against the oak and replays the events of his first day in his mind:

During lunch period, after having remained under the radar for most of the morning, he sets a strategy to find an empty seat in the back of the cafeteria and eat alone while waiting for the bell to ring to his next class—it's a solid plan which served him well at his previous school, and he feels comfortable employing it here at Cameron Creek.

After receiving his lunch from an unenthusiastic pimple-ridden worker, Teddy turns around and walks toward an empty table in the rear of the cafeteria. As he passes rows of tables on the way to his, he can see a group of eighth-grade boys and girls whispering and laughing amongst each other from the corner of his eye. He immediately looks away and maintains his head down, keeping his vision fixed on the tray of food in his hands. One of the boys out of the group notices Teddy's negligence and slowly sticks one of his feet out from under the table as Teddy passes. The boy's foot then connects with Teddy's, and Teddy stumbles forward.

The laughter from the group grows louder as Teddy desperately tries to maintain his balance before momentum finally takes over, and he crashes to his knees, losing grip immediately with his blue plastic lunch tray. Mashed potatoes, gravy, chicken nuggets, green peas, and a warm chocolate chip cookie all lie wasted, splattered on the ground with the other students cackling so loud he swears he can see the windows shaking.

Naroshi is still nibbling on some grass several dozen yards away into the pasture while Teddy remains sitting with his back against the oak. His head is sunk and eyes are closed as he rests his face in his open palms. The surfacing emotions aren't something he ever wants to deal with—not here nor out there. He shakes his head and tries to think of something else, but it's no use. The dam which has protected his mind from these negative feelings is finally breaking, and little by little, the emotions are seeping through.

He thinks about how he feels universally disliked at school and how he has not even one friend to talk with. He thinks about how much he misses his dad and how he regrets being so distant with him during his final days. He thinks about how much he wishes in this exact moment, to never wake up, to just stay here with Naroshi in the pasture forever.

He hates to cry, so chooses to squeeze his eyes shut to try and fight it off, but that only forces the release. One cold teardrop escapes from beneath his eyelids, streaming down his cheek and past his lips.

Naroshi finishes eating and trots toward Teddy and the oak. She brings herself down next to the boy in the tall grass, then rolls onto her side and rests her head in his lap. Teddy remains still with his head sunken while Naroshi closes her eyes and prepares to nap. A few moments pass before Teddy's lone teardrop finally arrives at the bottom of his chin. It hangs there suspended for a moment, dancing in the wind, before finally falling and splashing onto the nose of Naroshi. She looks up, puzzled and scanning the area, before finally understanding where it came from.

Teddy hears the horse exhale slowly through her nostrils then feels a slight nudge underneath his chin. He looks up and opens his eyes to find Naroshi's snout just a few inches away from him. The horse pulls back another inch, and Teddy sniffles while wiping away any more potential tears from his eyes. He then reaches over and rubs her nose. "You know, you might just be the only..."

He then drops his hand and physically jumps back. He and Naroshi have just locked eyes, and something isn't right.

Teddy's heart races as his brain works to register what he's looking at. A few more moments pass before his system calms enough to where he can lean forward again and get a better look.

Naroshi's eyes are of a color and glow which he's never seen in the real world, nor even imagines could exist in the real world. It's beyond visual and feels like something that a human body isn't wired to observe. They're deep and cyan green infused with a neon glow which makes you feel as if you're staring into everything that ever was, while at the same time absolutely nothing at all. The longer he looks, the less scared he feels.

"Were they... always like that?" He says in a low voice.

Something then snaps in the distance, and a gust of air blows past his head. He swings his focus off from Naroshi and looks up.

An orange feather sways downward and lands on the tip of his nose. A foot above that is the arrow lodged into the base of the oak from which it fell.

Zarmore

Naroshi speeds through the forest like a heat-seeking missile locked onto a target Teddy only wishes he knew. His right hand is gripped firmly to the reins while his left is raised in a defensive position, protecting his face from incoming pines, twigs, and branches. The sun has long fallen below the horizon and been replaced by a rising full moon and engulfing black clouds. Naroshi leaps over another ditch and turns a corner. The young roars of thunder echo through the ever-darkening forest, and Teddy feels something wet land on the top of his right wrist. He spares a glance upwards and grimaces. It's starting to rain.

"Easy girl!" he pleads but to no avail.

"Why isn't she listening to me? Where is she going?"

Teddy can't remember the last time he lost so much control in a dream. Perhaps it's the stress at school, or maybe it was finally giving in to his emotions and breaking down. Whatever it is, it needs to stop. This isn't fun anymore, and he's ready to call it a night. With that thought, he closes his eyes, takes a deep breath, and focuses all his intention on waking up.

As he slowly raises his eyelids again, he expects to see the soft daybreak of morning peeking through his second-story bedroom window, illuminating the towers of yet to be unpacked moving boxes. Instead, he's met with a *hard* smack to the face. Teddy's body jerks to the left, and he nearly falls off the horse and into the mud. He yanks the reins and pulls himself back up, causing Naroshi to squeal and shift her speed into an even higher gear.

Teddy spits out a few bitter-tasting leaves from his mouth then tosses the branch that's lodged over his eye to the side. As he works to resettle himself atop the horse, a blinding bolt of lightning shoots down from the darkness and strikes a tree in front of them. The ancient redwood splits at its base then crashes to the ground, sending a boom through the woods so powerful that both of them nearly go tumbling.

The rain is coming down in a torrent now, with clashes of thunder, lightning, and fallen trees every couple of seconds. A sea of black floods Teddy's vision, and he wonders how Naroshi is able to navigate through it all. He continues bouncing atop her back as he closes his eyes once more and refocuses his intent.

"Wake up. Wake up. Wake up."

The wolves decide to join in the chaos and howl into the storm, causing Naroshi to gallop even faster. Teddy clenches his teeth and reopens his eyes.

Sweeping gusts of wind work in tandem with the rain in drenching his face and blocking his vision. He squints, then runs several fingers through his long and soaked brown hair, slicking it backwards and out of his eyes. Terrified, wet, and cold, an idea comes to mind.

"I can just jump off...."

The high speed at which they're moving is probably enough to kill himself, thus allowing this nightmare of a dream to end and safe passage to his warm bed to begin.

He slowly loosens his grip on the reins while at the same time tightening the ones on his eyelids. Then he pauses.

Although he's died in his dreams countless times before and always woke up intact and secure, something about this moment feels different. This time it feels real... like *real* real.

More crackling of lightning followed by explosions of thunder nearly toss him off Naroshi again. He instinctively opens his eyes and grabs back hold of the reins.

"Naroshi, please!" He begs.

He has to let go but can't. He can feel the blood starting to pool and swell around his left eye from where the branch had crashed into his face. The muscles in his now callused hands are beginning to cramp from the prolonged gripping of the reins. His bottom aches as he bounces violently on the horse, trying to maintain atop. The authenticity of this pain is undeniable.

Naroshi hurdles over yet another fallen and lifeless tree as Teddy momentarily becomes airborne. He ricochets off her saddle on the landing and nearly flies headfirst over her body. His inner thighs wrap tightly around the base of her neck as he tries to regain position and control.

The full moon has now completely breached the horizon, illuminating the two as they gallop toward its center. The muddy path in front of him appears to be fading toward an abrupt end, and all he can see beyond it are the moon and its stars. Sounds of an ocean and crashing waves, somewhere in the less and less distant below, are growing louder. Not wanting to see what lies beyond the drop-off ahead, Teddy grits his teeth and yanks the reins as hard as his current positioning will permit, slowing Naroshi slightly, but not enough.

The smell of salt and fish permeates his nostrils now. Naroshi lets out a low whinny sound as she raises her head and picks up more speed. Teddy's thighs finally give in and lose their hold, causing him to slide down her back. His waning hands gripped to the reins are now the only thing keeping him affixed to the animal. He bounces hard on his stomach against her back, crushing his ribs and robbing the air from his lungs with each stride.

He tries to call out to her one last time, but there's nothing there. The muscles in his hands are now cramped, and he can feel the reins slipping from his grip. Breathless, he pulls himself forward and climbs up her wet and cold body. One hand at a time, he lets go of the reins and then uses his arms to hug around her upper chest with all the strength he can muster. The drop-off to the path ahead of them is now in clear view, and Naroshi isn't showing any sign of slowing down.

Teddy closes his eyes and digs his nose into her damp yet still soft white mane. Her hair smells like the honey his mom used to set out with French toast every Saturday morning.

That was always his favorite day of the week. He would wake up late, watch some cartoons, then maybe play catch at the park with his dad or do some skateboarding around the neighborhood until dark. He probably should've enjoyed it more.

Naroshi finally stops galloping. The sounds of the waves are now louder than his thoughts. It's time for him to go.

. . .

The warm sun shining through his closed eyelids makes him smile. He's alive, and the nightmare is over. And although he has much to think about it, he's happy that at least he's safe and back in his bed. Teddy rolls over onto his side and begins to fumble around blindly for his cell phone before a stabbing pain shoots across his ribs and halts his motion. He opens his eyes.

All he can see in front of him is green, thick grass, and nothing else. He raises himself onto his knees and sees that several hundred yards ahead of him are tumbling rows of rolling hills that grow in size all the way up until they become a tall range of rocky mountains. Towering forest green trees, similar to the ones he's just seen earlier, blanket both the hills and mountains, with many reaching so high that they shoot up and through the low hanging white clouds. At the pinnacle of the tallest mountain, a fiery red sun is just clearing the peak and casting a pinkish glow upon a large white structure which overlooks the entire valley.

Teddy swings his head around to see that behind him is even more grass-covered lowland and that further beyond that is another large formation of trees. However, these trees to his rear appear to be more akin to a tropical jungle than an evergreen forest and are cast in a heavy shade of darkness rather than lit by the warmth of a sun. A shiver runs down his spine as he listens to what sounds like monkeys and apes shouting from deep within the jungle's shadows. He turns his head back around and looks up toward the structure at the top of the mountain on the other side of the valley before a thought rushes to his mind, causing his eyes to dart from left to right.

"She's not here. Was that... Am I still... Is this a dream?"

He uses his hands to prop himself up to his feet. His hoodie and pants are soaked with water, and it's a struggle just to stand up. Once on his feet, he takes several sloshy and slow steps toward the hills. His socks squish out water with each passing movement, and for a moment he wonders why he has no shoes on before pausing and thinking to himself.

"Savages."

He sits back down on the grass and rips the tattered and wet pair of socks off from his feet. A gust of air then shoots down into the valley, breezing over several of his now exposed cuts and scrapes along the soles and heels of his feet. He shuts his eyes and clenches his teeth.

"Naroshiii!" The boy bellows out through the blankness while rising to his feet. The call echoes through the valley in all directions, but the only answer he receives back is some rabid chatter from the apes in the jungle behind him.

"What the hell is going on?" He thinks to himself.

A heavy and dark ball of fear takes root and grows in the pit of his stomach. He drops back down to his knees and bows his forehead into the tall grass while focusing all his intention once more upon waking up. When he finally looks forward and sees the same unfamiliar landscape again, he punches his fists into the ground, collapses onto his belly, and lets out a muffled cry through the grass.

His body aches and throbs, and for a couple of minutes, he just wants to lie there, face down in the center of the valley. To his rear, he can still hear the apes and their faint screams emanating from the shadowy jungle, while up the hill in front of him, birds chirp underneath a rosy sun. He waits another minute, then takes a deep breath, throws himself back up to his feet, and starts to walk toward the hills.

"This is going to suck."

The length of the grass is up to his knees, and the low-hanging clouds are beneath him when he finally decides to take a break. He sits atop a large rock that rests underneath the shadow of several giant redwoods and watches as a pair of purple and blue birds fight over a worm on the bank of a small pond. A couple of hours have now passed since he started walking, and what had initially seemed like an impossible task to reach the structure at the top of the mountain, now seems like just a matter of time. He looks down, lifts one of his feet up, and sees that the open cuts and scrapes are already closed and beginning to scab. He gives a pat around his ribs, which he was sure were broken back down in the valley, and notices that the pain is gone. Everything that was hurt before has now healed. Teddy furrows his brow for a moment, then stands back up from the rock.

The sun is directly above head when he finally reaches the summit. He walks out from underneath the canopy of the forest and squints as he tries to absorb all that's in front of him.

The large white structure which he struggled to make out back in the valley is colossal up front and makes him feel like an ant staring up a stone wall. Dark blue water trickles and skips over rocks in a moat which surrounds the entirety of it all. Nearly everything is constructed from stone, and there are dozens of circular towers spread about, all of which are finished with cone-shaped roofs in the color of a dark forest green. Out of the windows he can see, the majority are stained glass and emit somewhat of a rainbow gleam as the sun reflects off their surface.

"Of course it's a freaking castle," he says.

As he approaches the drawbridge which leads to the entrance and covers the moat, his attention is pulled away from the castle and toward a large oak tree that lies just in front of the bridge. It looks a bit out of place due to its location and is the only tree of its kind in the area. As he approaches further, he notices a door carved into its wide trunk on the side of the tree that faces the bridge and castle. The door's handle is missing. In the location where you would typically find it is a polished bronze ring knocker in the form of a lion's head.

Teddy walks closer until there's only a foot of separation between him and the tree. He reaches a hand closer toward the door's knocker as sensations of pleasure and well-being rush through his fingers and then onto the rest of his body.

"Uh, yeah ok, this is weird," he says to himself while dropping his hand away from the knocker and taking a step back.

Leaves rustle in the wind, and the breeze feels clean. He doesn't really care to knock on the door, but now it almost feels like he's being compelled to. Another gust of air blows by.

"Screw it," he says while returning his attention toward the tree and reaching a hand toward the lion's head.

"AKASHATAKAH!" Something screams from above the castle.

Teddy jerks around and looks up to see a dagger-wielding goblin dressed in knight's armor jumping from one of the circular watchtowers above. The miniature monster crashes hard on his landing, losing his sword in the process and nearly tumbling off the wooden drawbridge into the flowing water below.

"Son of a gargoyle, they don't pay me enough," he mumbles while working himself back to his feet.

"Caesar?" Teddy asks.

Quickly gaining his composure and into a fighting stance, the beast snarls and flashes his teeth at the boy.

"How dare you compare me to that good-for-nothing-never-worked-a-day-in-his-life-coward! I am Gobo, Guardian of Zarmore and Defender of the Drowsy. I demand respect and command you..."

He's cut off when a girl with blonde hair appears from behind Teddy. She's wearing a green plaid skirt that falls just above her knees and a white button-up shirt with a small patch on one of the collars. Her black socks are tall, and the skinny tie around her neck matches her skirt. Teddy immediately looks back and sees the door to the oak tree has opened but is now closing behind the girl. A hazy purple mist emanates from its inside.

"Hey Gobs, you giving the new kid a hard time?"

"Ah, Miss Bailey, you're late. Shocking," Gobo replies, still not lifting an eye off Teddy. "Now remain in the rear whilst I take care of this intruder. And would you please, for once in your life, address me properly."

"You're not doing anything, Gobsy Goo. I mean, come on, look at this kid. He's clearly a student here." She pauses and surveys Teddy's disheveled appearance. "A stinky one, but a student nonetheless. Now let us through," the girl says as she puts her arm around Teddy.

"But Miss, he does not bear the patch nor even the slightest resemblance of a proper uniform per Regulatory Standard 1254.24 (b), which states, all student attire must..."

"It's the first day, Gobs! None of the freshmen have uniforms yet. Come on; you know this."

"But Miss, I am sworn to..."

"Gobo, when was the last time this castle was attacked?"

"That would be the Chimp Uprise of 1994 AD, Earth-tethered."

"And before that?"

"Well, there hasn't been one, but that's no reason to..."

"We're coming in."

"But Miss, would you just look at the boy? I mean, for heaven's sake, he's got cow poop on his face."

"It's not cow, ugh," Teddy says before rubbing his face with the bottom of his hoodie.

The girl slowly removes her arm from Teddy's shoulder before continuing, "Gobo, if you don't open that door, then perhaps Dean Spear may just happen to find out that his favorite pair of dress shoes, which *mysteriously* went missing last spring, could've been found in your belly."

And with just that, the goblin closes his eyes and appears to be focusing on something. A split second later, the castle door creaks open.

"Thanks, Gobzilla!" The girl says before turning back to Teddy. "Come on, let's get out of here before he decides to cuddle us to death."

She smiles and winks at Gobo, who replies by growling and flashing her his barbed teeth.

"Uh sure, ok," Teddy says as the two cross the wooden drawbridge and make their way into the castle.

"I'm Ava, by the way. It's my second year here. I love giving Gobo a hard time. He's a sweetie, but don't be misled; those goblins can really mess you up if they want to."

"That's what I've been hearing. I'm Teddy."

She laughs. "That's cute. I still like Gobsy better, but your name's a close second now! So, what are you even doing out here?" Ava asks. "The rest of the first-year kids are all probably at lunch break by now."

"Kind of a long story."

"I get it," she begins. "I couldn't stand orientation day either. Like come on, we're supposedly farther away from Earth than humanly imaginable, yet we still have to be dragged through the monotony of PowerPoints and telling the class 'three interesting facts about ourselves and how we spent our summer vacation.' Give me a break."

"Um, yeah, so where are we exactly?" Teddy asks.

"Teddy Teddy Teddy, you're messing with me, huh? This is Zarmore! Now let's go get some lunch. I'll introduce you to the crew."

The dining hall which Teddy is led into makes the cafeteria at Cameron Creek look like feeding hours at the zoo. The food is all gourmet with plates laid out buffet style in the center of the room. Chandeliers lit by torches hang from the arched ceilings and fill the hall with an aroma of burnt pine wood. Scattered along the old cobblestone floor are dozens of round wooden tables where teenagers sit in groups and share meals.

Most of the girls in the dining hall are wearing similar uniforms as Ava's. Some have chosen to go with longer sleeves, while others have opted to wear black pea coats over their tops—however, it's all the same style and color. The majority of the boys are wearing black slacks or shorts and white button-up shirts. A few wear coats. Their green plaid ties match the girls, albeit theirs are a bit wider in size, and they have a similar patch on their collars. The rest of the students are wearing regular street clothes not associated with any uniform.

"They're all down in that corner. Follow me," Ava says as she continues to lead Teddy through the hall.

A strong boy with a blonde-haired buzz cut intersects the two near the buffet table.

"Hey Ava, didn't see you in tuning class today. Thought they might've wiped you."

"Oh, hey Sean. Nope, still here. Brain intact," she says while letting out a strained laugh and lightly knocking on the top of her head with her knuckles. "But if you'll excuse me, I have to meet up with my friends down there."

"Who's your new pet? He smells like he's been living in a barn," Sean says while moving more in front of them and further blocking their path.

"Well, actually," Teddy begins before Ava cuts him off.

"This is Teddy. He's my friend and new here. Now can you please move out of the way?"

"What happened to your shoes, Teddy? You have to bribe Gobo with them for him to let your pig wrestling bum face in here?"

"Enough, Sean!" Ava says as she grabs Teddy's hand and maneuvers them past the boy and his broad shoulders.

Sean scoffs as the two brush past him then shouts from behind a few seconds later. "Real improvement, Ava!"

"Ugh, I can't stand that guy," she says.

"What is that like your ex-boyfriend for this dream or something?" Teddy asks.

"Ew, he's far from dreamy. But yeah, we dated freshman year for a couple of weeks. That was until I realized HOW MUCH OF A SOCIOPATH HE WAS." Ava says, raising her voice toward the end.

Sean smirks then finds a seat with a group of similar-looking boys near the center of the hall.

A cute girl with dark and wavy hair is smiling as Ava and Teddy approach her table.

"Heyyy, there she is," the girl begins. "And only three hours late on the first day of class. Well done, my friend, well done."

Ava playfully punches the girl in the arm. "Some of us have real lives to live, Olivia."

"I'd hardly classify watching Netflix until six in the morning as living."

Ava laughs and punches her again before taking a seat. "Where's everybody else?"

"We're second-yearers now, dude. They're all doing the mentor thing with the firsts. That's why I got these two kids with me," Olivia says while motioning to the two dark-haired boys at the table.

"Oh crap, you're right!" Ava replies. "Ugh, Dean Spear is so going to feed my soul to those monkeys."

"III don't think that's how it works," Olivia says.

"No, hang on, I have my first-yearer right here!" Ava says while looking over toward Teddy. "May I present to you all—Mr. Ted... or Teddy, I meant... Mr. Teddy Tedster, everybody!"

"Uh, just Teddy is fine, thanks," Teddy says as he pulls out the last open chair and sits down.

"I was wondering who that guy was," one of the boys at the table says to the other before speaking up to Teddy. "Nice to meet you, Ted... or Tedster... or whatever. My little brother and I are new here as well. I'm Calvin, and this is Ronnie."

Ronnie looks over at his brother.

"Cal, do you really have to keep introducing me like that?"

"Like what?"

"Just call me your brother! You're only ten months older. And plus, I'm taller than you, so you just sound stupid when you say it like that."

"Hmm, uh yeah, no can do *little* bro. Unless you want to try and make me...."

"You really wanna do this right here, shorty?"

"Good to meet you both!" Teddy interjects, diffusing the situation between the two athletic boys.

Calvin leans back in his chair then ruffles his younger brother's short hair with a fist. Ronnie pushes him away then looks back toward Teddy.

"So how come I haven't seen you with the rest of the freshmen today?"

"He was dueling with Gobo on the bridge," Ava cuts in.

"Oh, hell yeah!" Calvin says, straightening back up in his seat so quickly that a few of his tied-up dreadlocks fall loose and are left dangling in front of his eyes.

"It looks like he kind of got the best of you though, huh?" Ronnie adds while gesturing toward Teddy's unkempt appearance and lack of shoes.

"Well actually, this was all from earlier. I'm not even really a student here, or whatever."

"What are you talking about?" Olivia cuts in with a mouth full of steak. "No one just *ends up* in Zarmore."

"Chew. Swallow. Breathe." Ava says to her friend before they go into a laughing fit.

"Yeah, well, I did," Teddy says. "And to be honest, I'm not even really sure if you guys are real or just something I'm dreaming up right now."

The table lapses into an awkward pause, and a few arched-eyebrowed glances are exchanged.

"And on that note," Teddy says before sliding his chair backwards and making a move back toward the entrance.

"Teddy, wait!" Ava says, flinging out of her seat and grabbing hold of his arm as he walks away. "What are you talking about?"

Teddy rubs his eyes and looks at the girl that's now affixed to his forearm.

"You know, I really don't know. One minute I'm part of some backyard goblin boy band, and the next, I got monkeys screaming at me and girls walking out of trees. My body still aches a bit, and this all feels real, for sure. But I don't know. I just really can't logically bring myself to believe that it is right now. And I think, what I need to do, is just find a way to wake myself up. So, as much as I'm enjoying our little thing we're all having right now, I'm going to go find a nice cliff to jump off of."

Ava pulls Teddy closer to her. Their noses are inches away from each other. Her large and almond brown eyes look concerned as she stares into his.

"Zarmore is real, Teddy. I'm real. Olivia is real. All this is real. I don't know how you got here, but if you leave, I don't think you'll be able to find your way back. We need to bring you to Dean Spear."

Teddy remains still for a moment, unable to break eye contact with the first person who showed him kindness in so long.

Olivia interjects back from the table.

"Teddy, if you do leave, can you do me a favor?"

"What's that?"

"Change out of that sweatshirt. It smells like my cat's litter box after I caught him eating a mouse last winter."

Ava turns around and raises her arms up toward her friend in a look of disbelief.

"What? I was just joking," Olivia says. "Sort of..."

"Ok, you know what," Teddy says before tearing his hoodie off and throwing it over his shoulder. "I'm out of here."

"No. Teddy, wait!" Ava says before a deep voice bellows from across the hall.

"Who threw that?!"

Teddy turns around to see Sean scanning the cafeteria while simultaneously wiping brown off his face.

"Crap," Ava says.

Sean looks over to see the two staring at him from a few tables away.

"Oh, it's got to be my lucky day," Sean says as he cups his right hand into a fist and cracks his knuckles.

The blonde-haired boy smiles and throws his chair to the side, causing it to tumble into the next table over. His eyes then lock onto Teddy as he walks straight toward him, like a Bengal tiger approaching some defenseless wild pig. Teddy returns the stare with a wide-eyed animal look of his own; however, his is more like a dog that just got caught eating out of the trash than one that's ready to fight.

Sean takes a few more steps forward and then stops. Ten feet separate him and Teddy now, but all the aggression and movement appears to be on hold.

"Um, alright," Teddy says as he turns back toward the exit. "I think I'm just going to..."

He leaves that thought unfinished as he sees a grin forming on Sean's face. The boy then chuckles and closes his eyes.

"Sean, no!" Ava shouts as she tries to move in front of Teddy.

Teddy looks around to see that the whole dining hall is now staring at him.

"Time to wake up, lover boy," Sean says.

Everything in Teddy's perspective starts to slow down, as if his subconscious is trying to give him one last opportunity to find a way out of this mess. Ronnie and Calvin are rising from their chairs while Ava is still mid-scream trying to move herself in front of Teddy. He can feel an almost gravitational pull emanating from Sean as the boy pulls his fist backwards.

Then, at the same speed as everything slowed down, it starts to ratchet back up. Sean's fist lashes forward, and the boy vanishes. Tables go flying, and trays of food crash into windows, but Sean is now nowhere to be found. Students run and scream in panic, and before Teddy can figure out what's happening, he feels something connect to his jaw, shattering it instantly. Then it gets quiet, and everything goes black.

The Outskirts

Something resembling the sound of an engine is revving, high and low, louder then softer. Teddy feels relaxed and at ease with his eyes still shut and vision black. His spine rests comfortably against a thick cushion, and he wonders if he might be sedated in an ambulance that's rushing him to the hospital.

"Does Zarmore have hospitals?" Another thought arrives. *"Or maybe that really was just some kind of strange deep dream, and I'm now just waking up... but why the noises?"*

The brainstorm is interrupted when he hears the engine shut off. Someone is walking toward him.

"How many times do I have to tell you to take your shoes off inside, Teddy?" A familiar voice asks.

His eyes shoot open.

"And I don't like you passing out on the couch either; that's what your bedroom is for."

His mother is winding up the cord to the vacuum cleaner by the outlet near the edge of the sofa.

"Huh," Teddy says.

"Huh to you too," she mocks her son. "Now you know you wouldn't be so tired if you played fewer video games at night and actually went to bed at a decent hour. Now get up; I'm trying to clean. Dinner will be ready in an hour and a half."

"An hour and a half?" Teddy thinks to himself.

"What time is it?" He asks.

"4:15," she says. "Plenty early enough for you to go upstairs and unpack your room."

It doesn't seem right. Cameron Creek lets out at 3:30, and it takes him at least fifteen minutes to skate home. Even if he had passed out immediately after that, there's no way he entered that kind of dream state so quickly and experienced all he had.

"What day is it?" He asks.

"Teddy, I'm too busy to play these games with you. Now please go upstairs and unpack your room."

He sits up on the couch with his brow furrowed and stares at the floor. A few seconds lapse into more before he raises his head and pats his hands around different sections of his body. His shoes are on, and white hoodie is in possession. Everything is clean and dry. The pain that consumed him earlier, now doesn't exist. He's left with one possible conclusion.

"I'm crazy," he says while rising to his feet then walking up the narrow staircase and into his bedroom.

He passes the next hour staring at his computer screen. Minute by minute, he types any and every keyword into the search engine that he thinks can give him even the slightest chance of helping make sense of what just happened.

```
: Accidentally found school in dream
: Shoe eating goblin/singer named Caesar
: Old man with crazy horse named Naroshi
: Door inside a tree next to castle
```

"Nothing," he says, slamming his laptop shut, then falling backwards on his bed and crashing his head into the soft feather pillow below.

He lies there for a moment, gazing at the ceiling, before suddenly sitting back up and opening his laptop again.

```
: Zarmore
```

There's one result.

Young Boy Who Claimed to Have Discovered Magical School in Other Dimension Falls Deeper into Coma

By **Charlie Davis** | **The London Leak**
June 19, 1944 [Archived]

Early Sunday evening Dorothy Armstrong confirmed via telegram that her fourteen-year-old son Henry has yet to wake. To those unfamiliar with the boy and his claims, he made headlines last week when he took to the streets of London and urged all citizens to evacuate, as death was certain and imminent. When confronted on how he was so convinced of these events, the boy spoke of having traveled to an academy through his dreams where children were being trained to use their minds in an effort to win the war. Henry asserted that he had already foreseen the destruction in his augury class at said school, which he referred to as Zarmore. He later went on to explain that humans have been attending this academy for hundreds of years, and many of the prominent leaders of our world are actually, in fact, alumni.

Now, this type of poppycock had obviously been accounted for as mere rubbish from the imagination of a whimsical lad. However, less than twenty-four hours later, as you all well know, our great city was indeed attacked. V-1 bombings from those Nazi scum still shower our city today as I type this article. So many dead. So many injured. But was it all preventable?

Journalists, reporters, and secret intelligence service MI6 combed the streets to locate and question the boy. His whereabouts were determined later that night, but no answers were to be had. His distraught mother answered the door of their marred home in South London. She told the press that her son had not woken up that morning and that doctors were not sure if he ever would.

She said that her rugby-loving son had been in perfect health, and she had no clue on how or why this had happened. The German bombings had mostly missed their home, and doctors confirmed that the coma was not induced by trauma.

"Henry came home Monday evening quite upset," Dorothy told reporters. "When I asked him what was wrong, he told me that no one believed him and then urged me to leave town with him and his sister Anna. I told him I couldn't. We had no place to go, and it was far too dangerous to be traveling during these times. That only infuriated him more. He said he wouldn't leave us alone to die and then rushed to his room and slammed the door. I should've believed him. We all should've."

When asked last week if her son had ever spoken of Zarmore before, she said he indeed had.

"Yes, he did always have a strange fascination with the idea of that school. At first, I felt that it was just playful fun, but as the months went on, he only became more adamant about it. I suggested that he seek the help of a psychiatrist, but he refused. He told me that I mustn't tell anyone of what he disclosed to me and that grave things would happen to him if anyone ever found out. I don't believe my son is insane, but he does need help."

Another reporter asked if she could describe any more details about the school, as it may assist in getting a better idea of what happened to her son.

"He described Zarmore as neither here nor there. He said that it was located in a place outside of time and that potential students were selected and then intercepted in their dreams to take an entrance exam. If they passed, they would be granted a small key of sorts, which would be infused into the base of their right ring finger, which under the correct light, would reveal a letter 'Z' superimposed over a triangle-shaped hourglass. Oh, how that infuriated me when he showed me that silly tattoo; I couldn't believe he would go to such lengths for a prank."

```
The reporter asked her to continue before
she went more off track.

"Yes, yes, he said that the key was tethered
to the student's soul or something and that
while it was in possession, would always
slingshot him or her to Zarmore after they
entered a dream state. He said the keys only
allowed access to the school between the
hours of 3:00 am and 11:30 am and that this
would correlate to a time on Zarmore as
something similar to 7:00 am to 3:30 pm."

One of the reporters asked what would happen
if someone failed the entrance exam.

"He said their memory of the event would be
erased or rendered so fuzzy that it could
only be summed up as a strange dream. I do
think this is enough. Please let me know if
you find out what's happening to my son."

That was the last intel we were able to
receive before she showed us the door.
```

"I knew it," Teddy says, a slight grin creeping up his face.

"I don't believe it," his mother says as she enters the bedroom, erasing his smile and causing him to slam his laptop shut. "What in the world are you even doing in here,

Theodore? You know what, I don't want to know. Dinner's ready. And listen, if I see even just one moving box remaining in this room tomorrow, I sure hope you like it, young man, because that'll be your new home!"

His mother exits the room and slams the door. Teddy waits until he hears that her footsteps are all the way down the stairs and out of earshot before opening his laptop again and bookmarking the article.

"It's real."

. . .

Nearly two weeks have passed, and the only dream he remembers is one where he couldn't find the bathroom.

"Maybe that's a subconscious correlation to my life at Cameron Creek, always on the run but never able to find relief," he thinks to himself while lying in bed with the lights off and staring at the ceiling. *"Or maybe I just drank too much water that night."*

He shakes his head, then sits up and turns on his laptop, as is now his evening ritual. The bright screen powers up and forces him to squint while his eyes work to readjust. A white glow illuminates his youthful face while the rest of the bedroom remains in shadows. He's preparing to scan once more over the Zarmore article in hopes of finding a clue on how he can return. However, each time he reads it, the less it makes sense. From the looks of things, he really had no business being anywhere near that school. He wasn't intercepted in his dreams by anyone to take an entrance exam, he had no key, and lastly, wasn't even sleeping during the supposed designated time period.

"If it weren't for that psycho horse, I probably never would have even ended up there at all," he thinks.

He pauses for a moment.

"Hmm... Would if..."

All this time, he's been focusing his intention on returning to Zarmore. That's what he's always done to experience a lucid dream before. He would envision the place he wished to visit before bed and intend on traveling there. But if Zarmore is, in fact, some sort of guarded and secret academy, then perhaps he's been going against some unseen defenses to maintain that privacy.

"Would if I just focus on finding Naroshi instead of Zarmore? Then once I do that, she can take me where I want to go."

He pauses again and looks down. *"I really hope I'm not going crazy."*

Teddy shuts his laptop and discards it to the desk aside. He then lies back onto his soft pillow, pulls the heavy white comforter over his body, and closes his eyes.

"Find Naroshi. Find Naroshi. Find Naroshi..." He repeats like a mantra in his mind until finally, he's asleep.

A clanging of cans and what sounds like a goat gargling water is what initially grabs his attention. Teddy slides the raggedy curtains to the side, walks across the flimsy platform, and further toward the sounds.

"What the hell?" He mutters to himself as he takes in the scene.

The place looks as if it's been hit by a tornado. Ash, wooden debris, and red aluminum cans emblazoned with the word "Mapsy's" litter the dirt floor while a cold breeze drafts in from the gaping hole near the entrance. Teddy can't nip the feeling of déjà vu as he continues scanning the destruction.

A few moments later, his eyes finally land on the source of the noise. Sitting next to a pile of empty cans and leaning against a stack of overturned hay is a small brown and furry creature dressed in black slacks and a white collared dress shirt with the buttons undone. The hair on top of the creature's head is a greasy mess, and his fuzzy white belly is covered in some sort of brown liquid. Teddy hops off the stage and approaches the animal, who doesn't seem to be bothered as the boy draws closer. When they're finally within a few feet of each other, a spark of recognition flashes across Teddy's face.

"C-Caesar?" he asks. "Is that you? It's me, Teddy. Are you... crying?"

The fellow continues to sob as he cracks open a new can of the unknown liquid. Teddy picks an empty one off the ground and reads the label:

Mapsy's

The Finest Maple Syrup in alllll of Slaybethor

Teddy tosses the can over his shoulder then slowly reaches for the one in the creature's paw. "I think you've had enough of these, bud..."

The miniature beast grabs Teddy by the wrist and looks up at him with his deep and jet-black eyes. His dagger-like teeth barely block the hot air that exudes underneath his growl. He then throws the boy's hand to the side before fixing his eyesight back onto the can and chugging the rest of its contents, crumpling, then tossing the aluminum into the pile afterwards.

Teddy takes a step back, unsure of how to continue, before Caesar finally speaks up. "Why'd you do it, Teddy?"

"I, uh... I don't know; I just thought you'd probably drunk enough of them by now. I was only trying to..."

"Not the Mapsy's, Teddy!"

"Oh..."

"You took the man's horse!"

"Oh... Oh yeah, Naroshi! Holy crap. Yes, that's why I'm here," Teddy says, more to himself than to Caesar. "Where is she? I need to uh, talk with her."

Caesar cocks his head to the side and looks up at Teddy.

"Where is she? You stole her!" he says, pointing a furry finger at the boy.

"Whoa, easy with the accusations. I was only borrowing that horse... with limited permission."

"Tell that to the old man," Caesar says.

"Wait, that old one-eyed farmer did this?"

Caesar doesn't reply.

"How? Why?"

Caesar cracks open a new can of Mapsy's.

"Because. You. Took. His. Horse," Caesar says. "Jeez, and they call goblins dumb."

"Ok, but..."

"Listen, after I selflessly saved your life and calmed down the crowd..."

"Briefly," Teddy interjects. "They still charged out the back door a few minutes later."

Caesar growls, and Teddy shuts up.

"Listen, kid. After everything went down and you rode off safely into the sunset, that old man returned to the barn and blasted a hole through that front wall. He pointed that stupid wooden staff at everyone demanding to know where the BOY and the HORSE had run off to."

"Ok, ok, wow. I'm really sorry," Teddy says.

"I know you must've thought you were dreaming, but this affects my real life, Teddy. It's not a game."

"Hang on, how would you... Caesar, are you... real? What is this place?"

"You know, you kids show up every so often. Sometimes you get eaten; sometimes we have some fun like we did. But I've never seen anything like this."

"I don't understand, Caesar. Have you heard of Zarmore?"

"This is Slaybethor, an outskirt city on the edge of time and what you Earth brats call reality. Half dream, half real world here they say. We're a colony of goblins and farmers who all have coexisted just fine for thousands of years until yesterday."

"Yesterday? Why did the old man wait so long to come looking for me? He couldn't have been that mad if he waited two weeks."

"Time moves differently here, Teddy. That was yesterday."

"Huh?"

Caesar takes another sip from his can of Mapsy's as Teddy looks ready to fire off another question.

"Wait, so when you were saying that this was our fifth gig in a month... How many times have I been down here?"

Caesar lets out a small laugh, the first non-threatening action since Teddy's arrival.

"I was just messing with ya, kid. It's not that often I catch a dreamer so close to the castle. I just wanted to have some fun. Those other goblins, they would have killed you though, believe that. Never take away a goblin's fun."

"Ok, the castle, so you do know of Zarmore! And I wouldn't have really died, just woken up, right?"

"Zarmore exists inside a kingdom called Egaria. It's enchanted with an ancient protection spell so that if you were to die there in Zarmore, yes, you would have woken up, just like any other regular dream. However, in the rest of Egaria or in one of these border cities, that's not the case. Here, it's lights out, Teddy baby."

Teddy's heart drops to the bottom of his stomach as he absorbs what he just heard.

"I was trying to wake up when that horse was galloping away from Slaybethor, but I couldn't. Is that because this place isn't a dream?"

"Like I said, kid. Half dream, half real world. In most areas of Slaybethor, you should have a fair amount of control as you would in any of your other regular dreams. However, the further you move away from here and the closer you get to Zarmore or Egaria in general, the less it starts to function like a dream and the more it starts to operate like you're accustomed to on Earth."

"Hang on, but I saw some things happen at Zarmore that could never have happened on Earth."

"I'm not saying it's impossible to live a dream-like existence over there. It just takes training. And actually, if you want to have any hope of surviving in Egaria, you'll have to develop at least a basic skill set. Anyway," Caesar says as he grabs another can of Mapsy's. "I guess I need to go warn the rest of my people that help isn't on the way since the idiot who stole the horse, also lost it."

"I know where she is," Teddy says.

"Excuse me?"

"I know where the horse is. She took me to Zarmore. She's probably still there. Do you know how I can get back?"

Caesar lowers his drink from his mouth and sighs.

"Yeah, I know a way," he finally says. "Just make sure to give my lousy brother Gobo a whack in the ribs for me when you see him."

Dean Spear

The sun is near set by the time the two finally arrive at the edge of the cliff. Crashing waves beneath them make it nearly impossible to hear one another.

"Yup, this is exactly where Naroshi took me last time!" Teddy shouts.

"Yeah, I figured!" Caesar yells back. "This is the only way I know to Egaria without a key! Anyway, you have to jump; just make sure to land beyond those first two rocks!"

"Wait, what?!"

"Or maybe it was in front of the set of rocks," Caesar mutters to himself.

"Hell no!" Teddy shouts as he looks down into the crashing white waves below. "There's got to be another way! My life isn't the greatest, but I'm not ready to risk it all on a jump!"

"What was that, Teddy? I can't hear a word you're saying!"

"I said, no freaking wa...!"

He's cut off when Caesar plants both paws into the lower section of Teddy's back. The boy gasps for breath as he shuffles his feet and waves his arms in the air, desperately trying not to step over the cliff's edge. Caesar then gives him one final kick, and the boy's knees buckle. Teddy swings his body around midair and tries to grab the cliff's edge, but it's too late. He falls back-first toward the water and can only watch as the short goblin with pointy ears cracks open a can of Mapsy's and walks back into the forest.

The sounds of breaking waves morph into a melody of chirping birds. It's hard to pinpoint when exactly the switch happened, or how, but when he opens his eyes, Teddy finds himself back in the center of the valley. The red sun has already risen over the castle on top of the mountain while the jungle behind him remains in a state of perpetual darkness. Teddy exhales, then helps himself up to his feet and looks around, a small smile inching up his face.

"It's actually real."

He spends the next couple of hours hiking up the mountain, choosing to follow the same path as his last visit. Once he arrives at the large rock which overlooks the pond, he opts once again to sit and take a break.

"Damn, this is cool," he says aloud to himself while looking around, his smile yet to escape him.

After a few moments, he stands and walks over to the bank of the pond. He inspects the water briefly, then crouches down and cups his palms together to form a small bowl. He then lowers his palms into the water, brings them back up to his mouth, and takes a sip.

A feeling of repulsion immediately overtakes Teddy's body, and he spits the water out.

"Oh God, that was a bad idea," he says, now on his knees and fighting off the urge to vomit. "Note to self: Pond water is still pond water, regardless of whatever planet I may or may not be on."

He pushes himself back up to his feet and is about to walk away but stops when he catches sight of his reflection in the water.

Teddy realized from the moment he arrived in the valley that he was barefoot, but it isn't until he sees his reflection in the pond that he notices he's also wearing the same black shorts and white t-shirt he had on when he went to bed. All his injuries from the previous visit have healed and are no longer affecting him, but there seems to be some connection between what clothes he wears to bed and how he's attired once inside Zarmore territory.

Teddy holds that thought as he turns away from the pond but then immediately drops it when a new question enters his mind.

"What's this crap doing on my throne?" He mumbles as he approaches the rock where he was just previously sitting. "That wasn't there before."

Fresh tree bark shavings cover the rock. Teddy glances up and sees that one of the redwoods which provides shade over the rock now has something carved into its trunk.

"Alright, that *definitely* wasn't there before," he says as he walks closer and brushes his fingers against the carving, which resembles something that holds the appearance of a sword or spear-like object being crossed out by a giant "X".

A branch snaps in the distance, and Teddy hears something scatter away.

"What the..."

Goosebumps shoot down his spine, and his heart pounds. Teddy freezes and waits for the next noise, but after several long moments, none arrive.

"Ok, I think it's time to check out of this spot," he finally says before stepping away from the rock and resuming his hike up the mountain.

Another hour passes before he arrives at the top and can see the castle. There are several groups of students talking amongst each other near the drawbridge.

"Oh my God, hang on," one of the girls says as he walks out from under the shade of the forest. "Teddy, is that you?"

"Ava," Teddy says as he recognizes the girl, unable to conceal a smile from his face.

"It is!" She yells as she runs up and wraps her arms around him. "But how?"

Before Teddy can say anything, he's flanked by a pair of goblins on each side of his body.

"To your knees, boy!" one of them yells.

"Huh," Teddy says.

"Knees!" the goblin says again, this time ramming the rear of his bayonet into the small of Teddy's back.

"Relax, Gobs," Ava says.

"All students to class!" Gobo orders.

"But..." Ava begins.

"Now!"

"You're going to be ok, Teddy," Ava says as she walks toward the drawbridge. "They're just taking you to see Dean Spear."

"As long as I'm away from these hounds," Teddy starts before another bayonet jams into his back.

"Shut up," Gobo says. "I knew you weren't to be trusted."

. . .

The team of four goblins march Teddy past the students gathered in the foyer, up a set of stairs, through a short hall, then up another staircase that overlooks the foyer and valley outside.

"Whoa, you guys think we can stop for a second to appreciate this view?" Teddy says before the rear of another bayonet is jabbed into his side and they turn a corner.

The goblins lead the boy down a hallway layered with red carpet. Doors line both sides of the corridor, and nobody stops walking until they reach a tall and intricately cut set of wooden double doors at the end. Once there, the goblin in front of Teddy's right rests his weapon against the wall, then jumps up and uses both paws to pull open the doors. A warm gust of air escapes the room and brushes past Teddy's face, ruffling his shaggy and curly brown hair.

"Sit," Gobo orders.

"You know, you're a lot different than your brother down in Slaybethor," Teddy begins. "Are you sure you weren't adopted?"

Gobo jams the rear of his bayonet into Teddy's stomach, causing the boy to fall back onto the wooden bench behind him.

"Hey, that's what he told me to do to you," Teddy says while letting out a flurry of coughs.

"Bring him in!" A voice bellows from behind another set of grand wooden double doors in the back of the room.

A bayonet thrusts into Teddy's back, and he jumps to his feet.

"Ok enough with the jabs, guys! Jeez, your hairball mother never sit on your eggs and keep you warm as a baby or what?"

"No courtesy for criminals," one of the goblins says before snarling at Teddy and pushing him into the dean's office.

Teddy stumbles through the entryway, and the doors slam shut behind him. Momentum carries the boy a few more steps into the office before he's able to come to a stop and regather his feet. He then dusts himself off and looks toward the large man sitting behind the ornate desk in the back of the circular room.

"Mr. Lancaster, I heard you had quite the first day at Zarmore earlier this month. I'm honestly a bit surprised to see you in my office today. Take a seat, please," Dean Spear says as he gestures to an open seat in front of his desk.

The room is warm but dark. There are portraits of older-looking men and women dressed in hats and wigs that line the candlelit and curved walls. A marred sword and some triangular coins are displayed on top of the dean's desk under a thick sheet of glass. Settled behind the man is a fireplace wider than the desk and taller than Teddy himself. Orange flames dance inside and emit a smell similar to the one in the dining hall.

The whole ambiance of the room doesn't particularly match the man who claims ownership over it. Although he's bald and clearly past his days as a student, Dean Spear still holds a youthful appearance. He wears thick glasses and a pressed collared gray shirt with the sleeves rolled up. His charcoal suspenders match his pants and run up tight over his shoulders, making his muscular build well noticeable underneath.

"How do you know my last name?" Teddy asks.

The dean chuckles. "There's very little we don't know about you now, Theodore. Your father is Maurice, correct?"

Teddy narrows his eyes and tilts his head slightly before looking down toward the wooden floor. "Yeah... he *was*."

"Yes, of course. I apologize. Your father was a great man."

Teddy looks up.

"Let's get to it, shall we?" The dean says. "What myself and the Council would like to understand is how exactly you managed to find yourself here in Zarmore."

Teddy hesitates for a second, scanning over the circular room again and wondering how much he should reveal.

For the next fifteen minutes, everything is explained to the dean, and throughout that entire relating, the man doesn't utter a word. He nods his head at certain points and gestures using his hands for Teddy to continue at others but never once is a question raised or a reaction given. The only moment where the man seems to be somewhat taken aback is when Teddy mentions Naroshi. Once he says her name, the dean appears to almost flinch. It's an ever so slight, hardly noticeable hesitation, and Teddy thinks for a moment that he's about to say something before the man quickly regains his composure and returns to his default expression.

"Interesting," the dean says once all is told.

"It's the truth," Teddy replies.

"Mr. Lancaster, in the past 1,000 years, do you know how many times a human has just simply appeared, by chance, in Egaria?"

Teddy shrugs his shoulders then opens his mouth to answer but is cut off before he can respond.

"10,988 times."

Teddy rubs one of his eyes. "*So much for a well-guarded secret,*" he thinks to himself.

"And do you know out of those nearly eleven thousand times where a human has found themselves by chance in Egaria that they then made it inside the colony of Zarmore?" Dean Spear asks.

Teddy shakes his head.

"Zero," the dean says. "Zero times in the history of this academy has a human, without specific granted access, managed to break through onto our grounds. And you succeed in doing it not just twice in two weeks, but from an outskirt city beyond the borders of Egaria. Not only that, you remember every detail of the experience."

The dean seems to be battling with a thought internally. He slowly spins around in his chair, then raises a hand toward his chin and stares into the flames of the large fireplace which rests behind his desk. For the next minute, neither of them say a word. Besides the occasional crackling of logs splitting underneath the heat of red and orange embers, the room is dead silent. Teddy clears his throat and is about to speak before the dean swings back around in his chair and places his elbows on top of the desk, clasping his hands.

"What I'm about to do is highly unorthodox and will surely put me in hot water amongst my colleagues due to your... *history*."

Teddy furrows his brow and watches as the dean stands up and walks toward a curved wall of bookcases to the left of his desk.

"But they'll come to understand me in time," the dean continues, seemingly more to himself than to Teddy. "I'd like to offer you an opportunity, Theodore. An opportunity that all human beings have, but very few see, and even less choose to take. You've known since you were little that your world is not all that it seems. You can sense it inside you; even in this very moment, you feel something deep in your core that wishes to expand, that wants to grow, that knows it is great. But you go through your life on Earth and everyone tells you that you're not good enough, that there is something wrong or uncool with being loving, and that having confidence and walking like a humble king amongst kings with the power of the creator burning in your core is a shameful trait that should be cut down at first notice. You tell them your goals and dreams, and they tell you why it'll never happen. They believe you must struggle and suffer through this life as they have, because that is the same lie that they've learned to believe as well. This is a fatal disease that has been spreading across the planet for thousands of years. It is a disease purposely injected into your mind to turn you into a slave rather than the master of your fate, which is your true and natural right.

The dean runs a finger across a row of books.

"Here at Zarmore, we will remove your shackles and train you to harness your life energies in such a way that you can create a world of good for you and for the planet Earth. We will remind you of a truth which you always knew before this life but may have forgotten."

Teddy remains silent, unsure of how to respond.

"I am aware that this is not an easy decision, but it is one that you must make now. I present you with two options."

One of the bookcases then creaks upwards off the wall and slides through the ceiling, revealing something which resembles a black mirror in its previous location on the wall. It's about the size of a door and, although dark at its core, gleams brightly in contrast to the dimly lit office. Its edges are surrounded by a thin metallic blue cloud that rumbles and crackles with neon white lightning. After a few seconds, the dark center of the mirror begins melting in toward itself, like a whirlpool sucking in everything connected to it until all that remains is an image of a poorly lit bedroom. There's a boy sleeping comfortably in bed, made visible by the light of the moon that shines through his window. Teddy quickly recognizes that he's actually staring and watching all this through one of the mirrors in the boy's bedroom and that the boy isn't just some random kid at all. It's him.

"You can walk through this gateway and reunite with your body, returning to your life as it currently is today. No harm will be done to you, I assure it. You will continue to live your life as you always have been, as ninety-nine percent of the human species does every day, believing that things just happen to them and that they have no control over it at all. And this is a perfectly reasonable way to live. For many people, it is easier to blame God, or the universe, or dumb luck for their circumstances. And there is nothing wrong with that. Taking ownership over everything that happens to you in your life is a heavy responsibility, and I would not judge you in the slightest if you choose to leave. Be that as it may, do know that once you pass through this mirror, you will have zero recollection of your experiences at Zarmore. You will still dream, and you may even see your goblin buddies down in Slaybethor from time to time. But you will *never* find yourself on this campus again. I promise you that. However, if you have the desire to live your life as you were born to, and as you always intended to, then there is another option."

The room brightens a little. The flames inside the fireplace increase in size, spiraling upwards like a small tornado and forcing a stack of papers to fly off the dean's desk. The blaze continues to pick up speed and height until finally reaching the ceiling of the tall fireplace. A hot gust of wind blows Teddy's hair into his face. He shuts his eyelids and tries to block out the heat, but the blaze is still well felt from underneath. The chair Dean Spear was sitting in earlier rolls to the side of the room and crashes into a bookcase. Teddy clenches his eyes even tighter as he sinks in his chair and covers his face with both hands. A boom of fiery wind blows across his body, upturning his seat from underneath him and throwing him onto his back. He nearly slams his head against the hardwood floor and then waits for the blaze to calm down before reopening his eyes.

The reverberation of the windows shaking makes the hair on his forearms stand straight in the now much darker room. All the candles that lined the office walls have been blown out, and there's a strong smell of pine and smoke in the air. Teddy gets up to his feet and looks toward the fireplace, which now has become something more. The fire has split into two, covering both sides of the fireplace's walls and illuminating a wide and long cobblestone path in the middle. The passage extends nearly twenty yards deep into the fireplace until finally arriving at the end, where a white door with a green knob lies.

Dean Spear puts his left hand on Teddy's shoulder and motions toward the flames with his right. "Or you can choose to follow the light and pass through the door at the end of the hall. The decision is yours, Theodore. Always has been, always will be."

The dean removes his hand and starts walking toward the entrance of his office, then stops midway.

"I must let you know though, if you choose option number two and walk through that door, there is no walking back out. Wearing this uniform is an honor few on Earth have ever known, but it is also one that turns you into a target."

The dean pauses for a moment while Teddy continues to stare into the flames. "There's much more to all of this than you're prepared to hear right now, but it is my aspiration that one day you shall learn."

One of the heavy double doors slams shut and sends an echo through the room. Teddy turns around and sees that the dean is gone. He then walks toward the set of the office entrance doors, places his right hand on one of the knobs, and jiggles it.

"This guy really locked me in here?" He mutters to himself.

He exhales, then turns around and makes his way back toward the fireplace. When he gets back to where they were sitting earlier, the blue cloud around the mirror is still rumbling to the side of him. He plops himself atop the dean's desk and looks into the mirror that rests just ten yards away.

"Well, he wasn't kidding; that's definitely me there," Teddy says as he stares into the mirror, observing his dormant body lying in bed. "Wow, do I always sleep with my mouth wide open like that?"

He leans forward and squints before standing up and walking toward the mirror to get a better look. A flash of white lightning then cracks off from the blue cloud that encircles the mirror and forces Teddy to flinch. His foot hits an object on the ground in front of him, and he stumbles forward. Panic overtakes his eyes as he starts to fall, gravely in search of balance. The mirror is now just six yards away. He reaches to his left and attempts to grab something to prevent the inevitable, but nothing is there. Three more steps. He swipes his hand to his right. Only air.

"*Crap.*"

The mirror is just three yards away now. Teddy closes his eyes as his body approaches the floor. There's a thud as his knees hit first. He throws his hands in front of his face and tries to curl up the rest of his body. Another thud arrives as his right shoulder hits the ground, and his body slides across the floor.

Teddy keeps his eyes closed. Everything still looks dark beneath his eyelids, and there's a rumbling sound just above where his head lies. His body tenses as he slowly reopens his eyes. CRACK!

Teddy's eyes jolt open, and a flash of neon white blinds his vision. He throws himself up off the floor then backpedals until he crashes into something and falls once again. He lies there still now, curled up and blinking incessantly. A minute passes before all the white blurs escape from his vision, and he's able to see somewhat clearly.

The fiery pathway inside the fireplace is just a few feet to the side of him; however, it looks a bit less tame than before. He grabs the edge of the dean's desk and helps himself back up to his feet.

"I need to chill," he says to himself as he closes his eyes and tries to calm down.

He takes one long breath in through the nose and then out through the mouth. There's a brief moment of silence before another crack of lightning shoots off and forces him to flinch once again.

He clenches his jaw, then takes another deep breath in and regathers himself.

"Stupid mirror."

He searches the floor to see what initially caused him to start tumbling in the first place. Not too far away from the mirror, he finds a thick leather-bound book.

"Stupid book."

He picks the text up and begins inspecting it, rubbing his thumb over its dry and cracked cover before a burning sensation overtakes his hands and forces him to fling the book to his right. It somersaults sideways through the air like a frisbee and toward the mirror.

Teddy grimaces and closes his eyes as he quickly realizes his error. He remains stiff while he awaits to hear the sound of shattering glass, but it never comes. He then opens his eyes and looks toward the mirror. There's a circular ripple of waves flowing outwards from its center. He slowly walks toward it but then stops when he hears an eruption coming from the fireplace.

The flames that line both sides of the walls have nearly doubled in size and are beginning to close in on each other. The white door with the green knob at the end of the cobblestone path is still well visible, but he knows that his time for making a decision is dwindling. He looks at the boy sleeping on the other side of the mirror and pictures how his life would be never knowing that Zarmore exists:

He would continue to drag himself to school every day for the next six years, where students would tease him ruthlessly. He probably would never make any friends, definitely never date anyone. Depression. Anxiety. His mom would eventually throw him out onto the streets after his grades started slipping. Probably would have to move under the freeway overpass and fight for bread in Central Park against the pigeons. The pigeons would always win though. They'd always win....

Maybe he's being too dramatic.

The fire roars even louder.

"Stop wasting time!" He shouts to himself.

He runs over to the base of the fireplace. The door is still visible at the end but now only barely. The fires have extended out to a point where the cobblestone path is now only a few feet wide. No more time to think. He sprints in between the walls of orange flames.

"*This isn't too bad,*" he thinks.

Then he screams. One of his sleeves is on fire. He slows his pace but continues to run—just ten more yards to go.

He screams a little louder. The blaze is moving up toward the neckline of his shirt, and sweat is dripping into his eyes, blurring his vision. He glances to his left and then to his right. The flames are closing in. He adjusts his body so that it's parallel with the fires, then rips what remains of his shirt off and over his head, tossing it into the inferno—five more yards to go. Smoke fills the tunnel as the fire eats into his shirt, but he can see the green knob. The path that would have fit a car earlier has now been reduced to less than a foot. A deathly cough overtakes him as he sidesteps through the final stretch. The fire roars into his ears. No need to check the gap anymore—just a little further. Something smells like burnt hair. *"Not going to cry,"* he says internally as he sticks his right arm out, a shaky hand hovering now just inches in front of the knob. He's beginning to feel dizzy and starting to doubt if he can...

"Got it!"

Teddy cranks the knob to the right, and a surge of electricity shoots up through one of his fingers that grip the handle. The jolt races up his arm and expands throughout the rest of his body like an eruption, making him feel like he's about to explode. Then it all reverses and contracts in on itself, feeling like trillions of little ropes are being fastened around each and every cell inside him. His whole body cringes as salty tears mixed with sweat run down his cheeks. He falls to his knees while still holding onto the green knob. There's a loud click as he hits the cobblestone. His eyes then roll to the back of his head, and his body falls limp against the door... which slowly creaks open.

That Which is Unseen

The room is bright. Teddy yawns and rolls onto his side while stretching his arms upwards and over his head. He then flexes his legs downwards, pointing and wiggling his toes at the end as he allows his ankles to crack softly. A gust of cool air sails through the window and brushes a few strands of hair in front of his eyes. He blows the stragglers away then runs his fingers through the rest. His cellphone is resting atop the wobbly black nightstand next to a small white lamp. He grabs it then presses the button on the side. 6:47 am. He's up before his alarm.

"*Maybe I actually won't be late today,*" he thinks to himself.

The bed creaks as he moves over toward its edge and tries to remember if he had any dreams last night. Probably not. Today would mark the two-week anniversary since his last lucid dream. Zarmore, perhaps it isn't real after all. The whole idea of it is starting to seem a little silly anyway, even if the memory still lives vivid in his mind.

He stands up and walks toward his closet. It's one of those weird box ones with a door and a knob.

"It's not a box, Teddy," he remembers his mom saying when they pulled over to the side of the road and loaded it onto the truck. "It's an *armoireee*." He told her that her fake French accent didn't make it smell any less like wet dog. They laughed. The two of them could have fun sometimes.

There's a heavy full-length mirror that hangs onto the front of it, but the thing can never stay put and constantly crashes to the floor if he shuts the door to the armoire too hard. He's thought to just leave the door open all the time, but the inside of it still smells really bad.

He looks at his bed in the reflection of the mirror as he approaches the closet. He'll have to remember to make that before she comes home. Ever since his mom started working twelve-hour graveyard shifts at the hospital, she hasn't been as fun.

He opens the armoire, grabs his clothes, then shuts the door slightly, making sure that it doesn't close completely just yet. He then starts changing and sits down on the edge of his bed after putting his khaki shorts on. His black socks slide comfortably over his ankles, and he stands back up and throws on his black t-shirt with a picture of a cat eating pizza on the front. He then walks over to the mirror and works on combing out some of the knots in his hair. Although he's beginning to care less and less about how people at school think of him, he knows that walking into class with this level of bedhead will ultimately bring him more attention than he wants. He takes a step back as the knots become undone and expose how long his hair has truly become.

It's near to his shoulders now and by far the longest he's ever grown it. His dad's was long too, but Teddy never grew it out when he was alive. People were always telling him that they looked enough alike without it.

After ten more seconds of combing, he tosses the brush on the floor and curses as he remembers the armoire still needs to be closed. He takes a pause, then a deep breath in, and grabs the knob, slowly turning it to the left. Once all the way there, he pushes the door in slightly then releases the handle back to the right. There's a soft click. He exhales, then turns around and starts to make his bed.

A few seconds later, he hears three heavy thuds and what sounds like papers flying. He turns around to see his mirror lying face-up on the carpet and his math homework littered around it and under his desk.

He clenches his fists as he walks toward the mess. "Stupid mirror."

Teddy takes a few more steps forward then stops. His grip loosens out of a fist, and he tilts his head to the side, lost in thought, gazing out the window. He then takes a few more steps toward the mirror and looks down into it.

"Stupid... mirror?"

He stares at the boy through the glass for a few moments until they both abruptly break eye contact with each other.

"No, no, no, no, no. I did dream last night!"

Teddy walks back toward his desk and sits down for a second before standing right back up again.

"NO!"

He shoves the chair to the ground then marches back over to the mirror on the floor.

"This isn't right. I did everything you said! Why am I here?!"

He looks away from his reflection and walks to the other side of the room. He stops after he passes his bed and thinks to himself.

"Crap! Did I choose the wrong one? No, no, no, no...."

He paces back and forth.

"No, that's not right either. I remember. Door was Zarmore. Mirror was crap. He said if I chose to leave, I would forget everything... But I remember... So why am I here?! Was it a trick?"

Teddy walks back over to the mirror and pokes it with his toe.

"Unless, it was just all a dream, and I really am crazy."

He walks over and sits on the edge of his bed, looking at his long hair hanging over his slouched body in the reflection of the mirror.

"Maybe I just miss dad and want it all to be real."

Tears pool up in his eyes. He sits still for a few seconds before pushing himself back up to his feet and speaking. "No. Zarmore is real, and this article proves it."

He sniffles, then walks over to his laptop and pulls open the browser.

"That's weird."

The article he had bookmarked is missing. He rubs his chin, then looks up at the ceiling for a few moments before beginning to type:

```
Your search Zarmore did not match any documents.

   Suggestions:
      • Check your spelling.
      • Use less keywords.
      • Use more keywords.
```

He tries another browser:

```
We couldn't find anything matching Zarmore.
Are you sure you didn't mean to type Lawnmowers?
```

Teddy slams his computer shut and dives onto his bed. He picks his phone back up off the nightstand and attempts to search on there:

```
0 results for Zarmore could be found.
Click here to receive $50,000.00 instantly!!
```

He stares at the empty search results for nearly thirty seconds before looking up at the time on top of the screen. He's going to be late for class.

. . .

Teddy hardly bats an eye when his English teacher hands him a red detention slip and the whole class bursts into laughter. He doesn't care—about anything.

"Nice shirt, loser," one kid says as they pass each other in the hall. His name is Jeremy Culver. He has red hair and is the strongest boy in school. He's also the meanest.

"I wonder how it looks covered in Gatorade."

Jeremy untwists the orange cap and dumps the purple sticky liquid over Teddy's head. The pointing and laughter arrive on cue, but Teddy keeps walking straight as if nothing happened. He hears a couple of students talking behind him after he passes by.

"You see that? He didn't even flinch when Jeremy doused him. That Teddy kid is freaking crazy."

That's exactly what Teddy's thinking as well.

His last class of the day is biology. Today is the day they're choosing lab partners for the first half of the school year, and Teddy's been worrying about it the entire past week. He's sure that no one will want to match up with him.

"Excuse me... Excuse me... Um, hello? Anybody in there?"

There's a girl sitting directly across from Teddy. He flinches as if someone just woke him from a long nap. "Huh, you talking to me?"

"Uhh yeah, we're kinda the only two people sitting at this table," she says with a half-grin. "And I'm literally just like two feet in front of you."

"Oh, sorry, I'm kind of... out of it today."

"Don't sweat it. I'm Kristi. Want to be lab partners?"

"WhAt?" Teddy asks probably too loudly, his voice cracking at the end.

Her smile widens.

"I said, do you want to be lab partners?"

Her long black hair shines under the bright lights of the classroom while her glasses tilt down toward the tip of her nose. Her eyes are brown and appear larger from underneath the thick round lenses of her spectacles. She continues to talk. "Yeah, well, I'm new here, and it seems like everyone else is already matched up."

Teddy's head sinks a little. "Oh."

"I didn't mean it like that," she adds. "I mean, I saw what that kid did to you in the hallway this morning, and I don't know; I guess I just thought you could use a friend."

Teddy almost laughs. He'd rather be alone than pitied.

"And I love your shirt," she says.

A smile tugs at his lips, and he looks away.

The two of them work together on gathering the supplies needed for the lab. Kristi picks up a couple of glass vials filled with green and blue liquids off the teacher's desk while Teddy grabs a microscope from the back of the class and brings it to their table.

"You know, Teddy, I can get you like a wet paper towel or something from the bathroom if you want. I mean, unless you like walking around with Gatorade glued to your face."

He hadn't even realized that he never cleaned himself up after the incident. There are too many other thoughts competing for his attention now. Zarmore isn't real. He's crazy.

Life sucks again. He opens his mouth to reply but is cut off when the teacher begins speaking to the class from the front of the room.

"I'm about to shut the lights off now. I want everyone to grab their blacklights and document what differences you notice in the organism's behavior once its light source is gone."

The classroom goes dark, and then one by one, neon blue bulbs of light pop into existence. Teddy grabs one of the vials as Kristi holds the blacklight.

"So are those tattoos real, or do they fade away in time?" She asks.

"What are you talking about?" Teddy replies.

"Your little triangle hourglass tattoo thingamabobber under your finger. My boyfriend had one just like that but got it removed. Or that's what he said at least, but I think it was just fake and faded away."

Teddy moves the vial to his left hand then looks at the palm of his right hand under the blacklight.

"Yup, that's the exact same one he had," she says. "So what's the deal? You guys get them from like a comic book or something?"

Teddy looks at the mark on the meaty part of the base of his right ring finger. There's a letter "Z" glowing in neon green against the backdrop of an hourglass. His heart races, and he notices the pulse of the "Z" pick up in speed accordingly. Without warning, the classroom lights flash back on, and the mark disappears.

"There are cleaning supplies in the closet, Mr. Lancaster," the teacher begins. "Now hurry and clean that up before someone touches it. And to the rest of the class, please hold onto your vials firmly. Don't be like Teddy."

All the students laugh. Well, everyone except Kristi.

"It's ok, Teddy; I shouldn't have distracted you. I'll help you clean up."

The two walk toward the closet as Teddy thinks to himself.

"Crap, did I really not even notice I dropped that or hear the glass shatter? But that was it! Right? That was basically the exact same mark that kid was talking about in the news article. But how?"

Kristi grabs some absorbent and cleaning spray while Teddy picks up a broom and dustpan. The teacher begins to talk about a diagram he drew on the board earlier, but all the student's eyes are still locked onto the two cleaning. Some look angry. Most continue to laugh. Kristi's face flushes red, and she puts her head down then starts scrubbing the green liquid off the concrete floor. Teddy then moves in to sweep, hardly even looking at the glass.

"Could it have been that wave of pain that went through my body after I touched the doorknob at the end of the fireplace? Is that what it feels like to have something 'soul-tethered' or whatever? I need to see it again."

Teddy finishes sweeping then dumps the shattered glass into the trash. They return to their seats with two fresh vials, and the lights shut off again.

"Do you want me to hold it this time?" Kristi asks.

"Uh, yeah. Sure," Teddy says as he hands her the vials then grabs the blacklight.

A few moments pass before Kristi speaks up again.

"Teddy, I can't see a thing. Can you shine that light over here? I really don't want to get in trouble again."

Teddy doesn't respond. He holds the light in his left hand and has his eyes fixed on the mark under his right ring finger.

"It's real," he says.

"You're looking at the tattoo?" Kristi laughs. "No way. Then why did my boyfriend's go away?"

"He didn't have one like this."

Kristi laughs again. "Ok, but come on, Teddy. Shine that light over here. We have to make some observations before class..."

The bell rings, and the lights flicker back on.

"Make sure to study your notes tonight!" The teacher shouts as the students rush toward the door. "You'll be writing a report on your observations next class!"

"Sorry," Teddy says as he looks up at Kristi.

"Don't stress it. I think I saw the thing move for a second or two. We'll be fine," she says as she smiles at Teddy and finishes packing her backpack. "See you tomorrow!"

Teddy says goodbye, then grabs his backpack and heads out of the class behind her. He looks down at his ring finger and smiles as he enters the busy hallway. "Tonight's going to be a good one."

Orientation

"Are you expecting a text or something, Mr. Happy Pants?"

"Mr. What? What are you talking about?" Teddy replies.

"Every time I walk in the living room, you pull out your phone, check it, then smile and put it back in your pocket," his mom says. "Meet a cute girl at school today? I told you that you'd eventually start making friends and having fun."

"Huh? No. That's not why I'm..."

He knows he can't tell her the truth.

"Teddy, I'm your mother. I can tell when you're in a good mood or not. Now spill the beans, kiddo. Who's the lucky girl?"

Teddy sighs and sinks deeper into the sofa, as if the depths of the blue polyester cushions can hide him from the incoming barrage of questions. Fortunately, a beeping sound goes off from the kitchen, and he's offered temporary refuge.

"Ugh, that's the lasagna. Dinner will be ready in fifteen, son. Feel free to invite your new girlfriend over. I made plenty," his mother says as she turns back into the kitchen.

Teddy sighs deeper into the couch, rubs his eyes, and pulls out his phone again. 5:30 pm. If that old news article from

London and his thoughts are correct, then class at Zarmore should begin around 10:00 pm when considering the time differences between England and New York—meaning just four and a half hours to go.

Teddy tries to remain silent throughout dinner, but his mom keeps probing him about his irregular upbeat mood earlier. Was it that obvious? He eventually tells her that there's a nice girl in his biology class, but she has a boyfriend, hoping that will get her to drop the subject.

"Well, Teddy, you know your father and I were just friends at first, too," she begins to say as she sets her fork down and gazes up at the ceiling with a smile. "Then one evening, he picked me up in his old red Chevy truck and drove me out to an abandoned parking lot to watch the sunset."

"Okkkk mom, I think I'm full, and you know what, I got this to report that needs to be written tomorrow, and I haven't prepared at all."

"But honey, you hardly even touched your lasagna, and I baked brownies."

"I'm just really not that hungry. Let's have them tomorrow."

"Aw, young love. I understand, Teddy. We'll save dessert for then."

He rubs his temples with his thumbs, then stands up and places his plate in the sink as his mom goes back to eating her dinner, seemingly lost in thought over something.

The hours pass like days as Teddy waits for night to fall. He tries to study his biology notes but can't stay focused for more than thirty seconds.

There's a bang at his door, and he looks up. It appears his mom's brief flame of happiness has burnt out as she remembers he didn't make his bed this morning. Teddy takes the scolding in stride as he's happy to have the subject changed.

When 9:00 pm finally hits, he climbs into bed and tries to fall asleep but only ends up tossing and turning for hours until finally around two or three in the morning, he feels as if he's drifting off. He pulls the heavy white comforter up and tighter around his chest while nuzzling his head deeper into the soft feather pillow. A faint smile creeps up his face as memories from Zarmore play out in his mind. The goblins, Naroshi. It's all real. He wonders what the other student's lives are like and if they're as amazed by it all as much as he is. Then at some point, he forgets what he's thinking about as his conscious thoughts mix with the unconscious. Soon after that, he's asleep.

. . .

The room is cold, and the floor feels sticky underneath his bare feet. He sits up straighter in the red velvet chair and cranes his neck upwards. The curtains on the stage in front of him match the seat he's sitting in. He looks to his left and then to his right. All the other chairs are empty. He then turns around and sees several more vacant rows of velvet seats and a tall set of double doors closed shut by the back wall. He scratches his head and tries to recall how he ended up here. Then he sees it. The pulsing green symbol is shining bright underneath the meaty base of his right ring finger.

"Holy crap, yes!" He shouts while jumping to his feet.

The double doors behind him creak open then slam shut a moment later, causing him to shudder. Something with a motherly and rushed voice starts to speak. "Oh no, no, no, please stay seated," the creature says as she walks down the center aisle between the rows of chairs and toward Teddy. "I am very very sorry to be arriving late to greet you. Well, actually, you're the one who's late, but we're not here to point paws! I'm Mrs. Suki." The creature finally arrives in front of Teddy and sticks out one of her dark brown paws up toward him. "It's a pleasure to meet you."

Teddy looks down at the short fox in front of him and furrows his brow. Mrs. Suki stands on her hind legs and is several feet shorter than Teddy. Her long gray dress extends all the way down to her exposed rear paws, and she's wearing a knitted gray sweater pulled over her top. Her fur is an orangish shade of brown, minus the white fuzz around her snout and neck region, and the amber in her eyes looks magnified from behind the lenses of her reading glasses. Her sharp gaze fixes onto Teddy.

"Um, nice to meet you too, Mrs. Suki," he says as he clasps his hand around her paw and softly shakes it. "I'm Teddy."

Her whiskers twitch, then she tilts her head to the side and smiles a toothy grin, causing Teddy to jump back.

"Oh no, dear, please don't flinch! I'm not a biter. Well, not anymore, at least. Or, I suppose it depends. Anywho, let's get started, shall we?"

She closes her eyes, and the lights dim. The curtains concealing the front of the stage open as Mrs. Suki turns away from Teddy's seat and walks toward the center aisle. She follows the path up and onto the stage, then approaches a wooden podium and taps the microphone twice. Teddy grimaces as two loud thuds echo through the speaker system inside the tall and vacant theater. Mrs. Suki smiles then opens her mouth.

"Welcome incoming students of Zarmore!"

Teddy looks around at the empty seats.

"Or student, that is. Sorry dear, I usually give this presentation to a much larger crowd. We'll make this quick, as you are already late enough as it is. As you know, my name is Mrs. Suki, and I have been tasked by Dean Spear to help acclimate all incoming first-yearers to campus. I am happy to see that you went to sleep with your clothes on last night, so we won't be needing to waste any time making extra visits to the locker rooms to change."

Teddy looks down and sees he's wearing the same blue basketball shorts and tank top he had on when he went to bed. When he looks back up, a large white projector screen has appeared behind the fox. She closes her eyes, and writing fills the screen.

~~~~~~

<div style="text-align:center">

Welcome *First-Yearers*

of

Zarmore

to

Orientation Day

with

Mrs. Suki :)))

</div>

Slide 1 of 472

~~~~~~

Teddy gapes as he reads the number of slides on the PowerPoint. This must be what Ava was referring to the first day they met on the drawbridge.

Mrs. Suki rubs her white and furry chin as she looks at the screen.

"You know what, dear, since it is just you this morning, I think I'm going to change things up a little for the sake of time."

The fox claps her dark brown paws together, and the velvet curtains behind her close shut, concealing the white screen. She walks down the stage's stairs and through the center aisle, stopping at Teddy's row, then turning to the boy and smiling.

"Let's walk and talk, shall we?"

Mrs. Suki turns back toward the center aisle and walks to the exit as Teddy stands up and follows. She arrives at the back wall of the theater then waits for the boy to catch up before pushing through the double doors and leading him into a vaulted hallway. Doors of all different sizes and styles line the hall, each one of them seemingly random and out of place. They continue to walk for a moment before Teddy glances back. He already can't tell which doors are the ones they just exited from.

Mrs. Suki resumes speaking. "I'm sure the dean has already explained to you what we do here at Zarmore, so I won't burn too much more time going over it again as I am only tasked to help you settle in, and that is all, dear. This is a school where you will learn to develop dormant abilities which all human beings possess, however few ever discover. Your first three years of study at Zarmore are dedicated strictly to mastering your basic core skills, while your final three will be focused on your dedicated path."

Teddy opens his mouth to ask a question, but Mrs. Suki continues to talk before he can get it out.

"There are five different paths a student can walk; however, only four of them are of your concern."

"Why not all five?" Teddy asks.

"The elemental paths one can walk are Earth, Fire, Water, and Air. Every human is born with a natural affinity to an elemental path. It is not imperative that you focus on this as a first-yearer, but it should be kept in the back of your mind as you progress through the program."

"Which path am I?"

"That will become more clear as you progress through the program," Mrs. Suki replies as she continues to lead him down the hall.

"What's the fifth path?" Teddy asks.

The fox glances back and smiles. "We're almost at the end of the hall, dear."

He sighs and continues to follow the fox.

"During your first few years, you will learn how to influence your reality by mastering the power of luck, mind control, and predicting the future, just to name a few skills," she continues. "Things happen quicker here at Zarmore. That is to say that this *magic*, or whatever you choose to call it, will take effect almost instantaneously when employed on campus. However, as you move further out into Egaria and beyond, we begin to deal with the concept of time, and therefore you will incur a delay in manifestation. You, being a being who lives on Earth, will often deal with a quite significant one."

They walk past a small black square door that Teddy isn't sure he can crawl through if he tries.

"I have another question," Teddy says.

"Go ahead, dear."

"Why is this place so secret? I mean, why not just let everyone know about this school and their own abilities?"

"It's a strong desire of ours at Zarmore that everyone could know the nature of their true being. However, as you will come to understand, you humans are much more powerful than you believe. If one is to acquire these skills, we must be sure that they are, firstly, learned in a safe and controlled environment, and secondly, that the student will only use said skills for the betterment of *all* life on Earth.

Teddy crosses his arms. "Yeah, I'm sure that jerk who punched me in the face is going to do great things for society."

Mrs. Suki stops and looks back at the boy.

"Mr. Teddy. Oh dear, I am quite aware of what you are referring to and am very very sorry about it. That truly was indeed a horrible incident. One that saddened me deeply to hear about." She adjusts her glasses and looks up, locking eyes with his. "But you must know that type of behavior is categorically forbidden here."

She then turns her head, and the two continue walking down the hall.

"So, is that some type of skill I'll learn to do here as well?" Teddy asks. "That vanish and punch thing, or whatever he did to me?"

Mrs. Suki's beady eyes expand as she glances back toward the boy. "Would you really want to? After all you went through?"

"Uh, I mean, it sucked being on the receiving end but, I guess it looked kind of cool."

Mrs. Suki exhales as she shakes her head. "It appears that Sean Becker has had previous training on several Air attack procedures. None of which were taught to him here at Zarmore, I must say."

"So he's an Air?"

"He is a nothing as are you and as are all students year three and below," she replies, raising her voice slightly.

There's a lapse into silence; then Teddy speaks up.

"So this place is kind of just like a dream as well. I only have to think about something, and it will happen?"

"Are you a fool or just not paying attention, dear? If that's how you think things work here, then please, by all means, create yourself a stick of deodorant, and save my nose from more suffering."

Teddy closes his eyes for a second, then reopens them and purses his lips after realizing nothing changed.

"You see," Mrs. Suki continues. "There is much more to it all than that. The more of which you will learn in your classes. But do know that Sean Becker has been banished from Zarmore, and had it not been for the amount of influence his family holds in Egaria, he would've been sent to the island where he belongs."

"What's the island?" Teddy asks as he briefly sniffs under one of his armpits then looks back up.

"You will learn more about that in time, dear. Now let's carry on, shall we?"

They arrive near a large stone door. Mrs. Suki undoes a heavy latch then slides the door open.

"Stick close," she says as she steps through the doorway and grabs a torch off the wall.

The staircase is wide, and the descent is long. Even with the flame-lit torch in front of him, Teddy can't stop his body from shivering. The further down they go, the colder it becomes.

"Watch your step, dear. The floor can sometimes get slippery down here."

There's a faint drip of water that echoes louder and louder with each step they take. Teddy's bare toes feel like tiny icicles that are on the verge of shattering by the time they reach the bottom.

"Why is it so cold down here?" He asks as he hugs his arms around his body and continues to shiver.

"Hold the questions for a moment, dear."

The cave is about the same size as the castle foyer on the floor, but the tall ceilings are incomparable. More flame-lit torches cover the walls while the drip of water echoes at full resonance. They start to walk in between several rows of wooden bookcases when something stringy falls onto Teddy's face. "Ugh!"

"Shh," Mrs. Suki whispers.

"I think I just ate a freaking spider web."

"Swallow it."

"What?"

"Shh!"

Teddy shakes his head then scowls as he brings the neck of his tank top up to his mouth and wipes his tongue.

They pass through the rows of bookcases then find themselves in front of four hospital-style beds dressed in white sheets. Each bed is neatly made and separated from one another by white curtain dividers. The fox leads Teddy through a clearing on the right, past the beds, and toward the back of the room. She then suddenly stops walking, and Teddy bumps into her from behind. "Sorry," he whispers.

Mrs. Suki doesn't respond.

Teddy looks up and sees why.

There in the back corner, just ten yards in front of them, is some sort of giant of a creature sitting in a steel chair far too small for his body. He appears to be working on something at his desk, although Teddy can't tell for sure as all he can see is the back of the beast's head and his broad back. His fur is white and wooly, and he has blue ears that twitch every so often. The equipment at his desk looks similar to the tools Teddy uses in biology class. The creature picks up one of the glass vials filled with a purple and steamy liquid and brings it closer to his eyes. Teddy is just about to ask Mrs. Suki what this is all about but freezes up when he hears the beast grunt and slam his blue fist onto the desk, nearly splitting it in half.

"Dr. Borut," the fox says softly.

The beast sets the vial down, then jerks around out of his seat and stands up. A loud growl rumbles through the cave causing the hairs on the back of Teddy's neck to stand straight. The creature turns around and faces the two. He stands at least eight feet tall and is wearing an oversized white lab coat that matches the rest of his furry and shaggy body. His eyes are icy blue and piercing behind his safety glasses as he stares down at the boy and the fox.

Dr. Borut takes several steps forward, and the ground shakes beneath his heavy white feet and blue toes. Teddy cringes and lowers his head as the beast now hunches over him. Hot and humid air emanates from behind his large and jagged teeth, moistening and warming Teddy's face.

"Yes, yes, sorry to disturb you, Dr. Borut," Mrs. Suki hurries. "I hope you received my letter this morning explaining that I would possibly be visiting you today with a new student?"

The beast grunts.

"Oh dear, I am very very sorry that you didn't receive that notice! I will follow up with the snails later today."

Borut grunts again and sticks his blue pinky the size of a cucumber down toward Teddy's face, causing him to flinch backwards.

"Yes, you are very busy, doctor. We'll be leaving now." Mrs. Suki swings her head back toward Teddy. "Please shake the doctor's hand, Teddy!"

Teddy arches an eyebrow toward Mrs. Suki, then looks back up at the blue finger dangling in front of his face. He leans backwards, and slowly grips the pinky then shakes it. Borut grunts, then pulls his finger back before marching toward his desk and plopping himself back into the chair. Mrs. Suki claps her paws together and looks back at Teddy. "Very well! You both now have been introduced. Let's leave Dr. Borut to his work, shall we? Hurry on, Teddy." She says as she touches the small of his back with her paw and pushes him toward the staircase.

Once up the stairs and out of the cave, Mrs. Suki slides the heavy door shut again and relatches the lock. She then lets out an audible exhale of air and leans against the stone as she smiles up toward Teddy.

"How will he get out?" He asks.

"Oh, don't worry, sweetie. Dr. Borut rarely ever leaves his cave, and when he does, it's usually for places deeper underground. He's not much one for the heat. Rest assured though; he can get out if he wants."

"So there are more caves like that under Zarmore?" Teddy asks.

Mrs. Suki smiles again. "To say the least, but that is nothing of your concern as a first-yearer. All you need to know right now is who Dr. Borut is and where he is located," she says as she leads Teddy further down the hall again. "He is our in-house doctor here at Zarmore and is extraordinarily gifted in the art of healing. We're very very lucky to have him. The grounds of this campus are enchanted with healing powers. That is to say; if you incur an injury here at Zarmore, the wound should heal within a matter of minutes. However, in the rare cases where that does not happen, we have Dr. Borut."

Teddy thinks about his past experiences at Zarmore while he follows Mrs. Suki further down the hall.

"Our doctor also specializes in all ranges of Time Disorientation Illnesses. If you experience any symptoms of such, do not hesitate to pay him a visit."

Teddy slows his pace and opens his mouth to ask a question, but she starts talking before he can get it out.

"Time Disorientation Illness or *TDI's*, result from crossing into universes or realms where time operates at a different speed, or as in Zarmore's case, it ceases entirely. A few common symptoms include nausea, confusion, loss of appetite, and manic behavior."

"I don't understand though," Teddy says. "Time feels like it's moving just fine right now. How can you say that it doesn't exist here?"

Mrs. Suki sighs as she presses the call-button for the elevator at the end of the hall and then faces Teddy while they wait for it to arrive. "Everything we do here at Zarmore is Earth-centered. Everyone here has ties to Earth, and all our students live on Earth. Therefore, when I speak of timelessness, I'm referring to your reference point as a resident of Earth. So yes, dear, we are moving through time here at Zarmore. There is a past, we are in the present, and we can see that there is a constant progression into the future. However, you are not physically here right now, are you? Your life energies or soul is here, but your body is still on Earth. Do you understand me so far, Teddy?"

He nods his head.

"Your Earth is only one planet out of an infinite number of planets in an infinite number of universes. All those planets are experiencing their own version of time. However, they all do it at their own rate, and it's not always simply a one for one swap in comparison to Earth."

She bangs the call-button for the elevator again. "When you look up into the night sky and see the stars, did you know that you are looking back in time? What you see is how those stars looked perhaps twenty or thirty years ago. That's because that's how long it takes the light to travel from those stars to your eyes. Now, when you travel through the cosmos, as your soul has done tonight to arrive at Zarmore, you do so at velocities around the speed of light. And when this happens, you alter time."

The elevator finally arrives, and Mrs. Suki opens the metal cage and steps onto the creaky wooden platform. After Teddy walks in, she closes the cage and presses a button labeled with the letter "F". She continues to talk as the elevator sputters upwards. "Perhaps another example will help you see it more clearly. Let's say you were to travel to a planet billions of light-years away from Earth and spend a couple of hours there. When you finally decide to return home, you may find that your house and everyone you've ever known and loved are long gone. Each minute you spent on the other planet may have been equivalent to decades on Earth. It all depends on what speed you travel at. The same is true for the opposite scenario. You could live a decade on another planet making friends, having a family, growing old, whatever, then return to Earth with so little time having passed that nobody would have even noticed you left. This is sort of the case with Zarmore. However, this is not due to Zarmore's distance from Earth, per se, as many like to believe, but rather with the enchantments bestowed upon the colony of Zarmore and the portals your soul travels through to get here."

Teddy rubs his forehead. "Enchantments?"

"Yes, dear. Zarmore's location in Egaria presents a formidable risk of time alteration for travelers from Earth. Therefore, to ensure that all the training that happens here has a minimal impact on the student's 'real life' while also maintaining the highest level of secrecy, the Council placed an enchantment throughout the entire colony of Zarmore. This ensures that no time will ever be lost on Earth while a student pursues their studies here. So to sum it up, yes, time is passing here at Zarmore; but in comparison to Earth, not one second is passing. As I'm sure you can understand, time is quite a fragile thing, and we work very hard here at Zarmore to ensure that none of it is lost or damaged during your travels out of body."

"Ok, but why not just let the students study here for an eternity then go back to the real world? No time would be lost, and they could learn everything."

The elevator shakes to a halt, and Mrs. Suki opens the steel cage again and motions for Teddy to exit out and into the hallway. She then turns around and closes the cage as she answers his question. "That would be lovely, dear. However, there is no free lunch when it comes to time manipulation. We have concluded that ten hours per day is the maximum amount of time a human brain can handle being in a state of timelessness before risking serious health issues."

"Ok, uh, health issues?"

"Complete loss of mental faculties, psychotic behavior, coma, and of course, death." Mrs. Suki says as they walk toward a large circular red rug in the middle of the empty foyer. Teddy looks up and sees the stairs that the goblins marched him up the last time he was here.

"How much time do students spend in Zarmore for their classes?"

"Eight and a half hours per day, more or less."

Teddy rubs one of his eyes. "That's pretty close to ten hours. You guys are kind of pushing it, don't you think?"

"As long as you obey the rules and exit through the oak immediately after class, you will be fine, dear. I promise."

"Okk, and what exactly is *the oak?*"

She turns to her left and motions toward the open castle door where Gobo is standing post. Teddy's eyes still haven't adjusted fully from his time in Dr. Borut's cave, and he's forced to squint as the fiery red sun shines down from outside and illuminates the drawbridge. Settled on the other side of the bridge away from the castle is the large oak tree that Teddy saw Ava walk out of during his first day on campus.

"The oak to my left will be your ticket to and from Zarmore from here on out. Every day after school, you will exit through there. To do so, you simply approach the tree and place your right hand over any of the lower hanging branches. Your finger key will be scanned, and the door will open to you. The sensation you'll feel in your marked finger may be a bit *unpleasant* at first, but I assure you that it will subside in time. After that, simply enter and find yourself reunited with your body back on Earth. This is the only exit out of Zarmore.

"So everyone here at Zarmore isn't *really* here? It's just their souls?"

"For the students, they are here, but they are also on Earth. For everyone else you meet here or in Egaria, they are only here. This is their home and their only existence. You appear as real to them as they to you. And this is true because whatever happens to your soul while out of body can have physical consequences to your body back on Earth." She pauses for a second. "And to be frank, your soul is the real you anyway. Your body is just pieces of Earth that you're borrowing which eventually needs to be returned," she says with a grin. "All you need to know though is that you are protected from any harm while studying inside Zarmore's campus. The rest of Egaria and beyond, however, the danger is valid and significant."

"Ok, noted. I'll steer clear of wandering into Egaria."

"As you should! It is strictly forbidden... *for first-year students.*"

Teddy sighs. "Ok, the way you say, *first-year students*, tells me that there's something else you want to say."

Mrs. Suki laughs. "I knew you were smart, Mr. Teddy. Yes, *if* you make it past your first year here, then you will begin to go on some highly secure and monitored field trips to other colonies in Egaria beginning your second year. These trips will be led by a few tutors and our most elite trained team of goblins. Egaria is a beautiful land with many charming and kind creatures. There are pockets of evil, sure, but the only real danger is overstaying your visit and getting lost in time. As much of a risk as that is, we feel that it's one worth taking. Egaria is a land which must be understood firsthand and plays a vital role in what we are trying to accomplish here by training you students at Zarmore."

"And what exactly are you trying to accomplish?"

Mrs. Suki smiles. "To help transform Earth into the kingdom of love, peace, and happiness it was designed to be and already is at its core."

"But what does Egaria have to do with Earth?"

"Quite a lot of questions for a boy who has yet to even put on a uniform."

Teddy sees something out of the corner of his eye and looks down. There's a giant green snail with a blue and silver swirled shell the size of a large dog by his feet. Mrs. Suki taps its back twice with the pads of one of her paws, and the shell opens up, revealing a green backpack wrapped in plastic wrapping. She then grabs the bag and hands it to Teddy before speaking again. "In this backpack, you will find everything you need for your first year here at Zarmore, including your sets of uniforms. Whatever uniform you're wearing once you exit through the oak each day will be what you will be wearing when you return the following school day. The temperature around Zarmore is quite mild all year round, so you may never need the coats. That is unless you want to add a little *pizzazzzz* to your look," she says as she smiles and tilts her head to the side while shaking both paws in the air like a jazz dancer.

Teddy forces a half-smile then looks down at the red carpet beneath him. "Hey, where'd the snail go?"

"Who knows," Mrs. Suki says as she puts her paws back down. "They come and go as they please and only do so when you're not looking at them. I've been here for many many years and still haven't figured out how they do it. Anyway, on top of your pile of clothes is your schedule where you can find the classes for which you are already very very late. Fortunately, we operate with the same twenty-four-hour clock system as on Earth, so there should be no confusion on class duration and time frame. Just know that you are only allowed access on campus through the oak between 3:00 am and 11:30 am London Time, which is equivalent to 10:00 pm and 6:30 am for you in New York. Campus opens at 7:00 am here at Zarmore, which is equivalent to 10:00 pm for you. Campus is officially closed at 3:30 pm, which will also be equivalent to 10:00 pm for you, as no time will pass while you're here at Zarmore. If you fall asleep early before arriving here, you will dream regularly until 10:00 pm. At that point, you will be slingshotted to Zarmore, where you will then enter through the oak. If you fall asleep late, you will show up at Zarmore however many hours tardy you fell asleep. Access is only granted during the weekdays and during these specific allotted times."

Teddy tilts his head. "Uh, can you say that again?"

"You'll figure it out, dear." She rubs the white fur under her chin and looks up toward the vaulted ceilings of the castle foyer. "Well now, I do believe we have it all just about covered. That was quick! Just remember to always follow and respect the orders of the staff and goblins. The jungle located on the other end of Zarmore is strictly prohibited, and you must maintain satisfactory grades in your school back on

Earth as well as here at Zarmore. And lastly, waking another student by knockout or death is categorically forbidden, as is revealing the existence of Zarmore to any persons. These are both considered high crimes and will result in immediate expulsion and a sentence to the island for no less than one lifetime. If a question ever arises, you can find me in Room 826, Tower G. I will also be your history teacher. Now hurry to the rest of your classes, dear. You're late."

The Arena

Teddy watches as Mrs. Suki rides the elevator up and out of sight. He then turns around and walks over to a set of brown leather lounge chairs resting near an old fireplace in one of the front corners of the castle foyer. He sits in the seat closest to the window and pulls the backpack out of its green and slimy plastic wrapping, then sets it on the small table which rests in between the chairs. His hands feel sticky, so he uses the inside seams of his basketball shorts to wipe them clean. He then picks the large and heavy green backpack up off the table and sets it on his lap. The zipper to the main pouch slides open with ease and reveals a large stack of clothes with a golden-colored envelope resting on top. To the front of the envelope reads his name written in cursive green ink, while to the back, a matching thick wax stamp seals it shut. He works to peel off the stamp using one of his thumbnails then carefully pulls out a single sheet of paper, thus revealing his schedule:

Theodore M. Lancaster
First-Yearer

Class Schedule

===================================

Time	Subject	Professor	Room	Tower
07:30 ~ 09:00:	*Egarian History* 100	Prof. Suki	826	G
09:15 ~ 10:45:	*Tuning* 101	Prof. Raldorthorch	001	E
10:45 ~ 11:40:	*Lunch*	N/A	Dining Hall	
11:45 ~ 13:15:	*Augury* 101	Prof. Mun	428	C
13:30 ~ 15:00:	*Physical Training* 1	Prof. Jones	Arena	

He hears the sound of something ticking and notices a large grandfather clock sitting beside the fireplace. Teddy glances up toward it, then back down at his schedule, then back up to the clock—1:41 pm.

"Arena? Mrs. Suki never mentioned that."

Footsteps are sounding off from somewhere above, and Teddy turns his head to the right. There's a tall boy with a faded black haircut and a Zarmore coat walking from the top of the main dual set of stairs down to the foyer. Teddy pushes himself up out of his seat and jogs over to the student, trying to catch him before he reaches the bottom of the stairs.

"Hey, excuse me! Do you know where I can find...?"

"What the hell, Teddy?" The boy says as he looks up, and the two lock eyes.

"Oh crap. Ronnie, right?"

"Yeah, man. That's so weird," the boy says. "I was just talking to the dean about you. Does he know you're here? Because listen, I don't know how you do it, but from what I'm gathering, I don't think it's safe for you to just show up and be roaming around this place. You really should go talk with Dean Spear before one of the goblins finds you."

Teddy smiles, then flashes Ronnie his schedule. "It's all good. I'm a student now."

"What?! How?"

Teddy goes on to explain his meeting with Dean Spear and what happened inside the office and fireplace.

"Jeez, you think that guy would mention that to me during one of my daily interrogations."

"What do you mean?" Teddy asks.

"Dean Spear has been all over me since Sean killed you, and not once did he tell me that you were going to be a student. I literally just walked out of his freaking office too."

Teddy laughs. "Hang on. Nobody *killed* me that day."

"Ok, yeah, maybe too strong of a word, but you sure looked pretty damn dead from my viewpoint. And he would've gotten me too had my brother not jumped in."

"Wait, Calvin fought Sean?"

"I fought Sean," Ronnie says, looking almost irritated. "Cal jumped in to pull me back after I went after the kid."

"You went... after him?" Teddy asks, almost smiling.

Ronnie laughs. "Yes, bro. I got your back."

"Wow... Thanks, man. Sincerely. No one has ever..."

"Don't sweat it," Ronnie says before Teddy can finish. "It was mostly just instinct. I've had my fair share of bullies as well growing up. Plus, from the sound of it, you need all the goodwill you can get. That's the roughest initiation story I've ever heard."

"Oh, with me and the fireplace and Dean Spear? You guys didn't have to do all that?"

Ronnie smiles and shakes his head. "Not like that! My mom was an alumna of Zarmore, so Calvin and I already knew what to expect. No fireplace or office for us though. We just made our decisions, then showed up to the theater and had some goblin clamp our fingers with a metal device."

Teddy shakes his head. "Wow, what the hell. But hang on, so your mom told you about it? Isn't Zarmore supposed to be kept a secret?"

"Alumni parents aren't supposed to talk about it with their kids until, or if, they take and pass the entrance exam. After that, it's ok. Although, I'm not sure how many of them actually follow that rule."

"So was that the entrance exam?"

Ronnie laughs again. "Hell no! Seems you actually lucked out on not having to take that one."

"Well, how about that," Teddy says, looking amused. "So what happens with Sean now? Mrs. Suki said he was banished from Zarmore, but what's to say he doesn't try to come back?"

"He won't be back. I think he knows better than to mess with Dean Spear. Plus, they say his memory got wiped the best it could, which is a lot apparently, and that his finger key was permanently removed. Long story short, we'll never be seeing that kid again."

Teddy scratches his head. "Wiped *the best it could?*"

"Yeah, that was my reaction too. I guess he still remembers a little. Supposedly if someone spends a long enough time here, you can't really erase all those memories. They're too deeply ingrained. So, what they're supposed to do with people like that is send them to the island where they'll live out the rest of their lives as prisoners or something. Apparently, that doesn't apply to Sean though. I guess he's just free to roam around back in his regular life."

"Yeah, what the hell is up with that? Why didn't they send him to the island if that's exactly what they were supposed to do?"

"Beats me. Probably has to do with his parent's influence in Egaria. I hear they're basically treated like royalty out there."

Teddy shakes his head. "Well, at least he's out of here, and I don't have to worry about seeing him again. I have enough problems in my real life as it is. What about you though? Are you getting into any trouble for your part in the fight?"

"I'm good. Dean saw my point of view, and I guess Sean had already built a pretty well-documented reputation of being trouble. Honestly, I think they were looking for a reason to kick him out."

"I can get on board with that decision," Teddy says while reaching back into his pocket for his schedule. "So hey man, you know where this arena place is at? Mrs. Suki never really got around explaining it to me."

"Heading there right now. Looks like we got that class together. You're going to want to change into your uniform before we go out there though. Professor Jones is a pretty chill dude, but I can tell he's not someone you want to make angry."

. . .

Teddy changes in one of the bathrooms on the foyer floor then meets Ronnie by the bottom of the stairs.

"We're going to have to hurry if we want to make it out there before the class heads into the forest," Ronnie says.

"What's happening in the forest?" Teddy asks as he follows Ronnie underneath the dual staircases and through a tall set of stained glass doors.

"We're picking horses," he says with a grin, looking back at Teddy. "Some wild ones roam out by the arena, and if we catch one, it's ours for the rest of our time here at Zarmore during racing seasons."

"Wait, what?"

"You'll figure it out. Just follow me."

Teddy raises his hands then mumbles to himself. "Why does everyone keep saying that?"

Once through the doors, they find themselves in an open courtyard surrounded by ivy walls and brimming with bright green and white rose bushes. A giant statue of a sword-wielding knight riding horseback encircled by a marble fountain that trickles with water highlights the center. Rose petals dance in the soft wind, several of which land and come to rest in the fountain's pool.

The two walk past the statue, and Teddy glances over at a pair of students studying underneath the shade of a small cherry tree by one of the walls.

When they arrive at the opposite end of the courtyard, Ronnie pulls open a pair of glass doors hidden behind ivy and they find themselves back inside a different area of the castle.

They then continue through more halls and down several flights of stairs before arriving in front of yet another tall, however this time wooden, pair of double doors.

"It gets a bit tricky after this part," Ronnie says.

"I don't even know where I'm at right now," Teddy replies.

Ronnie laughs. "Well, stick close then."

He pulls open both doors, and the sounds of the forest greet them. Towering trees nearly as wide as Teddy is tall cast heavy shadows onto the beaten dirt path ahead. Teddy squints while allowing the cool breeze to brush across his face. The smell of pine floods his nostrils, and for a moment, he thinks he's going to sneeze before the urge escapes him.

"It's just a few minutes down this path," Ronnie says as he takes the first step into the forest.

Teddy follows, and the doors to the castle slam shut behind them. Pine cones crack beneath their feet with every other passing step until not before long the density of the trees diminishes, allowing the light from the sun to shine through. Ronnie picks up his pace and points toward a large structure that has just come into view. "That's her."

The arena looks like something Teddy used to see in his history books about ancient Rome. It's a stadium-like structure at least five stories high and is made entirely from stone. Much of it is chipped and discolored, but the basic framework of it all still seems sturdy.

"Holy crap, this place looks ancient," Teddy says as they walk into the stadium underneath a raised iron gate.

"Yeah, the school's been operating for hundreds of years, but there's obviously a lot more to Zarmore's past than they're letting onto," Ronnie says.

Once inside, they find themselves in the spectator area of the arena, where hundreds of rows of marble benches circle and wrap around a U-shaped dirt racetrack that leads in and out of the stadium at both ends. The area in between the track is lush with green vegetation. Several goblins push lawn mowers near its center, filling the air with an aroma of freshly cut grass.

Ronnie looks at his watch. "2:13. Alright, so look, there's a classroom underneath that other iron gate over there on the other side of the arena, but everyone should be coming out this way soon for the horse hunt. They have to exit through the raised gate we just passed under, so we can just wait here and meet them when they come out," he says while taking a seat on one of the marble benches.

"Sounds good to me," Teddy says as he sits down next to Ronnie. "I don't remember if I mentioned it to you guys on my first day here, but the way I actually found myself in Zarmore was by riding a horse from Slaybethor."

Ronnie raises an eyebrow and looks over at Teddy.

"I'm serious," Teddy says with a chuckle. "Her name was Naroshi. She had a snow-white coat, was way stronger than a horse ever needed to be, and was lightning fast. I think she ran off somewhere down here, so I'm sort of thinking, or hoping, that maybe I can find her during this horse hunt."

Ronnie relaxes his expression and looks down out into the arena. "I guess you never know. If that's all true, then I don't see why you couldn't."

There's a short pause then Ronnie speaks again. "Slaybethor though, huh? That place sounds like some sort of twisted medieval pumpkin patch from what I've heard. We studied a little about it in Mrs. Suki's class the first week. Is it really just like a free society of goblins and Egarian outcasts?"

Teddy hesitates for a second, then responds. "Uh, yeah, I guess it seemed *something* like that, maybe. I really wasn't there too long, and from what I've been gathering, there's not much enthusiasm from the community for me to ever return either. Supposedly, I sort of sparked a feud there between some angry farmer and the goblins when I left with Naroshi."

Ronnie laughs. "Well damn, you definitely make your presence known wherever you go!"

"Yeah, unfortunately. So now I have this goblin Caesar on my back who is demanding I find the horse while at the same time a crazy old man who probably wants my head on a stick."

"Well, hopefully this horse hunt today will shine some luck your way and solve both your problems."

A rumbling of murmurs from down inside the stadium interrupts the two's conversation. They both look forward and see around thirty students exiting through an archway on the other side of the arena and walking across the grass in their direction.

"Hey! You were supposed to come straight back to class, little bro!" A boy with black dreadlocks shouts from below with a smile, his voice echoing through the empty stadium. "I'm going to have to send you detention now, young man!"

A few girls walking beside the boy giggle.

Ronnie shakes his head and looks at Teddy. "See what I have to live with?"

The group of students make it across the field then walk up the short set of stairs leading to the exit near where Teddy and Ronnie are sitting. Calvin jogs in front of the group then plops himself next to Ronnie on the marble bench, rubbing his hand in his younger brother's hair while doing so.

"Get off me, man!" Ronnie says as he pushes Calvin away.

"You know I'm just messing with ya, little bro," Calvin says, unable to contain his laughter and revealing a pearly white smile. "I wasn't trying to interrupt your date with... Whoa, Teddy? What are you doing here?"

"Oh, you didn't know?" Ronnie asks. "He's a student here now. I guess he only told his friends that aren't annoying as crap."

Teddy laughs, then rises from the bench, slaps Calvin's hand, and bumps it with a fist. "You guys are deadly with each other. Good to see you again, Calvin."

After several students walk past the boys, a tall man with thin-framed glasses walks up the stairs and approaches them. "Teddy Lancaster?"

"Uh, yes, sir," Teddy says as he turns away from Calvin and looks toward the voice.

The man stands in front of Teddy and sticks out his hand. "I'm Professor Jones. I'll be your teacher for Physical Training this year."

Teddy reaches out his hand and meets the professor's leathery and firm grip. The man appears to be in his fifties or so with a short and trim hairstyle that recedes in the middle. He's about half a head taller than Teddy and has an athletic build. He wears white and green running shoes with black shorts that run up to the middle of his bulging and hairy thighs. His green t-shirt is tucked into his shorts, and his sleeves hang loose over his arms, which aren't as muscular as his legs. Teddy can see he has a few tattoos near his biceps but can't make out exactly what they're of.

"Dean Spear informed me that you'd be joining my class today. We're happy to have you here with us, and you arrived at a great time. Today we're going to go out into the forest and see if any of you students can catch yourselves a wild horse. You'll have thirty minutes to do so, and the students who successfully mount themselves will be allowed to participate in racing season this year and all successive years at Zarmore, if they choose. You missed much of my lectures, so you'll be at a disadvantage, but just know that these horses here in Egaria aren't quite exactly like the ones you'd find roaming around on Earth," Professor Jones says as he winks at Teddy then turns around to face the class that's gathered behind him. "Alright, everybody, let's get out there and see what you kids got!"

Extracurricular

The students gather at the top of a small hill overlooking an open grassy area in between the forest. There's a small pond in its center and a couple of brown horses with black manes drinking water from its source.

"Last things," Professor Jones says atop the hill to the group of students. "No harming the horses and no approaching them from behind. I don't want to be filling out any death paperwork today."

A couple of the students laugh as Jones looks down at his watch and continues to speak. "Alright, your thirty minutes begin... now!"

For a moment, nobody moves. They just look at each other and then back toward the horses as if their professor just spoke to them in some sort of foreign language none of them understood.

"Screw this," Calvin says before raising his fist in the air then screaming and chanting like he's the leader of an ancient tribe about to go on a hunt. The horses near the pond stop drinking and look back toward the boy as he sprints down the hill.

Not too much time passes before half of the class is imitating Calvin. Teddy and Ronnie glance at each other then watch as the horses scatter in different directions away from the water.

"Idiots," Ronnie says.

Teddy notices something in the distance then narrows his eyes, looking past the open area where the kids are running, and deeper into the forest. "Whoa, you see that over there?"

Ronnie tilts his chin up and cranes his neck. "You said that Naroshi horse of yours was white, right?"

"Yup," Teddy says.

"You think...?"

"Only one way to find out."

The two jog down the hill, past the pond, and toward the trees. The majority of the class has already cleared the open area and is still chasing the original two brown horses deeper into the forest. Teddy and Ronnie pass a female student with strawberry blonde hair and freckles sitting cross-legged underneath a tree. Ronnie snickers as he glances back at the girl, who continues to sit with her eyes closed and hands up in a meditative position. The boys then enter the forest and stand in the shade as they watch the two white horses they spotted earlier, who are now eating grass just twenty yards in front of them.

"Alright," Ronnie says. "So, what's our plan here?"

"What do you mean?" Teddy asks as he walks closer toward the animals. "Let's just hop on them."

"Dude!" Ronnie whispers as he grabs Teddy by the arm and pulls him back. "I think we need a little more sophisticated plan than that. You weren't here during the professor's lectures, but from what I gathered, I don't think it's going to be that easy."

"Relax," Teddy says as he frees himself from Ronnie's grip and looks back toward the horse nearest him. "There were no issues the first time I hopped onto Naroshi's back. I'm sure there won't be any today."

Ronnie shakes his head.

"Don't worry," Teddy says as he watches one of the horses walk away from the other and further into the woods. "If I screw this up, it's on me. I'm only going after this one that's eating right here. You're free to try whatever strategy you want on the other horse."

Ronnie sighs. "Alright. You work on Naroshi, and I'll follow the other one. Good luck!" The boy then hunches over and shuffles through the trees out of sight.

Teddy watches him leave, then slowly inches closer to the horse several yards in front of him. "Psst. Naroshi! Hey girl. How's it going? It's me, Teddy. Wow, do I sure have a lot to talk to you about. Nothing bad. It's just been a crazy past couple of weeks, that's all."

He's now just five yards away. The horse maintains its head down as it continues to eat grass.

"Sorry for separating you from your owner and stuff. That guy kind of seemed like a jerk anyway though, am I right? I mean, not like you shouldn't go back to him or something;

because you definitely should, and that's where we're going. It's just that... I don't know. He's kind of throwing a big hissy fit over you and putting a lot of lives in danger and whatnot."

Teddy's standing right next to the horse now. He smiles as he rubs the back of his hand down her soft white mane. "So what do you say? How about we ditch these grouchy goblins, and you and I head back to Slaybethor?"

He presses his hand onto the horse's back as he prepares to prop himself on top but releases pressure when he hears her snort.

"Easy, girl. It's just me. No need to get all flustered," he says as he reapplies pressure on her back and raises a leg in the air. "I'm just going to slowlyyy hop on and..." Before he can finish his sentence, the horse is squirming and shrieking. Teddy's right leg is already over her back, but she refuses to calm down. His body slips toward the right, and he instinctively grabs a handful of her thick white mane with his left hand to prevent himself from falling and pulls himself back up. The horse screeches even louder then looks back at Teddy. Her eyes are jet-black, and she has two large black spots on the right side of her face with a small scar in the center of her forehead.

"Uh, you're not..."

The black in her eyes then melts away, and a pool of fiery neon orange takes its place. Teddy starts to feel like he's staring into the sun and looks in the other direction. "Crap. Uh, sorry, ma'am. I mistook you for somebody else. If you'll excuse me, I'm just going to climb down now and..."

But before he can hop off, he finds himself in a deeper part of the forest he doesn't recognize.

"What the...?"

The horse neighs and writhes her body for the second time before Teddy's scenery changes again.

"Teddy, you got her!" Ronnie shouts. "I didn't even hear you come up. How did you get all the way over...?"

Teddy's scenery then changes again as the horse neighs and twists her body. He hugs his arms around her neck as he tries to orientate himself, but before he can, he's somewhere else.

"Ugh, not fair!" He hears a chubby boy shout near the pond.

The horse starts to run toward the water but then takes a sharp turn and swings the rear of her body back toward the shoreline at the last second, causing Teddy to nearly fall off.

"Look, the new kid caught a shifter!" He hears someone say.

"A what?!" Teddy shouts. But before he can get a reply, he's gone again. This time he reappears near the top of the hill where they all started the hunt. The horse neighs and writhes her body some more. Teddy then hears the slow clap of two hands coming from somewhere behind him. Still being shaken and in a panic, he briefly looks over his shoulder and sees Professor Jones smiling.

"Very impressive, Teddy. I can't remember the last time a student caught a shifter."

Teddy's head whips back and forth as the horse shows no intention of letting up.

"Please... help!" Teddy shouts. "Before she..."

Teddy closes his eyes and prepares for another change of scenery. However, when he reopens his eyes, he finds himself still atop the hill. He looks down to see that the horse has relaxed and is now nibbling on some grass again. Teddy dives off her back and rolls through a patch of weeds. He then pushes himself up to his feet and backpedals away from the horse. His momentum stops when he crashes into Professor Jones. The smiling man grabs ahold of Teddy by the shoulders and prevents him from falling.

"You can relax now, Teddy. She's not going to run away again." The professor says as he points to some sort of small black sticker that's now attached to the horse's rear.

"It's not the running away part I'm worried about," Teddy says as he gathers his feet and moves himself out of the professor's firm grip. "How did you get her to stop? What is that thing?"

"It's called a neutralizer. It calms the horse down and prevents it from shifting to different locations. It's completely harmless. However, the effects only last twenty-four hours. After that, you'll have to reapply a new sticker."

Teddy walks up to the horse as it continues to chomp away at the grass. He leans over and sees that her eyes have returned to their original glassy jet-black color.

A commotion erupts from down the hill. Teddy moves away from the horse and looks to see what's going on.

"Ah, looks like you won't be the only one competing from this class, Teddy." Professor Jones says.

"Wahoooo!" Calvin shouts from atop what appears to be one of the brown horses from earlier. A large group of students is walking behind him and cheering as he darts past the pond and up toward the hill.

A few moments later, another brown horse trots out from the opposite end of the forest. Atop this one is the strawberry blonde-haired girl with freckles that Teddy had seen meditating underneath a tree earlier.

The professor looks down at his watch then cups his hands around the edges of his mouth as he counts down. "Three... Two... One... Time! Everyone, whether you have a horse or not, please return to the top of the hill!"

Teddy looks down at the crowd of students making their way toward the professor and tries to locate Ronnie but can't find him. After most of the class arrives back at the top of the hill, Teddy finally spots a hunched figure walking out of the forest. He's moving slowly and looking down toward the ground. There are no other horses in sight.

"All right, looks like we have mostly everybody here," Professor Jones says. "First off, I just want to express how extremely proud and impressed I am with the effort I saw out of all of you today. Now, not every one of you succeeded in what you set out for this afternoon, but I'm sure there isn't anyone here who can say that they didn't at least learn something today on how they can perform better in the future.

Remember, we do these hunts at the beginning of each school year, and everyone has an equal opportunity for success."

Teddy feels someone brush past his shoulder. "Ronnie!" He whispers.

The boy doesn't answer nor bother to look back at Teddy. He just keeps his head down and squeezes himself more into the crowd of students, who continue to watch as the professor speaks.

"Now, as you can see if you look to my right, we have three beautiful horses tied up to this tree. This goes to say that we have three students in our class who have defied the first-year odds and will be participating in the races this year at Zarmore. I'd like you all to give it up and applaud for your fellow classmates just as loud and proud as you yourself would like to be cheered for had it been you that had captured a horse today, ok? Now come on up, Calvin Whitaker, Victoria Addington, and Teddy Lancaster!"

Teddy's eyes grow larger as he listens to the eruption of cheers. "*Now this feels like a dream.*"

He squeezes his way through the crowd toward the front while students pat him on the back and congratulate him. His cheeks flush red when he turns around and looks at the smiling crowd of boys and girls, all on their feet and celebrating as if he had just scored the game-winning touchdown in the Super Bowl. Calvin smiles, then puts one of his arms around Teddy's shoulder while raising his other in the air and forming a number one sign with his index finger. Teddy looks to his right and sees the blonde-haired freckled girl, Victoria.

She smiles at the crowd of students without opening her mouth, then puts the palms of her hands together as if she's praying and does a slight bow.

"Very well, very well!" Professor Jones shouts over the roar. He smiles as he waits for the applause to diminish, then continues to speak. "Each of the students in front of me have proven that there is not just one way to catch a horse. Nor is there just one way to take charge and create anything you want in this life. You all have skills and talents that are unique just to you, and I urge you to find and cultivate those. However, there is one thing that all three of these students shared in common during the hunt today though. Can anyone tell me what that one thing is?"

"They're all cute!" One girl shouts before sinking back down into the crowd and giggling amongst her friends.

"Um, not the answer I was looking for. But yes, I do believe we have a very handsome and beautiful group of students representing our class this year. Thank you. Now, the answer I was hoping to hear was that they all *believed* that they would capture their horses today. They were confident and never allowed doubt to exist in their mind, not for one second. I want you all to think about that when you're back on Earth later today."

The students nod their heads.

"That's all we have for today. Beginning next class, I want you all to arrive in your gym uniforms instead of your typical Zarmore ones as we will start to introduce and practice some of the more physical aspects of this course."

There's a low rumbling of whispers between the students, but the professor continues to speak anyway.

"The locker rooms are located inside the arena by our classroom. As for Calvin, Victoria, and Teddy, you will spend the second half of every class training with your horses. They will be housed and cared for in the stable located underneath the west gate inside the arena. Prior to the next class, I want each of you to think of a name for your horse as a few staff members and I will be creating the racing schedule over the weekend and posting it on Monday. Ok, have a safe trip back to the oak, everybody. I'll see you all tomorrow!"

. . .

The students disperse and follow the wide dirt path back toward the arena and castle. Teddy congratulates Victoria then waits behind with Calvin by the tree as they try to locate Ronnie. It doesn't take long until they see him walking toward the back of the crowd. Teddy and Calvin do a light jog and catch up to him.

"I don't want to hear it," Ronnie says.

"You don't want to hear what?" Teddy asks.

"Not you, Teddy. My little big brother has something I'm sure he wants to rub in my face."

No one says anything for a moment. They just continue to walk the path until finally, after a minute of silence, Calvin speaks up.

"I'm sorry if I rag on you too hard sometimes, Ronnie. You're my brother and I love you. I hope you know that."

Ronnie raises his head a little but still doesn't say anything. Calvin then puts his arm around his shoulder. "It's still you and me against the world, just like when we were little. That hasn't changed, never will." Calvin looks over and notices Ronnie's trying not to smile, then adds. "Even if you did let a hippie chick capture a horse before you."

Ronnie laughs, then frees himself from under Calvin's arm. "Can someone explain to me how that girl captured a horse?! She wasn't even doing anything!"

"That's what I'm saying, man!" Calvin says. "What happened to you? We were supposed to dominate the races together here."

"I know, I know...." Ronnie says as his smile starts to fade. "I don't think anyone could've caught that horse I was following though. It was way too quick."

"Was it a shifter, too?" Teddy asks.

"I knew you had a shifter! That scared the crap out of me when you popped up out of nowhere in the forest. I'm not sure if mine was though. Her eyes were a pretty insane shade of green, so I guess she could've been."

Teddy slows his pace as he looks over at Ronnie. "Green eyes? Like cyan, neon sort of green?"

"Yeah, that's it."

"That was Naroshi," Teddy says.

"You think?"

"Had to have been. You see where she went?"

"Oh, she went deep in it. I had clear eyes on her one second, then the next she was just a blur of white, and then zoom, gone."

"Who's Naroshi?" Calvin asks as they pass the arena and head through the trees back to the castle.

"I'll explain when we get home," Ronnie says.

Calvin stops walking then sticks his left arm out, causing Teddy and Ronnie to crash into it.

"What gives, dude?" Ronnie says.

"Look," Calvin says.

Ronnie jumps a step backwards. "What the hell is that?!"

There's a giant purple snail with beady black eyes and a green and yellow swirled shell blocking their path.

"It's looking at you," Calvin says.

"No way, man! You're in front," Ronnie replies. "It's looking at you!"

The snail wiggles its tentacles then slides forward toward the boys. Calvin and Ronnie scream and run in opposite directions.

Teddy laughs. "You guys have been here for two weeks and haven't seen one of these yet?"

"I just go to the dining hall and attend my classes!" Calvin shouts. "I'm not here to play safari."

"Come on. He's harmless," Teddy says.

"Alright, you go talk to him then," Ronnie says, still a good ten feet away. "Tell him to slide his slimy self up and out of our way."

"Fine, I think he's looking at me anyway," Teddy says. "Let's see what he's got."

Teddy walks over to the snail and taps the back of its shell twice, just as he saw Mrs. Suki do before. The shell then opens up, and there's a small white envelope wrapped in a plastic bag atop the snail's purple and moist back. Teddy takes out the envelope then throws the slimy bag toward Calvin and Ronnie, causing the two boys to flinch and nearly jump into each other.

"Hilarious," Cavin mutters.

Teddy seems to think so, then looks down at the envelope. Its edges are crumpled, and there are brown splotches of some sort of sticky substance on the face of it. Teddy's name, although hardly legible, is written on the front. He squints and looks at the snail for a second, then proceeds to open the envelope and pull out a letter:

Teddy,

I need you to hurry up and find that horse. The old man showed up at the barn again after you jumped off the cliff and through the portal. I told him I didn't know where you were at, but he wasn't buying it. He said he's giving me 7 days to find you or else... I don't know what he meant by that exactly, but usually, when people say "or else," it's not something great. Anyway, hurry up with it, would ya.

- caesar

P.S. If you're out in Egaria, can you swing by a shoppe and pick me up a case of Mapsy's? All the stores are closed here in Slaybethor due to everyone still being spooked about what happened last night in the barn. You owe me.

P.S.S. The old man prefers to be called Ziruam rather than "stupid hillbilly cyclops". I learned that one out the hard way.

"After I jumped...." Teddy says. "That was a straight shove in the back."

"What kind of secret squirrel farm boy life you living when you're not here?" Calvin asks.

Teddy looks over his shoulder to see that the two brothers have inched closer and are reading the letter over his back. "Nice to see you guys conquered your fear of snails."

"That thing is closer to a Ninja Turtle than a snail," Calvin says.

"And it also slid backwards a little after you grabbed the letter," Ronnie adds as he looks back toward the snail. "Crap! Where'd it go?"

Both brothers jump back as their heads go on a swivel, trying to locate the animal.

"Yeah, they do that," Teddy says as he resumes walking down the dirt path toward the castle.

"Just pop out of existence?" Calvin asks.

"Yup."

"This place is weird," Ronnie says as he taps Teddy's shoulder from behind then points to the right. "It's this way."

"Thanks, man," Teddy says as he alters his direction at a fork in the path and continues into a darker part of the forest.

"So I'm assuming that's your goblin friend you were talking about earlier?" Ronnie asks.

"Yeah, I think I'm kind of screwed. There's no way I'll be able to find Naroshi in this giant forest. I mean, look, I can barely even find my way back to the castle right now. Plus, it's not like we have a ton of free time around here to go on our own quests."

"It's not safe either," Calvin adds from behind the two.

"I'm not worried about the snails," Teddy says.

"It's not just snails you have to worry about," Calvin says as he looks to his left then his right. "Even if they are probably plotting to kill us all at this very moment."

"He's right," Ronnie adds. "Not about the snails, but..."

"Don't act like you weren't scared of that thing too, Ronnie!" Calvin cuts in.

Ronnie shakes his head then continues. "There's a jungle down the mountain and across the valley where some not-so-friendly apes live, apparently. Mrs. Suki didn't explain it to us too much on orientation day, but I know for a fact that we're definitely not supposed to go over there."

"Well, I'm not planning to. Plus, you said you saw Naroshi in these woods, so I don't think I'd bother to check there anyway, even if I could," Teddy says.

"They roam around the castle too," Ronnie adds.

"What?" Calvin and Teddy ask at the same time.

"Yeah, Ava talked about it at lunch last week. She doesn't know exactly why, so don't ask, but she did say that when nighttime comes to Zarmore, some of the monkeys and apes spread out through these forests. It has something to do with them only being able to live in the shadows and some sort of dark force that hovers over the jungle. Then when the sun rises again, they go back into the jungle. That's all I know."

"Where was I when she said all this?" Calvin asks.

"I don't know, man. You were probably bragging about how good of a football player you are back on Earth to some chick at a different table."

"Yeah, I can see that," Calvin mumbles.

"That's strange," Teddy says as they finally reach the double doors at the rear of the castle. He pulls open the one on the right then walks in.

"No, you'd actually be quite surprised, Mr. Tedster. I'm pretty good," Calvin says as he catches the door that's closing behind Teddy and follows him inside. "A lot of people think I can play at the university level. You know, once I get out of secondary school and everything. I'm trying not to get too excited about it though, but I think if I can..."

"Not that," Teddy cuts him off. "The monkeys wandering outside their jungle part. I saw some sort of carving in a tree the second time I hiked up the mountain to the castle. I had no idea what it was then, but now I'm wondering..."

Calvin mutters something under his breath.

"A carving?" Ronnie asks. "A carving of what?"

"It looked like a picture of a spear with an 'X' crossed through it."

"Spear, like "*Dean* Spear?" Ronnie asks.

"That's what I'm thinking," Teddy says. "Maybe there's some sort of bad blood between the castle and the chimps."

"That might explain why they're so uptight about getting us out through the oak tree every day right after class," Ronnie says. "Are you going to tell the dean?"

"I think I have to," he says as they arrive at a split in the hallway. He stops, then turns around and looks at Ronnie. "Ok, I think I'm lost."

Ronnie laughs. "You were going the right way. We just have to follow this hall, then go back up that stupidly tall staircase, swing a left, a right, and then up the middle set of stairs by the portraits. After that, it's a straight shot across the hall and into the courtyard."

"I'll just let you lead."

"You'll eventually get the hang of it," Ronnie replies as he passes Teddy.

They keep relatively quiet as they work to climb the stairs then Ronnie speaks up again. "So what are you going to do about Caesar, the old man, and finding Naroshi? Are you thinking of telling Spear about that as well? He could be able to help."

"I already kind of told him everything when we talked in his office," Teddy says. "Well, at least the part about Naroshi and Caesar. It didn't seem like he found it too concerning."

"You didn't mention anything about the farmer wanting to kill you or the urgent need to find the horse?" Ronnie asks.

"Yeah, no. That part got left out. I don't want him thinking that I'm trouble or some sort of liability to have around. I'm afraid he would just wipe my memory and send me home to get rid of the problem."

"Yeah, I mean that is a possibility," Ronnie says as he pulls open the glass doors to the courtyard.

"I'm just not going to tell him that part," Teddy continues. "I really don't know what I'm going to do about finding Naroshi in seven days though. Thursday is just about over now, and then we can't come here during the weekend. So I basically only have four days to find and return her. And on top of all that, this city of Zarmore is massive."

"I think my professor said that it's a colony, actually," Calvin speaks up. "The campus is called Zarmore, but it's also located inside the colony of Zarmore."

"I don't think Teddy cares for a lesson in Egarian history right now," Ronnie says. "Real lives are at risk here."

"But it means he'll have more than seven days," Calvin says.

"What are you talking about?" Teddy asks.

"Wow, you know what, he's actually right," Ronnie adds as he pushes open the other set of double doors at the opposite end of the courtyard leading back into the castle. "Time moves differently in Slaybethor. For every one day that passes there, thirty days pass on Earth. And since Zarmore is enchanted to be intertwined with Earth's time, you can experience thirty days in Zarmore with only one day passing in Slaybethor."

"Oh crap. That's right, huh? Because when I saw Caesar for the second time, I thought that two weeks had passed, but he told me that it had only been a night."

"What time were you talking to him at?" Ronnie asks.

"Well, we were singing in the evening of the night before, so it was probably around late-morning or early-afternoon the next day when he told me about what happened after I left with Naroshi.

"Whoa, hold up. Did you say you guys were singing?" Calvin asks.

"Not now, Cal," Ronnie cuts in.

"So yeah, probably only ten or so hours passed in Slaybethor, but I experienced two weeks while I was on Earth," Teddy continues. "So one day there equaling thirty days in Zarmore and on Earth would actually make sense."

"So instead of a week, you have seven months," Ronnie says as they walk through the entrance of the castle and across the wooden drawbridge toward the oak."

"But I don't understand how hardly any time passed on Earth during the moments when I was in Slaybethor," Teddy says. "Being that one day there equals thirty days on Earth, shouldn't several days have passed on Earth if I spent a few hours in Slaybethor?"

"Time operates differently depending on if you're actually in Slaybethor or not," Ronnie replies. "Since it's sort of half dream, half real world there, time will appear to slow down on Earth when you're actually in Slay.

Teddy looks over at Ronnie, a confused look painting his face.

"Listen, it's difficult to explain. Just know that while you're in Slaybethor, hardly any time will pass on Earth. And when you're out of Slaybethor, roughly thirty days will pass on Earth for every one day that passes in Slaybethor," Ronnie says.

"How do you know all this stuff?" Calvin asks.

"Hurry up and get out!" A raspy voice shouts from behind them.

Teddy turns around to see Gobo standing next to the castle door in his knight's gear and armed with a spear.

"Quit the chit-chat and get out! All of you! Through the oak!" Gobo shouts.

Teddy shakes his head and looks down. "This guy... But ok, yeah, seven months to find Naroshi over seven days sounds a hell of a lot more manageable."

"Yeah, and don't worry, man," Calvin says as they approach the oak. "We'll help you find her."

"Or give you a hand with this farmer freak if he wants to try anything," Ronnie adds.

"Thanks, guys," Teddy says. "That actually means a lot to me."

"Don't get all emotional on us now," Calvin says. "Alright, you guys ready to get out of here? I'm starting to feel Gobo's eyes burning a hole through the back of my head."

"Let's do it," Ronnie says as he places his right hand on one of the lower branches of the oak. The large door with the bronze lion head knocker creaks open, and a purple mist accompanied by a melodic whistle sings from inside. Ronnie then lifts his hand from the branch and steps back.

"Is that the sound of a flute?" Teddy asks.

"Yeah, it means you're good to go," Calvin says as he places his hand on the same branch that Ronnie was previously. "Once you hear it, you're cleared to step in." The whistle sings again, and Calvin releases his hand. The brothers then turn their eyes toward Teddy.

"So I just... place my hand on it?" He asks.

Ronnie and Calvin look at each other and smile. "Yeah, it might hurt since it's your first time," Ronnie says. "But it'll smooth out after a few rounds."

"Uh, ok. Well, here goes nothing then," Teddy says as he places his right hand on the same branch Calvin and Ronnie had. A jolt of pain immediately shoots through his marked ring finger then travels through the rest of his body. He clenches his eyes along with his teeth as he hears the laughs from the brothers. The pain is similar to what he felt inside the dean's office, but this time only lasts a second or two before it's gone. The melodic whistle then sounds off from inside the tree, and Teddy lets go of the branch.

"Good job," Calvin says as he walks through the door and into the tree. "I really didn't want to watch someone cry again like I had to during Ronnie's first time. See you tomorrow!"

"Pfft, I didn't cry," Ronnie says as he watches his brother's body disappear into the mist then follows behind him. "There was something in the air, and I have sensitive eyes... Later, Teddy!"

Ronnie takes a few steps into the mist and then is gone as well. Teddy turns around. A group of older students is making their way out of the castle entrance and heading toward where he's standing. He turns back to face the oak, inhales a deep breath in, then exhales out and takes a step through. The purple mist feels cool and oddly familiar as it brushes against his skin before eventually covering his body whole. His body relaxes, and any previous apprehension or tension he had just falls off, like old useless scabs. His eyelids then droop heavy, and legs feel weak. There's a bright purple flash, and he closes his eyes. That's the last he remembers.

Detention

Teddy rolls over and hits the snooze button on his phone—7:00 am. A weak groan escapes his lips as he rolls onto his back again and stretches his arms overhead. There's a light breeze blowing in through his open window, and he can already feel that it's going to be a hot day. He closes his eyes and yawns as the memories suddenly pour back into consciousness, causing him to cough and nearly lose his breath.

"Oh crap!" He shouts as he sits up and throws his blankets to the side. "That actually happened."

He goes through his morning routine of getting dressed, brushing his teeth, and making his bed. He then picks up his skateboard, goes downstairs, and grabs a Frosted Blueberry Pop-Tart from the pantry. Usually his mom leaves him a note on the fridge to read, and today is no different:

Good morning sweetheart,

Please preheat the oven to 350 degrees F when you get home from class. I'm cooking meatloaf tonight. Also, you left your dirty dishes in the sink last night. I washed them, but I'm not going to do it again next time. Oh, and please remember to make your bed this morning! Seriously, Teddy. How many times must I tell you?

Have a nice day!

Love,
mom

Teddy shakes his head then walks toward the front door. He snags his black backpack off the coat rack and exits the apartment.

Although he didn't get much sleep last night, he feels generally upbeat and motivated throughout the morning. Then lunchtime arrives.

"They're out of cookies at the counter, so I guess I'll have to take yours," Jeremy says as he walks up to Teddy and his empty table.

"Hey! Come on, man!" Teddy shouts as he stands up and reaches toward the cookie trapped within the clutches of the red-haired boy's strong grip.

Jeremy pushes Teddy back into his seat with his left hand then bites into the chocolate chip cookie he's holding in his right. "Sit back down, idiot. You're not going to do anything. Don't make me embarrass you again today."

He's right. Teddy isn't going to do anything. He watches as Jeremy walks back to his table and high-fives a couple of friends who hardly try to contain their laughter. Teddy then puts his head down and returns to eating what remains of his lunch.

His mood and wakefulness are both on a steady decline throughout the rest of the afternoon. The last class of the day is biology, and he's dreading the idea of trying to write a report for which he's completely unprepared. He sits down at the same empty table as yesterday and pulls his class binder and a pencil out of his backpack. He then tosses the supplies onto the table and sighs.

"Jeez, try not to look too excited there, Teddy," Kristi says as she pulls up a seat across from him and sits down.

"Oh, hey Kristi," Teddy says with a weak smile. "Sorry, I'm just a little..."

"Out of it," she says. "That's what you told me yesterday. Have you ever tried sleeping at night? I think I read somewhere once that it helps."

Teddy tries not to smile. "Interesting theory. Maybe I'll test it out sometime. So, about the report. I didn't really get too much into preparing for..."

"Say no more. I got us covered."

"What do you mean?"

Kristi starts talking in some sort of old gangster Italian accent. "I said, ya ain't got nothin' to worry about, Teddy."

"What? Why are you talking and looking at me like that? I don't get it."

"Oh, you're no fun!" She says as she throws three stapled pieces of typed paper on the table.

Teddy picks up the small stack and leafs through them. "You did the report?"

Kristi smiles.

"Really?" He asks. "How? We hardly had time to make any observations.

"What can I say? I got skills."

"Teddy laughs and shakes his head. "You're awesome. That was just another thing at this school that was stressing me out."

"I knew it was. That's why I did it."

"Well, I don't know what to say. Thanks again. So, what are we supposed to do now for the rest of class?"

"I don't know. Chill? Text? We'll just tell the teacher we worked on and finished it together after class yesterday."

"Why are you being so nice to me?"

"Why would I be anything else?"

"I don't know. Most people just don't usually seem to do favors for others unless they want something in return."

"Look, school has always come easy to me. Don't overthink it, ok."

Teddy smiles, then looks down toward the floor. "Ok, yeah. Cool."

"So tell me, did you run across your arch-enemy again today? I hope he didn't give you another Gatorade bath."

Teddy goes on to tell her about the cookie incident at lunch.

"Ugh, what a jerk! Tell you what, why don't you come sit with me out by the picnic tables next Monday during lunch. I'm usually just out there studying by myself anyway. It would be nice to have some company to chat with for once."

Teddy feels his cheeks flush red, then ducks his head low and pretends to have a coughing fit, hoping she hasn't already noticed.

"Whoa, you ok there, Teddy? I didn't think the thought of eating lunch with me would repulse you that much."

After a few moments, Teddy feels his face return to a normal color and looks back up. "Sorry, I don't know what that was all about. Um, yeah, I guess I could come out there and keep you company."

She laughs. "Great!"

For the remainder of class, they pretend to study the textbook while secretly watching a series of "cat fail" videos from underneath their desk on Kristi's phone. Teddy's upbeat mood from the morning has returned and looks as if it's there to stay. When the bell finally rings, Teddy packs up his supplies and says goodbye to his lab partner. He's halfway out the door when he feels his phone vibrate. He pulls it out of his pocket, then turns the corner and walks toward the exit at the end of the hall.

REMINDERS	now
Detention @ 3:35 today	

"Son of a..."

The detention slip he received for arriving tardy to English class yesterday had completely slipped his mind. He does a one-eighty and moves back through the hall.

Teddy arrives in the classroom where detention is being held at precisely 3:35 pm.

"Sign the roster and take a seat," The skinny middle-aged man at the front of the class says as Teddy walks through the door. "No talking. No cell phones. No sleeping. You're free to leave when the bell rings."

Teddy signs the roster then takes a seat in the back-left corner of the class. For the most part, the room is empty. There are two basketball players on the other side of the same row whispering and chuckling about something amongst each other and a few goth kids grouped around the middle, playing a game of hangman. Teddy sighs, then leans the back of his chair up against the wall and lets his mind drift.

It feels like every few seconds his gaze wanders up to the round clock hanging above the blackboard at the front of the class. The minutes soon feel like hours, and his lack of sleep last night finally seems to be catching up to him. Around 4:00 pm, he notices the teacher in the front of the class must be feeling the same, as his head is now tilted backwards, and a low gurgling snore emanates from deep inside his throat. Teddy looks around the room and sees that a couple of the other students have fallen asleep as well. He finally decides to risk it and lets his eyelids rest... just for a minute or two.

. . .

"I already told you this morning; we haven't received any new shipments today! Until things calm down and our drivers feel that it's safe enough to travel and pick up orders again, we will be out of Mapsy's," an older female goblin wearing an antiquated white dress and a pair of oversized glasses says from behind the counter.

"A bunch of cowards! You know that?" Caesar shouts at the proprietor. "They move to Slaybethor for a couple hundred years and completely forget about what makes us goblins! If their ancestors could see them now..."

Teddy's sitting on a small wooden bar stool at a table next to the only window in the building. Lights to the low hanging and wobbly ceiling fans flicker off and on while a dusty radio plays some classic rock and roll on the rusty granite countertop. Teddy looks over toward the rest of the sitting area and catches a glimpse of a short and furry creature rushing out the door. He then looks over to his right and sees a couple of goblins with grayish-brown hair playing a game of chess and returning his gaze.

"You got a traveler, Miss Butts," one of the men says as he slides a chess piece across the board, then taps a timer and looks at the goblin sitting across from him. "Your move, old man."

The female goblin behind the counter seems confused for a second, and then her eyes expand when she sees Teddy. She runs into the back and grabs a wine glass and a menu, then rushes over toward the boy. She lays the menu out in front of him and sets the empty glass on the table. "Welcome, welcome, welcome, traveler! What type of wine can I get you started with?" Or perhaps some steak? Actually, we're out of steak.... But we do have Animal Crackers and sardines!"

She picks up the wine glass and cleans off some of the dust with her dress. "You know what, I'll just bring out a tray of our finest delicacies, and you can decide from there! We accept rubies, diamonds, gold, or anything else you clever travelers can pull out of the air."

She smiles then runs back behind the counter and into the kitchen.

"Teddy, Teddy, Teddy," Caesar says as he smiles and walks toward him. "I knew I could count on you, boy. So, where's our horse? You got her tied up out front?"

Teddy rubs his eyes. He's still trying to process what's going on.

"Why am I in Slaybethor?"

"Uh, to deliver my horse, I hope."

"No, that's not it... Is this a... Yeah... This is a dream. Well, not like a normal one but... nevermind. Caesar, I'm really sorry, man, but I have to go. I don't have the horse yet, but I'll find her. I promise."

"What are you talking about?! Then why are you here? Do you at least have my Mapsy's?"

"I don't know. I'm in detention right now, and I guess I fell asleep. I really can't afford to get caught and be in trouble again."

"You've gotta be kidding me," Caesar says as he raises his short arms in the air and walks back toward the counter.

"Sorry, Caesar, I'll try and write!" Teddy says as he closes his eyes and focuses on waking up.

When his eyes reopen, he finds himself in the same spot as before. Caesar is standing in front of him while clapping his paws together. "Bravo, kid. Doing Zarmore proud."

"What the...?" Teddy closes his eyes and tries again.

When he opens them, he sees his surroundings still haven't changed. "Why can't I wake up?!"

"Not my problem," Caesar says as he walks toward the saloon doors, then pushes them open and exits the tavern.

Teddy stands up out of his chair and hits his head on the ceiling.

"Ugh."

He then lowers his head and almost has to get on his knees to avoid the ceiling fans as he follows Caesar out the doors and onto a sunlit dirt road.

"Caesar!" Teddy yells.

His voice resonates loud and clear through the deserted street. Teddy brings his arms closer to his body and starts to shiver as he continues following the goblin. He's never seen this part of Slaybethor before. Colorful wooden shacks with rusty tin roofs line both sides of the road. They all stand not much taller than Teddy himself, and each one appears to serve a different purpose. He reads the signs as he passes them by:

Pub.

Barbershop.

Disco.

"*Maybe goblins and humans have more in common than I thought.*"

Sneaker Snacks.

Fight Club.

Boot Buffet.

"*Maybe not.*"

Teddy puts his head down as the wind kicks up and a flurry of dust rushes toward his face. He calls out to Caesar again. "Listen, man. I'm sorry! I'm going to find Naroshi, believe me. My life is in just as much danger as yours. I just need a little more time."

Caesar stops and turns around. "What about the Mapsy's?"

"Dude, I don't even know what that stuff is, even less where to buy it!"

Caesar looks away, then brings a paw to his chin. "Yeah, they probably wouldn't even sell it to you, come to think of it."

"So, are we good?" Teddy asks.

Caesar hesitates for a moment, then smiles. "Yeah, we can still be friends, Teddy baby." He forms his paw into a fist and raises it toward the boy.

Teddy returns the smile, then makes a fist of his own and bumps it against Caesar's. "Cool. So why can't I wake up?"

"Like I told you before. Half dream, half real world here. Sometimes your little sleep magic works. Other times it doesn't. The closer you get to Egaria, the more real life gets."

"Ok, so, how...?"

"You popped up pretty deep in Slaybethor today. We're only about thirty minutes from Egaria's border right now. If we head back toward the countryside, you should be able to wake up. I would let you use my motorcycle, but I think you're too big."

"So we're walking?"

"We're walking. But it's not too far. All we need to do is go..." Caesar stops and squints his eyes.

"Go... where?" Teddy asks.

"Shut up," Caesar says.

"Uh, what happened to us being friends again?"

"Shut... Up."

"What's going on?" Teddy asks.

"He's coming," Caesar replies. "Get back in the tavern... Now!"

"What are you talking about? Who's coming? I don't see anybody."

"The freaking cyclops farmer that wants to kill us. Now get back inside! Tell Miss Butts that Ziruam is coming and she needs to hide you."

Teddy looks down the road where Caesar is staring. There's a small cloud of brown dust meandering in the distance, but besides that, Teddy doesn't see anything alarming."

"I don't think anyone is coming, Caesar. Maybe you're just stressed out, or..."

Caesar turns around, then jumps up and grabs Teddy by the collar of his shirt. The boy falls to his knees and meets the gaze of Caesar's deep and dark black eyes. "Goblins can see things far beyond what a human can ever even dream of. Now get inside. If he sees both of us out here together, we're dead."

Caesar releases Teddy's collar then turns back toward the dust.

"Ugh," Teddy grunts as he works himself back up from his knees and runs toward the tavern. He then lowers his head and pushes through the creaky saloon doors. Miss Butts is carrying a silver tray of food out from the back kitchen.

"I was worried you left, young man. Look here. I have a wide variety of cuisine for you to choose from."

"I need you to hide me," Teddy says.

"Excuse me?" Miss. Butts replies.

"Uh, Zumbum is coming."

"Who?" She asks. "Is that some friend of yours? Does he have rubies as well?"

"No! Zimbomrom... or Zir... Zirgothrop! No... Damn it. What was it?"

"Ziruam is coming," Caesar says as he pushes through the saloon doors.

"Oh my!" Miss Butts shouts.

Chess pieces go flying as the two older goblins stumble out of their seats and grab their canes resting against the table. They shuffle over toward the exit, and then before walking out the doors, one of them turns around back toward the group. "We were never here."

Caesar shakes his head then directs his attention toward Teddy. "Get behind the counter!"

"Yes, dear," Miss Butts says. "Hurry, hurry! Get underneath here, and I'll stand in front! Caesar, you take a seat there and just act natural."

"That would be a lot easier if you guys could keep your inventory in stock."

"Oh, would you just shut up about the Mapsy's already!"

Teddy moves to under the bar and lays himself flat, pressed between the wooden front wall of the counter and the sides of Miss Butt's furry legs. A damp mop and a dirty iron skillet rest by his face.

"I think I'm going to barf," Teddy says.

"Shut up!" Caesar shouts. "He's coming."

A few moments pass before Teddy hears the saloon doors creak open.

"Pardon me, sir," Miss Butts says. "But this area of town is really only designed to accommodate goblins. Your capital is certainly welcome. However, I feel you would be more comfortable around your own type in the main district. It's really not too far away from here. You just need to..."

"Hi, Caesar." The old man says. "I thought after our little talk earlier today that you would be more motivated to find Teddy and my horse."

"You told him my name?" Teddy whispers.

Miss Butts kicks him in the stomach.

"Can a goblin grab a bite to eat, Ziruam?" Caesar says. "Jeez. And what are you doing in this part of town anyway? Don't you have some cows to milk or something?"

Ziruam laughs. "You goblins always have been known for your sarcasm. No, you're right. I usually do avoid this area of town. However, a young goblin approached me in my stable just a few minutes ago. He said a boy matching the description of Teddy was here."

"Michael," Miss Butts grumbles.

"What was that, ma'am?" Ziruam asks.

"Sorry. I had something in my throat," she replies.

"Listen, Ziruam," Caesar says. "I've been here for the past twenty minutes, and I promise you that no human has come through. Goblin's honor."

"Hmm... Well, I guess that young goblin lied to me and I should just get going then, huh," the old man says.

"Yup, that's probably your best bet," Caesar replies. "I'll let you know if I see anything suspicious."

Teddy hears footsteps moving away, then the saloon doors creak open. He exhales and prepares himself to move out from under the bar counter but stops when he hears someone walk inside.

"Or perhaps I should just take a look around and see for myself," Ziruam says.

"No, no, no! I don't think that's necessary," Caesar replies.

"Oh, please. No need to stand up, Caesar," Ziruam says. "With a goblin's honor and all, I'm certain I won't find anything."

"Caesar, look out!" Miss Butts shouts.

Something that sounds like a laser gun shoots off, and a couple of wooden tables crash against the wall.

"Oh my!" Miss Butts screams again.

"Oh hush, you old hag," Ziruam says. "If I wanted to hurt him, I already would have."

"Well, how about you adjust your pirate patch and watch where you're pointing that thing then, you overgrown piece of..." Caesar shouts before calming himself down. "Listen. Ziruam. How about you and your super neat little wooden staff there go outside and stretch your legs for a bit. I'll walk around in here and double-check to see if there are any naughty boys hiding in this establishment. Sound good?"

"Ah, you're too kind, Caesar," Ziruam says. "But I'm sure I can make some room."

There's another boom and a crash.

"Oh my! Those ceiling fans took forever to install...." Miss Butts says.

"You know, it's funny," Ziruam says as he approaches closer to the counter. "All this commotion going on, and you haven't moved a muscle."

Miss Butts clears her throat. "I'm not sure what you mean, sir."

"Oh, but I think you do," he replies.

He takes two more steps toward the counter. The old man can't be more than a foot away now.

"But sir, why would I move? You're quite large and very intimidating. I'm not sure there is much I can do to stop you."

Ziruam laughs then taps his staff on the granite countertop. "Yes, but with so many objects flying through the air, one would at least expect someone to duck for cover. Even our mighty Caesar here tried to hide underneath a table. But you, a poor old goblin standing right next to a hard-surfaced counter, and you don't move."

Miss Butts stutters, "Si... siir, like you said, I'm an... ol... old woman. Plus, there's no room under there."

"Is that because there's a boy hiding underneath?"

"Of... of course not!" She shouts.

"Great. Why don't I just take a little peek for myself then."

Teddy can now see the old man's boots walking past the side of the counter. He clenches his eyes shut and scrunches his body tighter into the fetal position as his heart pounds so hard against his chest, he's sure Ziruam can hear.

"Wait, no! There he is!" Miss Butts shouts. "Behind you! Out the window!"

Teddy opens his eyes and sees the boots turn in the opposite direction. A furry paw with painted red nails then reaches underneath the counter. Miss Butts grabs hold of the dirty iron skillet with both paws then twists her body backwards. "Sorry Teddy, I hope this doesn't kill ya," she whispers.

When he looks up, the base of the skillet is flashing toward him. He closes his eyes then feels a heavy thud across the side of his face. His head bounces off the front wall of the counter, then slides down onto the wooden floor and next to a moist mop. His vision gets blurry, and voices are screaming. He tries to lift his head, but it's too heavy and crashes hard onto the floor. Then it gets quiet, and everything goes black.

Restricted

Teddy awakes, gasping for air. "Miss Butts!" He shouts.

The teacher in the front of the class wakes up mid-snore and nearly falls out of his chair. His head darts left to right as he tries to locate the source of the noise. He then calms down and fixes his attention onto Teddy. "You," he says as he points at the boy. "Detention again. Monday after school."

A few of the other students laugh while another imitates him. "*Miss Buuuuutttsss.*"

Teddy sinks into his chair then looks up at the clock—4:03 pm.

The bell rings about thirty minutes later. Teddy grabs his backpack, goes outside, and skates home. The postman is in front of his mailbox when he arrives. "Michelle Lancaster live here?" The pot-bellied man asks.

"Yeah, that's my mom," Teddy says.

The postman hands Teddy a small stack of mail then goes back on his way.

Teddy walks inside and notices his mom is already in the kitchen. He sets the mail on the small table by the coat rack and tries to walk upstairs without being noticed.

"Why are you just now getting home?" She yells. "Did you not read my note this morning?"

Teddy stops midway up the staircase. "Sorry, mom. I had detention."

"You had *what?!*" She marches out of the kitchen and into the living room, still in her light blue scrubs from work. Her hands are covered in raw meat, and she looks as if she hasn't slept well in weeks. There are dark bags under her eyes, and her brown hair is tied up in a loose bun. The sun glaring through the window makes her squint, accentuating the light wrinkles on the sides of her eyes.

"Yeah, I arrived tardy to class the other day."

"But you've been so good at going to bed early. What's going on? Are you not sleeping well?"

"No, mom. I am. I just... I was just late, that's all."

Water boils over a pot in the kitchen producing a loud sizzling sound. "We'll talk about this at dinner," she says, then turns around and hurries back into the kitchen.

It's seven o'clock when he finally finishes eating his meatloaf and talking with his mom. He brings his plate to the sink, washes it, then goes upstairs and crawls into bed. He usually doesn't try to sleep this early, but he wants to go back and see if they're ok.

He closes his eyes and focuses all his intention on Slaybethor as he drifts to sleep. When he awakes, it's 9:34 pm.

"*Did I make it?*" He wonders.

He sits up and stares at the shadowy image of himself in the mirror across from his bed. Cool air drafts through his open window, and a couple of dogs bark in the distance.

"*I don't even think I dreamed.*"

He sighs, then slides back down, rests his head on the pillow, and closes his eyes. It isn't as easy for him to fall asleep the second time around. He tosses and turns up until around 2:00 am before he finally manages to drift off.

His body feels at ease as a cloud of purple sweeps over him. He raises his eyelids and watches while the door to the oak creaks open and the mist slowly dissipates, revealing a light blue sky and a sunny day.

"I don't know what the dean sees in you," Gobo says as Teddy exits the oak and steps onto the wooden drawbridge.

"Good to see you too, Gobo."

"Dirty, ill-mannered, and now tardy," the goblin continues as he spits out the side of his mouth into the moat beneath the bridge.

"Come on. I'm not looking that bad today, am I?" Teddy asks as he straightens his green plaid tie and continues to walk across the drawbridge toward the open castle door. "I was only dirty those other times because I was coming from Slaybethor."

"Whatever. Get to class."

Teddy stops for a moment then looks over at the goblin. "Hey, do you ever talk to your brother Caesar?"

"Excuse me?"

"Your brother, Caesar, do you ever..."

"Shut up!" Gobo shouts as he slams the butt of his spear into the ground. "Who told you that clown was my brother?"

"Um... He did. He and I are friends, actually. I just ask because I heard that some bad stuff is happening in Slaybethor right now, and I want to make sure he's alright."

Gobo stares at Teddy for a few seconds then growls as he reaches into his pocket and pulls out a crumpled piece of paper. "If you would show up on time, you would have been briefed," he says as he throws the ball of paper at Teddy. "Now, get to class."

Teddy reaches down and picks the paper up off the drawbridge, then walks through the castle door. He sits in one of the leather chairs next to the fireplace in the corner of the foyer and unwrinkles the document:

Zarmore Academy
The Office of Dean Spear
Zarmore, Egaria

September 22nd

MEMORANDUM FOR ALL FACULTY AND STUDENTS

FROM: Dean Spear

SUBJECT: Slaybethor Travel Restrictions

As of 0130 on September 22nd, all faculty and students are hereby restricted from traveling to the border city of Slaybethor. Finger keys have been updated to not allow access for students, and immediate termination will be imposed on all faculty members caught traveling in said zone.

In the past twenty-four hours, there have been a series of attacks carried out by an individual who goes by the name of Ziruam. His target victims have been goblins, but there are reports that he is looking for humans as well. The motive behind these attacks is still unknown.

Slaybethor resident, Nancy Butts, has been reported missing. While a former Egarian citizen, Caesar Luna, has been brought into custody for questioning. Any suspicious activity or information regarding these incidents should be reported immediately.

H. Spear

H. SPEAR, Zarmore Academy Dean

. . .

"Wait, so you're saying that you were in **Slaybethor** when that goblin chick got kidnapped?" Olivia asks as she spreads more grape jelly onto her toast.

"I think the official term is goblinapped, Olivia," Ava says.

"Her name is Miss Butts, and I already told you that I wasn't there for that part," Teddy says. "She knocked me out and woke me up before all that went down. She could be dead for all I know."

"Well, at least she was smart enough to do that," Ronnie says. "Who knows what would've happened if that Ziruam guy would've caught you."

"Yeah, you don't know much about what it's like to catch something, huh, Ronnie?" Calvin says.

"Keep it down, junior," Ronnie replies. "We're trying to have a grown-up conversation over here."

"Here we go again," Olivia says as she looks toward Ava.

"You seem to forget that I'm older than you, *little bro*."

"By ten months, and you're shorter," Ronnie says.

"By one inch, dude!"

"Two."

"Alright, guys, relax!" Ava says, then looks toward Teddy. "So what's up with your friend Caesar? You think he's working with this Ziruam guy?"

"No way, Caesar hates him," Teddy says. "I don't understand why they arrested him though. Or even who arrested him, actually. I didn't think Slaybethor had a police force."

"They don't," Ava replies. "But if someone calls in and the situation seems bad enough, Frostlepeak will send a squad to check it out."

"Frostlepeak?" Teddy, Calvin, and Ronnie all ask in unison.

"It's another colony in Egaria," Ava says. "It's located high in the mountains and is the closest city to Slaybethor. They don't have a large population, but their warriors are fierce. Imagine Gobo but ten times bigger and ten times meaner."

"Yiikes," Calvin says.

"Yeah," Ava replies. "So, are you going to tell Dean Spear?"

"Tell me what?" A deep voice arises from behind them. Dean Spear is holding a piece of carrot cake on a shiny white plate and appears to have been heading toward the exit before stopping behind their table.

The students gasp then straighten themselves in their chairs. "Sorry, sir, I didn't see you there," Ava says. "You usually don't come down..."

"Yes, yes, Miss Bailey, I usually do not come down to the dining hall during the student's lunch hour. However, I've had quite a lot to deal with today and wanted to enjoy a piece of cake. Now, what is it that you need to tell me?" The dean asks as he looks toward the group.

"Uh..." Teddy begins.

The dean slices through the white frosting on the surface of the cake then scoops it up with a fork and brings it to his mouth.

"Uh, I wanted to tell you that... um..." Teddy says as the dean chews and looks toward the boy. "I saw something strange in the forest the other day. There was a carving on a tree with a picture of a spear crossed out by an 'X'. I just thought you should know that maybe someone is looking to hurt you or something. I don't know."

The dean smiles then proceeds to laugh. "I am aware of those markings, and there is no reason to be concerned." He swallows the piece of cake in his mouth then wipes the corners of his lips with a napkin. "There's a small group of apes that believe if I wasn't in charge here that they would be ruling all of Zarmore. And I can assure you that is far from the truth. Back after the chimp uprise last century, I signed a treaty with their current leader, Kortan Chaquarius III. They don't bother us in the light, and we don't bother them in the dark. It's natural for a few members of their population to still be resentful, but it is nothing I'm worried about. All students are safe while here on campus. I promise." He looks back down at his plate. "Now, was that all you wished to tell me?"

"Uh, yes, sir. Thank you," Teddy says.

"Very well," Dean Spear says. He smiles, then scoops up the remaining piece of cake with his fork and walks toward the exit. "Have a wonderful day."

They wait until he's out of earshot before talking again. "Why didn't you tell him that you were in Slaybethor last night?" Ava asks.

"I just got here, and I'm not trying to get wiped already. You think he wants a horse thief in his academy?"

"Hmm, I don't know Teddy. He might be able to help," Ava says.

"I'm not getting kicked out of here," Teddy says. "I won't let that happen."

The bell rings, and students start to leave their tables and scatter throughout the dining hall.

"Ok, Teddy," Ava says. "I just worry, you know."

He smiles. "It'll be fine."

"So what class you got next, Teddy?" Ronnie asks.

"Let me check," he says while pulling his schedule out from his pocket. "Looks like I have Augury with Professor Mun."

Ava snorts. "Good luck!"

"Why do you say it like that?" Teddy asks.

"You'll see!" She says as she tosses her backpack over shoulder and heads toward the exit. "At least Olivia will be there with you for moral support. See you Monday, guys!"

He waves goodbye then looks toward Olivia. "I thought you were a second-yearer. What are you doing in Augury 101?"

"Oh, you know, I'm just pretty dumb," Olivia says. "I have to retake it."

"Don't fall into her trap, Teddy," Calvin says. "She's the in-class super nerd there. Tutor/teacher's aide."

"Ugh!" Olivia says as she smiles and pushes Calvin. She then looks back toward Teddy. "We should probably head over there now though. Professor Mun usually likes to begin class early, and you really don't want to start out on his bad side."

They all walk toward the exit, and Teddy glances over his shoulder at the two brothers. "What about you guys?"

Calvin is still laughing at Olivia's push attempt, so Ronnie speaks up. "We have the same class but with a different professor."

"Ah, lame," Teddy says as they walk through the open passageway leading to the main foyer.

"Yeah, man. We'll see ya in PT though!" Ronnie says.

"Yup. Later, guys!" Calvin adds as he and Ronnie turn the corner and mix within a crowd of students.

Teddy and Olivia turn in the opposite direction toward the elevator. Olivia scans Teddy from his belt up to his face then smiles. "Much better shirt today."

Full Moon

The professor is already into his lecture when they walk through the door. Teddy avoids looking in the voice's direction then sits at an empty desk toward the back of the room next to a curved window while Olivia takes a seat in the front by the blackboard facing the students. The classroom doesn't seem much different than any of his at Cameron Creek. Neatly filed rows of individual desks line the room while the familiar expressions of less than eager students fill their seats. Teddy reaches down into the front pouch of his backpack and pulls out a notebook and pencil. He sets the supplies on his desk then looks to his right out the window. The class is located in one of the taller towers and permits him a chance to look down upon the valley from a view which he's never seen before. He narrows his eyes and tries to see if he can make out anything past the blackness of the jungle in the distance, but it's no use. For all he knows, that shadow of mystery will remain forever cast. He then rests his chin in his hand and wonders how much more to life there is that he doesn't yet understand.

"Quite a bit," a deep voice says from the front of the room. "And I wonder how it's possible that I manage to receive all the most incapable students in my class, year after year."

Teddy stops gazing out the window and looks forward. *"Was that... Professor Mun?"* He thinks to himself. *"He couldn't be talking to me."*

"Yes, it is, and yes, I am talking to you, *Teddy*. And although my name is spelled M-u-n, it is pronounced as moon. Like the one you were just trying to find instead of paying attention to today's lecture."

The rest of the students turn around and stare at Teddy while Olivia smiles and shakes her head from the front of the class. *"What? No way. I'm not even opening my mouth. How does he know what I'm thinking?"*

"Because your mind is more open than a boot buffet in Slaybethor on Thanksgiving. Now, if you would pay attention, just maybe you'll learn how to close it, Mr. Lancaster."

The class laughs. Teddy inches up in his seat and raises his chin to try and locate the professor but can't find him. All he can see is some sort of stuffed animal resting on top of a long desk.

"Class, you are not going to believe what your fellow student just called me. Get up here, Mr. Lancaster!"

"Oh crap."

Teddy rises from his seat and walks up the center aisle toward the front while Olivia's smile grows in size, and she shakes her head again. The closer he gets toward the desk, the more he recognizes his error. It appears that what he thought was a stuffed animal might just be the professor himself. He's a gray cat with black stripes, a chubby white belly, and light blue eyes. He stands on his hind legs and is wearing a blue collared shirt that's tucked into his neatly pressed black slacks. For Teddy's credit, the cat truly is no bigger than a stuffed animal. The boy continues to walk toward the front of the class as his mind drifts to the thought of a prize he once won at the state fair several years ago. The cat taps the bottom of his rear right paw against the surface of the table on which he stands while he awaits Teddy's arrival.

Teddy tries to conceal his smile before he makes eye contact with the cat.

"Oh, is that so?" Professor Mun asks.

"Huh?" Teddy replies.

"You know what you thought," he says. "Roll up one of your sleeves and stick out your arm."

The class laughs. Teddy looks around, then pulls up his right sleeve and lowers his arm in front of the cat. Professor Mun looks Teddy in the eyes then wiggles his whiskers. He raises his left paw in the air then swipes down and across the boy's exposed skin, leaving four red gashes across his forearm. Teddy grimaces and stumbles backwards as the class laughs even louder.

"What the... ouch," Teddy says.

"Still think I'm cute?" Professor Mun asks, then signals for Teddy to return to his seat.

Teddy rolls down his sleeve and applies pressure to the newly formed cuts. The blood seeps through his white collared shirt and morphs into one big blotch of red. He then sits back down in his chair and closes the drapes to the window next to him.

. . .

Calvin can't stop laughing as Teddy relays the story to him and Victoria during their walk from the arena's classroom out to the stable.

"It's not funny, dude," Teddy says. "Thing stung pretty bad until it healed. And now I'm always worried he's in my head, listening to every single thought that runs through it."

"He can only do that within a twenty-foot radius, and if you lock your mind, he can't do it at all," Victoria says.

"Lock my mind? What does that even mean?" Teddy asks, then directs his attention back to Calvin. "And could you relax a little? It's not *that* funny."

Calvin smiles and wipes a couple of tears from his eyes. "Sorry, man. I just wasn't even aware that we had cats teaching classes here. I'll stop laughing, I promise. Just let me get it out of my system."

Victoria smiles then looks back at Teddy. "When your thoughts are organized and focused intensely on something, you can lock your mind. If everything in your head is all jumbled up and you're bouncing from thought to thought, it's pretty easy for someone to come in and influence you. You're lucky he spoke to you out loud. If he really wanted to mess with you, he could've pretended to be the voice in your head and implanted whatever thoughts he wanted in there, making you believe that they were your own."

"Uh, ok. That's a little dark," Teddy says. "Is that what you did to capture your horse?"

Victoria laughs while playing with her strawberry blonde hair. "Yeah, horse thoughts are funny. I pretended to be his own voice in his head then made him think that I probably had some food for him. He walked straight up to me after that."

"Oh. Cool. I guess. Just promise not to do anything like that to me, please," Teddy says as they walk underneath the raised gate toward the stable of horses.

"Oh, trust me, I won't," she says. "Boy thoughts are gross. I learned my lesson to stay far away from your minds a while ago."

"That's a little reassuring," Teddy says. "So can you eavesdrop into people's minds back on Earth as well?"

"Eh, not really. I can sort of feel their emotions, I think. But that's as far as I've ever got. Dean Spear seemed impressed with the little I can do though, and says if I stick with the course here at Zarmore, I'll improve."

The stable is now within view, and they can see the back of a tall man wearing blue overalls tending to three horses. Goosebumps run up Teddy's spine. The man hears the group approaching, then turns around and looks at the students. Teddy flinches backwards and stumbles into Calvin.

"Whoa," Calvin says. "You alright? Professor Mun talking to you again?"

Teddy gathers himself. "I'm fine. I just... I just thought that was going to be somebody else."

The young man with a clean-shaven face and straw hat approaches the students. "Well, howdy y'all! Great group of horses you caught the other day!" He stops and shakes everyone's hands. "Now, which one of you here is the one that caught themselves a shifter?"

Teddy looks around then raises his hand.

"Well done, boy! As you'll see, I've fixed her up all nice and secure with an ol' neutralizer, but you're gonna want to take a pack of stickers with you every time you ride, just in case it falls off."

He hands Teddy a small silk pouch containing four stickers.

"My name is Dickie Clayton, and I'm one of the horse caretakers here on campus. All we have planned for you kids today is to get y'all better acquainted with your horses and the racetrack so that on future practices, you don't need to always come and find me to handle your business."

Dickie opens the stable gates then turns around toward the students. "Oh, and one more little thing! I got to remember to get all y'alls horses names for Professor Jones before we leave today."

Dickie mounts himself on top of a large black horse while Victoria, Teddy, and Calvin get settled on the ones they caught the previous day. The group then trots in a single file line behind Dickie out the west gate from which they entered previously and onto the track.

"So this is where y'all will begin and end every race this season," Dickie says. They're looking out toward an archway in the stadium that the racetrack runs under. "As you can see, our track inside the arena is shaped like a letter 'U', and we're just about at one of the two tips of said 'U' right now. However, as you'll also see, there's a lot more track to be run outside the arena."

Calvin's horse bumps into the back of Teddy's, causing a fuss between the two recently domesticated animals. Dickie stops talking and looks back toward the students.

"We're fine!" Calvin shouts.

"You sure?" Dickie asks. "I can..."

"Nope! We're good!"

"Ok, anyway," Dickie says as he turns his horse around to face the students. "So here's how a typical race will go. There will be four horses here, all mounted by students from your same grade level, facing the outside area of the track."

"Wait," Victoria says.

"Yes, Miss Addington?"

"So you're saying we only get to race against students from our own class?"

"No. Well, yes. But no. See, listen here." Dickie says. "There are many other first-year classes taking place on this campus with students who have all caught horses just as you three have. For the entire season, you'll only race amongst each other, as the second-yearers will only race amongst the second-yearers, and the third-yearers will only race amongst the third-yearers, and so on. However, during the season, we'll be keeping standings. A first-place finish earns you five points. A second-place finish earns you three points. A third-place finish earns you two points. And if you finish fourth-place, also known as last-place, you will lose two points. In the case of a tie in the standings, the higher ranking will go to the student with the fastest course finish time. At the end of the season, the top two students with the highest number of points will advance to the Zarmore Cup, which will consist of one single race between the top two students from each grade level. The winner will then have their name etched into the golden cup for all of eternity."

"So the final race will be twelve horses all at once?" Victoria asks.

"That's right," Dickie replies

"Cool," Calvin says.

"But I reckon it's highly unlikely that any of y'all will fare too well in the Cup if you happen to make it there," Dickie says. "In the nearly three-hundred-year history of the races, there has only been one first-yearer that has ever won it all. So don't get too excited about it, ok? This year is really just to get you kids accustomed to racing and learning how to better influence the situations and circumstances in your physical and inner surroundings."

"Screw that, I'm going to win," Calvin says as his horse bumps into Teddy's again.

"I like the enthusiasm," Dickie says. "I didn't say that there isn't at least a chance. Now, let me continue explaining how the races will go. So the four horses will start from here, facing toward the outside area of the track. Oh, and let me say another thing before we continue; throughout the entire race, inside the arena and out, you will and must always stay on the track. Remember that, please. Now anyway, so y'all will be facing toward that archway. There will be a stable out here to park your horses until the gun shoots off. Once that happens, the gates will be released, and your horses will begin running out of the arena. Once through the archway, the track will take y'all on a left through the woods for several miles. After that, there'll be another left, and y'all will cut down the mountain and into the open valley."

"What about the monkeys?" Teddy asks.

"Don't worry. The turn into the valley happens far before you ever get close to the jungle," Dickie replies. "Now, after you cut through the valley, you will race up another side of the mountain range and eventually turn another left back toward the castle. From there, you will continue racing through the forest until you hit one last sharp left. I advise y'all to slow down for this final turn. I've seen many well-run races lost here by being overzealous. Once you complete that turn, you'll find yourselves moving under the other arch of the stadium at the opposite tip of the 'U' inside the track. From there, you just follow the course down and around until the finish line, which is where we are right now. The temporary stable that was used in this spot at the beginning of the race will have been removed."

He makes eye contact with each of the students then smiles. "Any questions?"

No one says anything.

"Great!" Dickie says. "Now, normally, we'd do a ride-through together with our horses, and I'd show you the entire track in person. But it looks like we're just about out of time for today, and we all know that if I don't get you kids home through the oak before dark, they'll have my head."

The group of students follows Dickie back into the stable. Teddy and Victoria hop off and say goodbye to their horses. Calvin is struggling to get his back into the stable, so Dickie has to help him out. Teddy and Victoria laugh until Calvin's horse finally calms down, and he's able to hop off.

"You guys won't think it's so funny when I'm holding the Cup nine months from now," Calvin says. "Let's get out of here."

The three walk back out underneath the west gate and into the central area of the arena.

"How do you know how long the season is?" Teddy asks.

"I've been prepping for this ever since my mom told me about it after I was accepted," Calvin says. "The season runs up until May, and the Cup is on the last day of class in June."

"Wait!" Dickie calls out from back in the stable. "I need to get y'alls horse's names before you leave."

Calvin turns around and shouts, "Skull Crusher!"

Teddy and Victoria look at each other and laugh. Dickie seems like he's trying to hold back a smile as well, "Ok, Calvin Whitaker and Skull Crusher." He says while writing on a piece of paper attached to a clipboard.

Calvin looks at his two classmates. "Shut up."

"Ok, and for Miss Addington?" Dickie says.

"My horse's name will be Gemini," she replies.

Calvin bursts into laughter. "Gemini?! Are you serious?" He looks over at Teddy. "Can you believe that?! Gemini?"

Teddy shrugs his shoulders. "Sounds fine to me."

Calvin looks toward Dickie to see if he's laughing. The horsekeeper writes down the name on his clipboard with a neutral facial expression.

"You guys suck," Calvin says.

"And for Mr. Lancaster?" Dickie shouts.

Teddy hasn't really put much thought into naming his horse at all. A few moments pass before the horsekeeper looks up from his clipboard. "Mr. Lancaster?"

There's another pause, and then Teddy finally speaks up. "Call her Miss B."

Déjà Vu

A basketball crashes into the side of Teddy's leg, causing him to nearly lose his grip on his lunch tray and trip onto the black pavement. He looks to his left and sees a group of eighth-graders laughing. "Miss Buuuuuttttttssss," one of them calls out.

Teddy clenches his teeth then continues walking toward the grassy area where the picnic tables lay. Most of the seats are taken, none of which seem to be by the person he's looking for. "Figures," he says.

He turns around and prepares to walk past the basketball courts again when she calls out to him. "Teddy!"

He turns back around. Behind a few rows of crowded tables, he sees a hand waving in the air. "Back here, man!" she yells. "I saved you a seat!"

Teddy walks back into the grassy area and sees Kristi sitting at a small picnic table underneath a tree. She sets her textbook to the side and smiles as Teddy approaches. "Almost thought you weren't going to show," she says while adjusting her round eyeglasses.

Teddy smiles, then sits down next to her and looks back toward the basketball players. "Oh yeah, my friends are really bummed that I'm not hanging out with them today."

She laughs a little, then looks down toward her brown paper lunch bag and reaches inside. "So, it's my little brother's birthday today, and my mom made him some treats to bring for his classmates," she says as she pulls out two vanilla frosting cupcakes with rainbow sprinkles and sets them on the wooden table. "I made sure to grab one for you."

Teddy locks eyes with hers. "You serious?"

Kristi smiles.

"Wow, man. Wow. Thank you."

She starts to laugh. "I didn't buy you a car, Teddy. Relax."

"I'm sorry," he says. "It's just that. This kind of stuff never happens to me."

"Well, cheers to happier days then!" she says as she picks up one of the cupcakes and raises it in the air toward Teddy.

He laughs, then picks up the other cupcake and lifts it into the air toward Kristi's. "Cheers to that."

They touch the frosting-covered tips together, then bring them down and take a bite.

"Well, that was cute," a familiar voice says from somewhere nearby.

Teddy and Kristi swivel their heads.

"Oh, hey Sean!" Kristi says as she stands up and hugs the strong boy with a blonde-haired buzz cut. "What are you doing here? I didn't think you were coming to visit me today."

"School was boring, so I ditched," he says. "What's going on here? Who's your friend?"

"Oh, sorry!" She says. "Yeah, let me introduce you guys." Teddy, this is my boyfriend Sean that I was telling you about the other day. He's in the eighth grade and goes to McNair Middle School. It's a private school on the other side of town."

Teddy's eyes grow larger as he swallows the piece of cupcake in his mouth then sets the rest on the table.

"Teddy, you look familiar," Sean says as he walks closer toward him. "Where do I know you from?"

"Maybe you guys have seen each other in the comic book store or something," Kristi says. "Teddy has one of those same glow in the dark tattoos that you used to have."

Sean turns around and glares at Kristi. "I thought I told you not to tell anyone about that!"

"But Sean, it's the exact same one!" She says. "And who cares? It's just a little fake tattoo."

Sean looks back toward Teddy, stares at him for what feels like an eternity, then turns around and faces Kristi again.

"How did you see it?"

"See what?"

"The tattoo!"

"Oh. Relax. It was in biology class," she says. "I saw it under a blacklight. It's the same one. Like a letter 'Z' superimposed over an hourglass."

Sean squints then looks back at Teddy. A few moments pass before a spark of recognition flashes across Sean's eyes.

A smile grows on his face as he massages his knuckles. "What are the odds?"

Teddy looks down at the cupcake on the table.

"The odds of what?" Kristi asks.

"Seems you remembered to wear your shoes today, *Teddy*."

"What's that supposed to mean?" Kristi asks.

Sean laughs. "It means that my brain is more resilient and stronger than that old Spear gave it credit for."

"I don't get it," she says. "What are you talking about?"

"Don't worry about it," Sean says as he snags the cupcake Teddy's staring at, then takes a bite and turns his back.

"Hey! That's Teddy's!" Kristi yells.

"Oh really?" Sean says. "You bring cupcakes for some random nerd at school but none for your boyfriend?"

Kristi doesn't reply.

"I'll see ya around, Teddy," Sean says as he takes another bite and walks away. "Nice to meet ya."

. . .

The sound of static rumbles from the loudspeaker above the blackboard and Mrs. Suki stops talking, raising one of her brown paws in the air until the noise dissipates and a deep voice takes its place. It's Dean Spear.

"Good morning, students. I hope you all enjoyed your weekend. Hard to believe we're already nearly one month into the school year, isn't it? As a reminder, you are all expected to maintain a high GPA in both your classes here and on Earth. I've already had to dish out a few punishments for failure to comply with these standards, and I don't want to give out anymore."

"How is someone already failing one of their classes?" Ronnie whispers to Teddy.

Mrs. Suki looks toward the back of the class at the two boys and growls.

"Whoa," Ronnie says as he sinks down into his chair.

The dean continues to speak. "Our Physical Training professors have finished creating the schedule for the horse races this year and will be posting it on the bulletin board in the foyer later today. For those students who will be competing in the races, a snail should be delivering your personalized schedules to you right about now."

Teddy squints, then looks down. There's a large blue snail with a green and purple swirled shell sniffing through his backpack.

"Hey!" Teddy whispers as he pulls his green bag away from the animal.

The snail retreats backwards then opens its shell, revealing a manila-colored envelope wrapped in plastic. Teddy reaches down and grabs the document, then sets it on his desk. He then turns back to close the snail's shell, but by the time he looks down, it's already gone. He shakes his head then separates the slimy plastic wrapping from the envelope.

"You can read it after class, Teddy," Mrs. Suki says, then points her paw back up toward the loudspeaker.

Teddy sighs, then wipes the blue slime off his hands using the inside seams of his slacks.

"And in final news," the dean continues. "The travel restriction to Slaybethor is still in effect. One of the main suspects, Caesar Luna, has confessed to working with Ziruam in the goblinapping of Nancy Butts. However, he refuses to disclose any more information than that and therefore is being held without bail in Frostlepeak Cavern, one of the most secure prisons in all of Egaria. The other suspect, Ziruam, still remains at large. As stated previously, all suspicious activity and any possible relevant information should be reported immediately. Have a great week, everyone!"

"I thought you said your buddy Caesar was one of the good guys," Ronnie whispers.

"He is," Teddy says. "I mean... I don't know, man. None of this still adds up."

"Ok, class!" Mrs. Suki says. "Now, with your morning brief out of the way, let's get started! We have a lot planned for today, so I need everyone to pay extra attention. If you all could please open your textbooks to page sixty-seven, we're going to continue our discussion on the Battle of Edonao during the year 972. Egarian-tethered, of course.

Ronnie raises his hand.

"Yes, Mr. Ronnie?"

"I thought you said we were going to learn about the island this week."

"I'm sorry, dear. We actually don't have much time for that, and it's really not part of the first-year curriculum."

There's a collective groan from nearly all the students.

Mrs. Suki looks around for a moment then a tiny smile creeps onto her face. "Alright, alright—but just because you're all so darn cute. I'll answer a couple of questions about Trinovern Reef. Or as you all like to call it, *The Island*."

A loud cheer erupts from the students.

"Ok! But keep it down, would ya?" Mrs. Suki says as she looks toward the door. "Don't get me in trouble over here. Now, what do you want to know?"

Ronnie's hand is the first to shoot up. "Is it true that if someone gets sent to the island, they die on Earth?"

"No, not exactly, dear. Although that is usually the case. You see, throughout all of Egaria, there are several natural phenomena that alter and play with time. For the beings who live here, it isn't much of a problem as this is our only home. Time feels like it's passing just as normally as it does on Earth. However, being that you all are out of body visitors in Egaria right now and your real bodies are back on Earth, these natural phenomena can have a drastic impact on your life. This is why the Council approved to enchant the colony of Zarmore many many years ago. It is also why first-year student travel inside the Kingdom of Egaria is strictly forbidden and travel for students in subsequent year levels must be highly supervised."

Mrs. Suki walks over to a map on the side of the room. Teddy never gave it a second glance before as most of its areas are blacked out minus one small area of green in the top left corner. He squints then spares a glance toward Ronnie on his right. The boy looks back at Teddy and shrugs his shoulders.

The fox looks toward the door, then picks up a pointing stick and traces around the edges of the map. "All of what you see here is Egaria. As you may notice, most of the land is blacked out as you can only see that which you know and that which is true, and with this being only your first year, that isn't much. The more you learn about Egaria, the more the map will reveal itself to you." She raises her wooden stick and points to the upper left-hand corner. "This area here is where we are located right now. This is the colony of Zarmore."

There are some murmurs amongst the students as the professor lowers the stick and traces another circle around a smaller section in the middle of the map. She pauses once finished then turns back around toward the class. "If I reveal something to you all, can you promise not to tell anyone else that you can see it? I won't get in big big trouble, but it can turn into a little headache for me with administration here." Smiles grow on the student's faces as they nod their heads. Mrs. Suki sighs, then taps the middle of the map with the tip of her stick. The blackness in that specific area slowly fades away, and a circular island surrounded by a large body of water appears in its place. "This piece of land, right in the middle of the Crimson Sea, is called Trinovern Reef."

Ronnie smiles then looks over at Teddy. "The Island."

Mrs. Suki nods her head. "Yes, dear. More famously known as simply, The Island."

"Now, what I'd like you all to focus on is the swirl hovering above this island on the map. This dark force, mist, cloud, whatever you wish to call it, perpetually hovers over and casts a shadow on the island. Some scientists have referred to it as a black hole after probes sent into its center vanished without a trace. However, others argue that since it doesn't have a gravitational pull, it shouldn't be considered a black hole. The truth is no one really knows where they came from or what happens to an object that goes inside one."

Teddy raises his hand.

"Yes, dear," Mrs. Suki says.

"You mentioned that no one really knows where *they* came from. Are you saying there are more than one of these things floating around in Egaria?"

"That's right, Mr. Teddy. As I said, there are several natural phenomena that affect time throughout Egaria. These black holes, if you wish to call them as so, are just one of those mysteries inside this kingdom."

"So, how many black holes are there?" A chubby boy near the front of the class asks.

"There are two," Mrs. Suki replies. "And please raise your hand next time, Mr. Tommy."

She points her stick toward the edge of the map over Zarmore. "The other black hole is actually located right here inside the colony of Zarmore and is similar to the one that hovers over the island in many respects except for the fact that it isn't stationary and it has the ability to expand. The scientists are calling this particular black hole *Egaria SQ26*. For about twelve hours of the day, it hovers directly over the jungle across from the castle. Then as the sun begins to set, it expands and eventually casts its shadow over all areas of Egaria except for the Crimson Sea. Once the sun rises again, it recedes back to hovering only over the jungle." She notices Teddy raising his hand from the back of the class. "Yes, Mr. Teddy."

"Why can't the chimps and monkeys ever leave the shadows, and do they travel to other colonies in Egaria when it gets dark?"

"That's another subject which is not on our first-year curriculum. However, I will tell you that all the apes never leave the colony of Zarmore. They are a very territorial species and have no interest in what they do not believe is rightfully theirs. Now let me finish explaining to you children what you need to know about these black holes so that I can properly answer Mr. Ronnie's question, ok dear?"

Teddy exhales and slides down into his seat.

"Each of these black holes acts differently in how they move and their effect on beings traveling out of body," Mrs. Suki continues. "In regards to Egaria SQ26, the black hole which hovers over Zarmore's jungle by day and expands to the rest of Egaria by night, what we have learned is that anyone can safely conduct their regular life underneath its shadows, and time will continue to pass normally. Even after the shadow retreats or one exits from underneath it, no time will be lost, gained, or affected in any way."

She pauses for a moment, then continues to speak. "That is unless that being is traveling out of body. In that case, she or he would not notice any difference in time while *in* Egaria, out or inside of the shadows. The issue would only arise when they try to return to their bodies back on Earth. What we have learned about this particular black hole is that while a student traveling out of body is underneath its shadows, time appears to speed up on Earth significantly. The calculation is that for every hour a traveler spends in the shadows, 4.169 years will pass on Earth. Another way of saying that is if a human of Earth spent one night in the shadows, which is roughly twelve hours, when they return to their bodies on Earth, they would find that fifty years would have passed. This is true even if the time spent under the shadows was inside the colony of Zarmore, as the time enchantment spell cannot overcome the power of these phenomena."

"Doesn't sound too bad to me," Ronnie says. "I'd be cool with living in the future."

"You'd be an old and confused man if you were lucky, Mr. Ronnie," she says. "Back on Earth, it would appear as if you had fallen into a coma. Your best hope would be that your loved ones would have enough money and faith to hook you up to machines in a hospital for several decades until you could exit from Egaria and return. However, even if that were the case, eventually, you or them would die waiting for that possible day. And even if miraculously that day arrived, your likely old and feeble brain would have long withered away, and you would have no clue of what's going on or what happened once back inside your body on Earth."

"Oh," Ronnie says.

"So yes," Mrs. Suki continues. "You could spend a wonderful night in Egaria, but your time on Earth would be over."

"Wait, but what about when your body dies on Earth?" A girl in the middle of the class asks as she raises her hand. "What happens to the part of you that's still in Egaria? Your soul or whatever. Does it die too?"

Mrs. Suki pauses, then glances at the door before speaking. "If a human's body dies on Earth while their soul is in Egaria, their soul will remain here and carry out its life until termination."

A loud clamor arises amongst the students before Ronnie speaks above the rest." Hang on, hang on, hang on! So you're saying I can die on Earth but continue to live my life here?"

Mrs. Suki rubs her forearm then adjusts her glasses as she looks back over at the classroom door again. "Well, yes, dear. If your Earth body died while you were traveling out of it inside the Kingdom of Egaria, you would live out the rest of your life in Egaria until your natural or *unnatural* death arrives to your Egarian body."

The chatting amongst the students reaches an even higher level.

"Quiet!" Mrs. Suki shouts.

The side conversations cease, and Teddy raises a hand.

"Go ahead, Mr. Teddy."

"So there are dead people in Egaria?" He asks.

"From an Earth viewpoint, yes, there are some. But from an Egarian viewpoint, no. They are still very much alive here. However, everyone's time does come to pass. Eventually their Egarian body will die as well, and their soul will finally move on to the next stage of life... One way or the other."

"But time moves a lot differently here, right?" Teddy asks. "I've heard of people living thousands of years in other parts of Egaria."

"It is true that Egarian citizens age much slower than what you humans are accustomed to on Earth. And it is also true that there are many clever beings in Egaria who have learned to extend their lifespan even beyond that. However, they are all still mortal. Some other beings, like myself and anyone who lives or works inside the colony of Zarmore, are affected by the time enchantment spell, and we do not physically age while inside this colony. But always keep in mind that everyone's time eventually does run out."

"And then what?" Teddy asks. "What happens after that?"

"After what, dear?"

"After someone dies both here and on Earth. Where do they go?"

"That, Mr. Teddy, can only be experienced and never described. But I assure you that there's nothing to fear. Now back to our original conversation. All those potential outcomes to humans traveling out of body are due to the black hole that expands from the jungles of Zarmore all the way to the edges of the Crimson Sea each night. The other black hole, which is stationary and always has its shadow cast over the island, acts in a very different manner for travelers out of body *and* citizens of Egaria. As the black hole we just discussed speeds up time on Earth, the one that floats above the island slows down time on Earth while also speeding up time on the island."

Mrs. Suki looks at the students and smiles to see that they are all quiet and paying attention. "You see, if you were ever punished to the island, you would find yourself in somewhat of a mountainous jungle-like terrain cast in perpetual darkness surrounded by crashing waves of nearly fifty feet and the worst of the worst criminals. The black hole over this island is known as *Trinovern RT43*. While on this mass of land, your life and years would feel as if they were passing just as normally as they do on Earth. You may live seventy, eighty, possibly one hundred years there. Or maybe you wouldn't make it through the first night. No one is really monitoring the situation on the island or how all the prisoners are getting by. Nevertheless, eventually, if you were lucky, you would grow into an old woman or man and die. And when this happens, the moment your Egarian body dies here, your body on Earth instantly dies as well."

Mrs. Suki pauses to see she still has everyone's attention then continues to speak.

"Now, the interesting thing is how time is affected underneath the constant shadow of this particular black hole. What we have learned is that for every fifty years spent on the island, only one day passes on Earth. So let's say you were fifteen years old when sent to the island and spent seventy years there; only about one and a half days would have passed on Earth. You would be eighty-five years old on the island but still only fifteen years old on Earth. Your loved ones would have no idea what's happening to you, and it would appear as if you had fallen into a coma for a day or two. Then, once you finally pass away in Egaria, your body on Earth would instantly die as well."

There are some whispers amongst the students, but Mrs. Suki continues to speak. "This time ratio of fifty years on the island equating to only one day passing on Earth also holds true for the rest of Egaria as well. Better said, for every fifty years spent on the island, only one day will pass on Earth and in Egaria."

Ronnie raises his hand then speaks up. "Couldn't that be used for better objectives? I mean, these people on the island, they're living like, way into the future sort of. Couldn't that island be used for more productive purposes? We could study there and learn a hundred year's worth of knowledge with only one weekend passing on Earth."

Mrs. Suki smiles. "Very astute, Mr. Ronnie. I always knew there was a wise boy hiding underneath that tough demeanor of yours. I hope you continue to participate like this in future lessons."

Ronnie sinks into his chair.

"But yes, you're correct," Mrs. Suki says. "If one were to spend some time on the island and then return to Egaria or Earth, the advantage they would have would be unfathomable. However, that's not possible. And we have tried dutifully.

Ronnie tilts his head.

"If you remember from orientation day," Mrs. Suki begins. "The most amount of time we can have you kids learning here is ten hours per day. Any longer than that and serious health issues start to arise, one of which being death. Your brains just simply cannot handle that much information coming into your consciousness in one jump after returning from Egaria."

"But what about Egarians?" Ronnie asks. "At least you all could benefit from it since you're not traveling out of body."

"Yes, this is true. We could leave the island and come back to the rest of Egaria with all of the new information intact. However, unlike you travelers, this is our only body. So we wouldn't be returning as our young selves again but rather as the old beings we grew into on the island."

"Oh, I guess that would kind of suck."

"A bit," Mrs. Suki says. "So what the Council has concluded is that leaving the island as so is best. We can send prisoners there so that they have a chance to live out their lives while at the same time we can protect the secrecy and security of Zarmore and all of Egaria." She sees Ronnie raising his hand again and motions for him to speak.

"Is there like a handout or something that explains all these time differences? I don't want to get lost one day and end up being some dinosaur's lunch or something."

"Of course, dear. You're actually sitting right in front of one. And don't be disheartened if you're having trouble grasping all of this right now. This is a complicated subject which you'll spend much more time on in the coming years."

Ronnie turns around and notices a series of blank posters thumbtacked on the back wall. The sound of Mrs. Suki clapping her paws together echoes softly through the room, and then writing appears and fills the placards:

> *Basic Time Conversion Table for While Under the Shadows of the Following Black Holes*

Egaria SQ26

<u>Egarian Citizen</u>:

1 hour in shadows = **1 hour** having passed upon return out of shadows **(no effect)**

<u>Out of Body Traveler</u>:

1 hour in shadows = **1 hour** having passed upon return out of shadows **(no effect)**

1 hour in shadows = **4.169 years** having passed upon return to Earth body

Trinovern RT43

<u>Egarian Citizen</u>:

50 years in shadows = **1 day** having passed upon return out of shadows

<u>Out of Body Traveler</u>:

50 years in shadows = **1 day** having passed upon return out of shadows

50 years in shadows = **1 day** having passed upon return to Earth body

Basic Time & Travel Conversions

Basic Time Conversions
Standard:
1 **day** passing in Slaybethor = **1 day** passing in Egaria **(no change)**
1 **day** passing in Slaybethor = **30 days** passing on Earth
1 **day** passing in Egaria = **30 days** passing on Earth
1 **day** passing in Zarmore, Egaria = **1 day** passing on Earth **(no change)**

Basic Travel Conversions

Standard:

Egarian Citizen **Traveling** in Slaybethor:

1 hour in Slaybethor = **1 hour** having passed upon return to Egaria **(no change)**

Out of Body Traveler **Traveling** in Slaybethor:

1 hour in Slaybethor = **2 minutes** having passed upon return to Earth body

---

Out of Body Traveler **Traveling** in Egaria (while not under shadow of black hole):

1 hour in Egaria = **4 minutes** having passed upon return to Earth body

---

Out of Body Traveler **Traveling** in the Colony of Zarmore, Egaria (while not under shadow of black hole):

1 hour in Zarmore = **0 minutes** having passed upon return to Earth body

Egarian Citizen **Traveling** in the Colony of Zarmore, Egaria:

Not permissible. All Egarian citizens working or living in Zarmore shall do so until their death. Only out of body student travelers and those of the goblin species are permitted to enter and exit.

> *Calculations are estimates. True experience may vary.
>
> **If return from shadows of Trinovern RT43, death or complete mental faculty loss is assumed for out of body travelers.
>
> ***Refer to Placard 127-B for all other non-listed time conversions.

"Sorry, Mrs. Suki," Ronnie says as he raises his hand. "I'm looking at these charts. "So you, Dean Spear, and all the teachers here really can never leave this place?"

"That's correct, dear. All the faculty here have volunteered to do so. We may never get to leave the colony of Zarmore, but we all believe that what we are doing here is much bigger than our lives individually."

"Wow," Ronnie says. "Well, at least you guys are like immortal now, right? I mean, how old are you anyway, Mrs. Suki?"

"Didn't your mother ever teach you to never ask a woman that?"

Ronnie stutters, then Mrs. Suki continues to speak.

"All the faculty here, apart from some of our goblin colleagues, are the same physical age they were when they took their jobs. And although we have the potential to live very long lives here in Zarmore, we are not immortal. Like I said earlier, everyone's time eventually does run out."

There's a brief pause then Ronnie raises his hand again.

"Yes, dear?"

"Back to the charts. So when us humans are traveling in Slaybethor or Egaria, time slows down on Earth?"

"During the day and out of the shadows, yes, it would appear as so, that's correct. And now perhaps you can understand why it can be enticing for out of body travelers to try and stay in Egaria for more time than recommended. They believe they can live full lives inside the Kingdom while losing hardly anytime on Earth. And this is technically true. However, eventually, they stay too long and experience fatal time disorientation illnesses or catch themselves underneath the effects of a black hole. And remember, you don't need to spend too much time in the shadows of one of those before the months begin to pass on Earth, and you're no longer in control of that body."

"Hmm, they should just stay in Slaybethor then," Ronnie says. "No black holes there, and you can live as long as you want."

"Not quite," Mrs. Suki says. "You still run the risk of catching a TDI if you stay too long. Also, the outskirts cities aren't as regulated and safe as inside the Kingdom of Egaria. And although Slaybethor is sometimes advertised as a peaceful town, it is still very much lawless. Just look at what's happening there now. Another thing one must remember is that if you die in Egaria or in most areas of Slaybethor, you die on Earth as well."

Ronnie looks over at Teddy. "I don't ever want to leave Zarmore."

Mrs. Suki sets the pointing stick down and walks back to the front of the class. "So, bringing it all together and answering your original question, Mr. Ronnie. It's not that because someone is sentenced to the island that they die on Earth. But rather due to the effect of the black hole above the island that manipulates time. Now, if there are no more questions, I'd like for you all to open your textbooks up to page..."

The bell rings, and everyone begins to clear their desks and pack their bags.

Mrs. Suki grimaces. "I want you all to be prepared to learn about the Battle of Edonao first thing tomorrow morning!"

Ronnie smiles as he looks over at Teddy and finishes zipping up his backpack. "That was pretty cool, huh."

"Hard to wrap my head around it all," Teddy says as he tosses the plastic that was covering his horse schedule envelope from earlier into the trash. "But yeah, pretty cool."

"Let's check out that schedule," Ronnie says. "I need to know the exact date you're going to beat my brother."

Teddy laughs, then wipes the slime off his hands and opens the manila-colored envelope on top of his desk. "Alright, let's see."

Theodore M. Lancaster
Regular Season
Zarmore Racing League Schedule.   First-Yearer

====================================

October 8th:

10:00 a.m.

Runner Info	Jockey
Bum Bum Bum Blam!	*Joshua Holstead*
Sunny Days	*Courtney Ackerly*
Miss B	*Theodore Lancaster*
Von Schnickerlonger Jr.	*Connor Graham*

====================================

November 12th:

<u>*09:00 a.m.*</u>

<u>Runner Info</u>   <u>Jockey</u>

Gemini   *Victoria Addington*

Sunny Days   *Courtney Ackerly*

Miss B   *Theodore Lancaster*

Skull Crusher   *Calvin Whitaker*

===================================

December 10th:

<u>*02:00 p.m.*</u>

<u>Runner Info</u>   <u>Jockey</u>

Miss B   Theodore Lancaster

Zarmore's Finest   Antonio Young

Von Schnickerlonger Jr.   Connor Graham

Jake   Jake Milbourne

===================================

January 14th:

<u>*10:00 a.m.*</u>

<u>Runner Info</u>   <u>Jockey</u>

Rumpy Frump   Katie Berringer

Skull Crusher   Calvin Whitaker

Not Last   Asmita Lee

Miss B   Theodore Lancaster

===================================

February 11th:

11:00 a.m.

Runner Info	Jockey
Bum Bum Bum Blam!	Joshua Holstead
Rachel is Fast	Rachel Redburn
Miss B	Theodore Lancaster
Dream Machine	Alice Torbett

===================================

March 11th:

<u>*01:00 p.m.*</u>

Runner Info	Jockey
Skull Crusher	Calvin Whitaker
Miss B	Theodore Lancaster
Von Schnickerlonger Jr.	Connor Graham
Sunny Days	Courtney Ackerly

April 8th:

09:00 a.m.

Runner Info	Jockey
Miss B	Theodore Lancaster
Sunny Days	Courtney Ackerly
First-Place Freddie	Fredrick Townsend
Jake	Jake Milbourne

May 13th:

<u>*11:00 a.m.*</u>

<u>Runner Info</u>　　　　　　　　　　　　　　　<u>Jockey</u>

Bonfire in the Rain　　　　　　　　*Giovanni Ginesi*

Gemini　　　　　　　　　　　　*Victoria Addington*

Not Last　　　　　　　　　　　　　　*Asmita Lee*

Miss B　　　　　　　　　　　　*Theodore Lancaster*

==================================

"Alright, November 12th is the first one, Teddy. I'm counting on you, man," Ronnie says.

Teddy laughs as he folds the schedule up and slides it into his pocket. "I'll do my best. So what class you have next? It looks like I'll be tuning with Professor Raldorthorch. Whatever that means."

"Nice," Ronnie says. "He's good. I have tuning class as well but with Professor Richardson."

"Ah, well, I guess I'll see you at lunch then?"

"Yes, sir! We're always sitting in that same spot as the day when ol' Captain Zarmore knocked you out."

"Oh, I actually have a story to tell you about that guy."

"I can't imagine it being more interesting than the one he told you on your first day."

Teddy releases a half-grin, then shakes his head. "I'll tell you all at lunch, man. You're not going to believe me."

Ronnie laughs then bumps fists with Teddy. "Alright. See you then."

Ronnie walks out of the classroom while Teddy reaches down and zips up his backpack. Mrs. Suki approaches his desk and smiles. "So how has everything been going so far, Mr. Teddy? I appreciate the participation and interest you showed in class today."

Teddy looks up toward the fox, then rises from his seat and tosses his backpack over his right shoulder. "Oh, thanks. Yeah, everything has been great. Everyone is really nice here."

Mrs. Suki continues to smile. "I'm happy to hear that. You're a sweet boy, so I'm not surprised. I'm sure you have a lot of friends back on Earth as well."

Teddy laughs. "Yeah, they really love me there."

Mrs. Suki's smile falls into a frown as she tilts her head to the side. "Is that sarcasm I detect?"

"Sorry, Mrs. Suki. I've just always had a bit of a bully problem at my schools on Earth."

The fox shakes her head. "Pitiful bullies. You should feel sorry for them, you know."

"Sorry?"

"Yes, dear. They live miserable existences."

"Um, I don't know, Mrs. Suki. They look like they're having a pretty fun time when they're tormenting me or stealing my lunch."

"They may appear that way in the moment, dear, but you don't know how they truly feel inside. I can assure you that it's not great, especially later when they're all alone with their thoughts."

Teddy sighs. "Yeah, but..."

"Let me ask you something, Mr. Teddy. When you're having a great day, and you're really happy, aren't you nice to just about everyone you come into contact with? Does the world not seem like a better place when you're happy and feeling good?"

Teddy looks up toward the ceiling for a moment. "Hmm, yeah, I guess."

"And when you're having a bad day, perhaps you slept poor and people have been being rude or mean to you; you're not such a nice person during those moments, are you? The world looks like a much darker place when you're not feeling good inside, doesn't it?"

"Um, yeah, if I'm cranky, I'm not a very great person to be around."

"So you see, when you feel good inside, you do nice and beautiful things. And when you feel bad inside, you do mean and nasty things. The truth is that these students that are picking on you do not have a very great self-image of themselves. And although they may pretend to be happy people, deep down, they don't feel very good at all. If they did, there's no way they would be doing such cruel things to others."

"I guess I never really thought of it like that."

She smiles then places a paw on the side of one of Teddy's arms. "Most humans on Earth are obsessed with *appearing* to be nice, cool, or 'good' people. However, they'll go about their day doing mean things, gossiping, and not even flashing a smile toward anyone."

Teddy nods his head. "Yeah, that's true."

"What I'd like you to practice is to just focus on feeling good all the time. No matter what's happening around you, you must learn to master your emotions and never allow anything or anyone to determine how you feel inside your own body. When you take charge of your emotions, body, and energies, you will see that, almost like magic, your whole world will begin to change. It will seem like a much better and happier place. And in fact, it will be because when you truly feel good on the inside, you do beautiful and kind acts on the outside and toward others which reinforces them to also feel good on the inside and be kind toward others as well. Do you see the cycle? And can you see how doing the reverse has only created negative emotions, feelings, and an opposite circuit?"

Teddy nods his head again, and Mrs. Suki continues to speak.

"So the next time you come across a bully who is doing mean things, just smile, because now you understand how he truly feels inside and that he's experiencing life through a very sad and ugly lens."

Mrs. Suki lowers her paw and smiles. "You're a good kid, Mr. Teddy. Now hurry on and get to your next class. I'll see you tomorrow morning."

Vibrational World

"But why such large wings if he can't even fly?" Teddy whispers to Victoria.

"Penguins can't fly either," she responds.

"Yeah, but come on, they're like, you know... fat."

Professor Raldorthorch is handing out sheets of paper to the students in the front of the class. "Take one and pass it down," he says, his voice sounding like that of a man who should have quit smoking cigarettes after his second episode of lung cancer.

"Does he at least breathe fire?" Teddy asks.

"I don't know. He didn't really give us a list of his character attributes on the first day of class."

The student sitting in front of Teddy turns around and hands him a stack of papers. Teddy takes one and sets it on his desk, then turns around and passes the remainder to the boy behind him. "I guess I just always thought that the day I would meet a dragon would be different. I mean, he's not even much taller than me."

Victoria finishes passing a stack of papers to the boy behind her then turns toward Teddy again. "You've been expecting to meet a dragon in your life?"

"You know what I mean."

"Um, not quite."

"Ok, class," Professor Raldorthorch says. "As I was explaining earlier and for these past few weeks, we must master the basics before we go any further."

He turns around and erases chalk from the blackboard. Teddy notices the professor's long and spiky thick green tail extending out from his gray slacks then looks over at Victoria. "Do you think they make their own clothes here or there's like special dragon and cat boutiques out in Egaria?"

The professor turns around and starts talking again before Victoria can answer. "Now, can anyone tell me some differences between this blackboard here and, let's say, this student sitting in front of me. What's your name again, young man?"

"Uh, Tommy," the chubby boy with a bowl cut replies.

"Very well," the dragon says. "Can anyone tell me the difference between this blackboard behind me and your fellow classmate, Tommy?"

The professor notices a boy's hand in the air. "Yes, you in the back."

"The difference between the blackboard and Tommy is that the blackboard at least gets some of the answers right from time to time."

The class erupts into laughter. Tommy crumples up his piece of paper on his desk and throws it toward the kid.

The professor doesn't seem to mind the chaos. "And how about between this apple on my desk and the classroom door?"

There's no reply.

"Or let's say between this stack of papers and the stapler in the back of the room? What is the difference?"

Still no answers.

"What you students must first understand if you wish to have any true success here at Zarmore or back on Earth is that everything in your existence is exactly the same. We know scientifically that all matter on Earth and in the entire universe is composed of atoms. Even deep space comets that have landed on your planet are made of the same atoms. Everyone here knows what atoms are, correct?"

A few students shake their heads no.

"Atoms are the building blocks for all life. Every physical thing you see in this universe is made up of atoms. There is no exception. All atoms are composed mainly of three separate things. Protons and neutrons make up a nucleus head which is encircled by an electron cloud. These electrons that circle the nucleus are known to be the smallest part of the atom and have therefore been recognized as the smallest particle in the universe. However, if you look deeper into an atom with super microscopes, as scientists have done both here and on Earth, you will see that the atom is really not even a particle at all. It's just a high-speed vibration with many holes in it."

The dragon starts pacing back and forth from the front of the classroom as he continues the lecture. "So what does this mean, you may be asking. It means that everything you see in this physical universe, at its core, is not actually physical at all. In Egaria, on Earth, everywhere. Everything, including your own bodies, is nothing more than just atoms. And atoms, at their deepest core, have been scientifically determined to be mostly just empty space. They are just a vibration of energy. The only thing that makes this blackboard look different than this student or this chair look different from that piece of paper is the structure of their atoms. Depending on how many neutrons, protons, and electrons they have, determines how they will look *physically*. But if we look beyond the physical, everything is simply just a vibration. This is not theory. It's science."

The professor stops walking and looks toward the class. "Is everyone still with me so far?"

The students nod their heads yes.

"Now I understand this may be a little difficult to start looking at your world and your own bodies as vibrational instead of physical, but if you wish to continue and have success with your studies here at Zarmore, you must begin to come to terms with this truth."

The professor resumes pacing. "Now, knowing that everything in your universe is simply a vibration rather than separate physical objects, you are better equipped to understand frequencies, which is the basis for all subsequent subjects in this class. Every physical thing you see, which you now know is just a vibration, also emits a specific frequency. This book on my desk is emitting a specific frequency, as is this chair, and as is your own body. This can all be measured with scientific instruments and confirmed."

Professor Raldorthorch picks up a remote control and walks over to a small flat-screen television sitting on a tall table in the front corner of the class. "Now why am I explaining this all to you, and why is it important for tuning class? First, let me ask all of you a question." He turns the television on, and there's what appears to be a soap opera playing out between a male and female dragon. The female is holding what looks like a baby goblin in her arms and screaming at the male dragon something about this being his son.

"What the...?" Teddy mumbles.

The professor quickly changes the channel. A commercial showing a goblin in a bikini pouring hot cheese over different styles of sneakers and high heels starts playing.

Professor Raldorthorch clicks the television off and tosses the remote in the corner of the classroom. "What's playing on the television isn't what's important. What I would like to know is if anyone here truly understands how it works. How is it that I can press a button on a remote, and images and sounds from something many miles away instantly appear on the screen? Or how is it that you can tune a radio to a specific channel, and out of nowhere, music begins to play?"

The room is silent.

"Well, the answer is because of frequencies. This television is requesting a certain frequency that it wants to receive for each channel. That frequency is being sent out by the TV cable company and travels through the sky while bouncing off satellites until it finds the matching frequency that your TV is requesting. The result is what you see on the television."

"And what exactly were we seeing on the television?" Teddy asks.

The professor continues to speak as if he hadn't heard him. "Frequencies are very specific and reliable. You don't turn your radio to 98.1 FM and ever hear 1630 AM, do you? Now just like this television or a radio can emit a specific frequency and call into itself a matching frequency, so can your brain. The only difference between your brain and a radio is that your brain is much more powerful and doesn't need to bounce off satellites to reach its destination. And as a radio signal can only travel a certain distance, the transmitter in your head can travel all the way across the universe, instantly, and without any training whatsoever. Every waking moment of your life, you are emitting frequencies, whether you know it or not. Now, you may be wondering what's the benefit of having such a powerful transmitter and receiver in your head. Are you going to be learning how to dial your brain toward radio stations and be listening to music in class instead of paying attention?"

A few students laugh while the professor continues to speak. "Well, that answer is no. In this class, we will begin to study some of the more unexplored abilities that lay hidden beneath your skulls. The first and most fundamental being the fact that your brain does emit frequencies, and when this happens, it alters and affects physical matter."

The professor glances at the clock then walks back over to his desk. "Now, I'd love to start digging into this, but it looks like we're already close to running out of time for today, and I still haven't assigned you all your homework yet."

There's a low groan from the students.

The dragon smiles, looking more menacingly than friendly. "Relax, I won't be grading it, and I think you will enjoy the experience. What we're going to practice on is awakening and sharpening your tuning abilities. You all are already considered masters of dreaming. Otherwise, you would not be here in this academy. That being said, this task should not prove to be too difficult. What I'd like for each of you to do is pick a partner with whom you would feel comfortable sharing a dream with. Your homework will need to be attempted once you exit through the oak today and return to your regular dreaming back on Earth. Once asleep and back on Earth, I would like you to meet up with your partner in the same dream. I am not talking about dreaming *about* your partner. I am saying that you must both meet inside the *same* exact dream. The experience should feel as vivid and natural as our experience right now. To do this, you need to both create your own specific frequency. This is done by the two of you coming up with and deciding on a unique thought which you believe no one else in the universe is thinking of. You will hold this thought in your mind as you drift to sleep. Or in today's case, as you exit through the oak and return to your regular dreams on Earth."

The dragon raises a scaly and pointy green finger in the air. "A few tips. The more weird and unique your thought is, the better. This reduces the chances of anyone else thinking of the same thing and creating resistance or traffic. If you can envision images or scenes with specific emotions attached to them, there will be an even greater advantage, as emotions are more important than the thought itself. And finally, keep your mind completely clear of any thoughts other than the one you and your partner have agreed upon. That's all I have for you. Good luck and I'll see you next class. Once you decide on a frequency with your partner, you're free to leave."

The room immediately floods with conversations amongst the students. Teddy looks over at Victoria. "Partners?"

"Sure," she says. "Have any ideas on what frequency you want to use?"

"Um, I don't know. He said to try and invoke some emotions so maybe let's think of something we're both scared of?"

"Eh, how about we try for some happy thoughts instead. What's an experience that brings you a lot of joy?"

Teddy pauses for a moment, then thinks about the first time he rode Naroshi. "Um..."

"Well, for me," she says. "I love hot air balloons. My parents own a couple, and I get to ride up on them quite a bit."

"Ok," Teddy says. "I've never been on one, but I guess I could imagine myself being happy doing that."

"Great!" She says. "But I don't know if that's really unique enough to be an individual type of frequency. We have to come up with something that no one else is thinking of to make it work."

"Hmm," Teddy says. "How about the hot air balloon is actually a hollowed-out orange, you know, like a fruit, and it's singing songs while we fly through some snowcapped mountains."

Victoria blinks a few times and opens her mouth but doesn't actually verbally respond.

"I mean," Teddy starts. "He said to make it weird, right?"

The bell rings, and students pack their bags and head toward the exit for lunch.

"Ok, um," Victoria says. "Yeah, let's just go ahead with that idea. So, when I'm leaving the oak today, I'll think of eating oranges in the balloon as it begins to snow?"

"No, you don't eat the orange," Teddy corrects her. "The orange is the hot air balloon itself. We'll be traveling in it through some snowcapped mountains, you know, like the Alps. And then while we're doing so, the orange will be singing songs."

Victoria sighs then tosses her backpack over her left shoulder. "Ok, you might have to explain it to me one more time during PT later today." She pulls the other half of her backpack over her shoulder and adjusts the straps. "See you then!"

· · ·

"Wow, you all really do sit in the exact same seats every day," Teddy says as he approaches his friends while holding a golden tray of food in his hands.

"Mr. Teddy Tedster, everybody!" Calvin announces.

Ronnie and Olivia burst into laughter as Ava furrows her brow and looks toward Calvin. "Hey, only I can call him that!"

"Do I have any vote in this?" Teddy asks as he sets his tray down and takes a seat.

"No," the group says in unison.

"And in regards to our seating arrangements," Olivia says. "We've officially claimed this table as property of House Tilly. You're welcome to join our clan if you wish."

"Wait, why is our clan named after you, Olivia?" Calvin asks. "If anything, it should be called House Whitaker since there are two of us here."

"Are you challenging your queen, peasant?" Olivia asks.

"Peasant?" Calvin says as he looks toward the rest of the group. "Please tell me you guys heard that."

Teddy looks over at Olivia. "So what happened to your other friends? I thought you guys were all just sitting together for that mentorship thing you had to do."

"Well," Olivia says. "We were initially, but after seeing Ava's first-yearer nearly get killed right in front of us, we all kind of bonded a little."

"Plus," Ava says from the seat next to Olivia. "All of our other friends have boyfriends now, so we're trying to steer clear from that kind of toxic environment."

"Enough of that though," Ronnie says as he grabs a french fry off of Calvin's plate and takes a bite. "What's this crazy story about Sean that I'm not going to believe?"

"You're asking for trouble, little bro," Calvin says.

Ronnie smiles as he chews the french fry then looks back toward Teddy.

"Wait," Ava says. "Sean? As in 'Sean' Sean? Like, our Sean? The same Sean that..."

"Relax and give the kid a chance to answer, Ava," Olivia says as she reaches over and grabs a french fry off of Calvin's plate as well. "Jeez."

Calvin raises his hands in a look of bewilderment.

Teddy goes on to explain everything that happened by the picnic benches with Kristi and Sean the other day.

"Definitely sounds like the same 'Sean' Sean to me," Ronnie says.

"It is," Teddy replies.

"Ugh, I'm so stupid sometimes," Ava says.

"Relax," Ronnie says. "I was just teasing you."

"No," she continues. "I should've told Teddy that Sean lived in New York as well. It didn't even cross my mind that they could possibly run into each other in the real world. It's just that; sometimes when we're down here, I forget that we have other lives.... Why couldn't Dean Spear just wipe that jerk completely as he would've done to anyone else or send him to the island?

"Seriously," Olivia says as she finishes chewing the fry she stole from Calvin, then cuts into a piece of turkey on her plate.

"By the way, Teddy, I'll be visiting New York with my parents next summer, so be prepared."

Ava shakes her head. "I mean, how important is his family in Egaria that he gets to receive such special treatment?"

"It's fine," Teddy says. "I've dealt with bullies my whole life. I think I'm getting pretty good at ignoring them now."

Ava forces a smile then looks down toward her food. "Still...."

"Well, in lighter news," Calvin says. "One of those creepy not so little snails came by my class today and delivered my schedule. Looks like I'll be racing Mr. Tedster here on November 12th."

Ava glances up and smiles. "I'll be looking forward to watching that."

"Just make sure to get to the arena on time," Calvin says. "I have a feeling I'll be finishing prettyyy early."

"Yeah, probably because they'll have to disqualify him before the race even starts since he doesn't even know how to properly mount himself on the horse," Ronnie says as he grabs another fry off Calvin's plate. "Victoria told me how practice went the other day."

"Alright, man," Calvin says. "You take one more fry..."

"What?" Ronnie says. "You going to tell mom your *little* brother is picking on you?"

"Hey, Teddy," Olivia interjects. "What's up with your friend Caesar? I heard he confessed to working with that farmer guy or whatever."

"Oh yeah," Ava says. "I heard that too! What's going on? I thought you guys were in a band together or something. Why is he teaming up with that Ziruam guy now and kidnapping other goblins?"

"Um, the term is actually called goblinapping, Ava," Olivia says, causing her friend to laugh and playfully punch her in the arm.

Teddy shakes his head as he stares down at his tray. "I have no clue what's going on with all that. I wish I could talk with him and find out."

"Yeah, I don't know if they even allow visitors in Frostlepeak or how you would get there if they did," Ava says. "The only part of Egaria I've seen so far is Zarmore."

"Buuut," Olivia says with a grin. "We might get to find out next week since we're finally making our first supervised trip off campus!"

"Yes, yes," Ava says, smiling from ear to ear toward her friend. "I'm excited too." Her smile then fades a little when she looks back at Teddy. "But we're not going to be visiting Frostlepeak, unfortunately. We'll be taking a tour of the capital colony, Praidora."

"It's fine," Teddy says. "I don't think going on a suicide mission to Frostlepeak just to try and ask Caesar a question is a great idea anyway. I'll just wait it out and keep looking for Naroshi."

"How's that going, by the way?" Ronnie asks.

"It's only been a couple of days. I'm keeping an eye out for her during my practice sessions in the arena and told Calvin and Victoria to as well."

"Yup, Detective Whitaker on duty," Calvin says as he bites into a cheeseburger. "If anyone can find your horse, it'll be me."

Ronnie shakes his head then looks back at Teddy. "Yeah, well, at least you have plenty of time. Ziruam gave you a week to find her, which is like seven months for us here."

"Well, he didn't actually give *me* anything," Teddy says. "He gave Caesar a week. But now that he's locked up, I don't really know what's going to happen. I assume Ziruam could come looking for me at any moment now."

"Well, I wouldn't worry too much, Teddy. You're safe here," Olivia says. "Dean Spear isn't going to let anything bad happen to you while you're on campus."

Teddy sighs. "Yeah, you're probably right."

Frosted Sweets

Teddy pulls his red cotton beanie down over his ears then zips his thick ski jacket up past his neck and over his mouth. Even with nearly three layers of clothes on, he can't get his body to stop shivering. He looks down. His legs have nearly sunken past their kneecaps in the midst of the thick white powder, which is acting more like quicksand than snow. He clenches his teeth then works to pull his right leg out. The three seconds it takes him to do so feels like thirty, and once his boot is out and leg is free, he takes a heavy step forward and sinks back into the frost again. He exhales, then looks back toward his left leg and repeats the process. "*What am I even doing here?*" He thinks to himself as he looks up through the blizzard and toward the pinnacle of a mountain.

    A flurry-filled gust of wind whips across his chest. He sways his hands in the air and desperately tries to find his balance, but with his feet fixed and locked into the snow like freshly poured cement, he has nowhere to go but backwards. He falls on his rear then rolls flat onto his back, slowly sinking into the snow once again. Another gust of flurries sweep in and run across his body and face, quickly piling fresh powder atop the boy. He spits some snow out of his mouth then tries to roll over on his side and prop himself back up to his feet, but the powder is too soft. Every effort he makes to free himself only causes him to sink more and become further entrapped. He looks up to his right to see if there's anything he can grab to help pull himself out and then grimaces when he sees that there isn't.

He clenches his eyes shut as another prolonged blast of flurries rushes in and adds one more layer of snow atop his sinking grave. He shudders underneath the added weight and tries to control his breathing. "*Is this really how I'm going out?*" He thinks. "*Killed in a blizzard in search of... I don't know. Something important? Maybe? Seriously, what am I doing out here?*"

The speed of the wind slows down, and he opens his eyes again then looks to his left. A few clouds move away from the others, revealing the pointed snowcapped pinnacles of three more mountains. "*Why do I feel like I've seen this place before?*" Before he can answer himself, another gust of white flurries rushes in and blocks his view, burying him yet deeper into the snow. He returns his gaze to the sky above him. The yellow glow from the fiery sun is shining bright in between a newly formed cluster of clouds. He squints, then looks away. Never in his life has he been so close to the sun. Never in his life has he been so far away.

He continues to shiver underneath the bright glow from above. For some reason, the thought of his father comes to mind. "Go with the light," the man would always say to him before he went to bed each night.

Teddy thinks of laughing, but it's physically impossible.

Then within a matter of seconds, it gets dark. He can't see the golden glow anymore, and his body is cast in shadow. "*This is it,*" he thinks to himself as he closes his eyes.

"Grab it!" Someone yells from above.

"*The angels are here,*" he continues inside his head. "*Take me away, my friends. Take me away.*"

"Teddy, come on!" the female voice shouts again. "Look up and grab the rope!"

Teddy's eyelids spring open. There, just a few inches away from his face, is a ladder made from rope. It's affixed to a large basket of what appears to be a hot air balloon hovering just below his view of the sun. A girl with strawberry blonde hair and a green beanie is staring back down at him.

"If Te Te Te Te TeddYYY is not re re re re ReadYYY
How we going to FlYYY high up in this SkYYY?"

"Please stop singing!" Teddy shouts. "It's not helping! And I can't reach the rope! My arms are already buried too deep!"

"It's not me singing!" The girl shouts from above through flurries of snow. "It's your freaking orange, man! He won't shut up! This is a dream, Teddy! Now grab the rope and get up here!"

"All you gotta do is BeliEvEEEEE, Teddy Teddy Teddy
Then you can get up with EasEEEEE, Teddy Teddy Teddy"

"Oh crap, we did it."

Teddy closes his eyes and envisions his jacket being powered by the warmth of the sun. But nothing happens.

"It's not working!" He shouts while sinking deeper into the snow.

"We're in a shared dream, Teddy. We both have to agree on something to make it happen!"

"Warm my jacket!" He shouts.

"Ok, I'm ready!" She says.

He closes his eyes again, then relaxes as the snow above and below his upper body melts and his teeth finally stop chattering. His arms are now free, but he's still sinking.

"Hurry, Teddy!"

He clenches his jaw as he reaches his shaky right hand up toward the rope. A few moments pass, and just when he thinks he isn't going to be able to reach it and that his arm is going to fall out of its socket, his fingers finally grasp around the thick thread. He yanks the rope toward him and pulls himself out of the snow. The ladder sways in the wind as he climbs up and into the basket. Once inside and secure, Victoria smiles and wraps her arms around him. "We did it!"

"Weee areeee the championsssss
WEEE AREEEE THE CHAMPIONSSSS"

Victoria shakes her head and looks up toward the balloon. "Ok, you keep singing, and I'm cutting off your gas and letting us crash. I found Teddy, and now we don't need to be here anymore. So unless you want to be orange juice on ice, I suggest you shut it, Mr. Balloon."

"Ohhhhhh, WHHHYYY do you MAKE me SO blueeeee? Baby, IIIIII don't WANT to HURT... Whoa whoa HEY THERE!"

Victoria just cut off the gas to the hot air balloon, and they're now in a free-fall toward the center of the valley.

"Ok, OK!" The balloon shouts. "I'll chill off the singing!"

Victoria turns the gas back on and the fall stops, allowing them to fly at a more steady and comfortable pace.

"Jeez, I figured you guys would like that last one," the orange says.

"Well, you were wrong," Victoria replies.

Teddy laughs, then walks over to one of the edges of the basket, placing his glove-covered hands on its brim and looking down into the white drenched valley below. The snow flurries have lightened up, and he can see the wide and steadily flowing blue river clearly beneath him now. He smiles as he turns back around and takes in the rest of the scene from above. It's nearly just as he imagined in class.

"What do we do now?" Teddy asks.

"I guess whatever we want," Victoria says. "It is a dream after all."

"Do you guys like tacos?" The orange asks. "I could kill for some right now."

Victoria's eyes grow larger as she looks at Teddy.

The boy just smiles, then turns back around and points toward another mountain in the distance. "Well, it looks like there's a cave over there. Want to check it out?"

"Not really a fan of the dark, kid," the orange says. "Plus, come on, Teddy. Let's focus here. Tacos, Teddy, tacos. Tacos, Teddy, tacos."

"Tacos, Teddy, TaccOOOOsssss
Tacos, Teddy, TaccOOOOsssss"

Victoria rolls her eyes then cuts the gas off again.

"For the love of..." the orange shouts. "Ok, I'll shut it!"

Victoria turns the gas back on. "Yeah, cave sounds fun to me."

The orange imitates Victoria in a squeaky and mocking voice. *"Yeah, cave sounds fun to me."*

"What was that?" She says as she looks up and puts her hand back on the knob which controls the gas.

"Nothing!" The orange squeaks.

"Whoa, what's that over there?" Teddy asks as he points toward the direction in which they're flying.

It looks as if another hot air balloon is traveling straight toward them.

"That's strange," Victoria says. "Do you think it's a real person or just another dream character like this crazy orange here?"

"Listen, lady," The orange says from above. "You're the one who keeps flirting with death every ten seconds, not me. If anyone is crazy, it's you."

"I don't know," Teddy says. "It looks like a regular hot air balloon, but I think there's someone inside. I can't tell for sure until it gets closer."

A few minutes pass before they can finally make out who's inside the other balloon.

"No way," Victoria says. "Is that a...?"

"Horse," Teddy finishes.

The two balloons slowly approach each other like cars on opposite sides of the road. The distance between them shrinks to about forty feet before Teddy speaks up. "That's her."

"That's who?" Victoria asks.

"Naroshi!" He shouts, his voice echoing through the valley.

The distance between the balloons shrinks another ten feet. Teddy walks over to the edge of the basket and grabs hold of one of the larger ropes attached to the balloon. He grasps it firmly, then pulls himself up and steps onto the brim of the basket. His feet wobble as he tries to remain balanced.

"What are you doing?!" Victoria shouts from behind him. "Are you crazy?!"

"I'm going to jump over when she passes by," he says, not bothering to look back at Victoria. "I have to."

"But Teddy," she says. "I don't think that horse is real. And even if she was, what good does it do if you're both riding on a hot air balloon in some weird dream? Plus, Mrs. Suki told us during orientation to never just assume we're dreaming and risk our lives!"

The orange snorts. "Coming from the girl who keeps assuming she's dreaming and risking our lives."

"I wasn't really going to let us crash! I just needed you to shut up."

"Oh really?" The orange says.

"Shut up!" Victoria shouts.

Teddy pays them no attention as he continues to focus on the slowly approaching hot air balloon. "And what if this isn't a dream? Or what if this is one of those places like Slaybethor where it's half dream, half real world? Maybe Naroshi and I can land the balloon, and I can ride her back to her owner from here."

"Well, if this is one of those kinds of places, then you definitely shouldn't risk it! You can die, Teddy!"

He doesn't respond. The balloons are now almost parallel with each other.

"Ugh," Teddy says. "This gap is a lot further than I expected!"

"Then don't do it!" Victoria shouts.

Teddy looks forward and sees the strong white horse standing in the basket nearly ten feet across from him. The horse turns her head toward Teddy, and the two lock eyes. A soft waterfall of ease and calm rushes down Teddy's spine as he stares into the warm and deep cyan green eyes of his old friend. He smiles, then crouches down and bends his knees atop the brim of the basket and waits. Once the balloons are parallel with each other, he springs upwards and into the frigid air toward the other balloon.

"Teddy!" Victoria shouts.

White snowflakes rush across Teddy's face as he extends his arms out toward the other basket. After what feels like an eternity, his fingers finally crash against straw-like material, and he grabs hold of its edge, causing the horse to neigh and the basket to wobble. He hears an audible sigh of relief behind him from Victoria.

Teddy starts to pull himself up, but with only the tips of his fingers wrapped around the brim of the basket, his grip is too weak. His right hand slips completely and falls to his side.

"No!" Victoria shouts.

Teddy winces as he tries to gather a tighter grip with his left hand. In the middle of his struggle, he feels something cold and coarse press down on the top of his fingers. He looks up and sees Naroshi looking down at him with one of her hooves up and placed firmly on top of his fingers. "That's it, girl," he says. "Help me up."

They lock eyes once again. Teddy smiles as she applies a little more pressure above his fingers. "There ya go, girl. Now just let me get my other hand back up here."

Then something changes inside Naroshi's eyes. The green melts away into a shade of fiery red.

"What the...?" Teddy says.

Her snow-white hair darkens into a heavy coat of midnight black. The horse releases pressure off the top of Teddy's fingers then slides her hoof to the side of his hand. A look of bewilderment overtakes Teddy's face. "Naroshi..."

She winks at the boy then swipes her hoof across Teddy's fingers, separating them from the basket. Tears glaze Teddy's eyes as he loses his grip and falls backwards toward the light blue river in the center of the snow-white valley, his left arm still extended out toward the basket.

He hears a faint and fading scream from Victoria as he descends. Then another rhythmic voice emerges from above.

> "Cream cheese taste better in DREAMsssss
> Teddy just died, and Victoria SCREAMeddddd"

. . .

The toaster makes a dinging sound, and Teddy sits up from the table then walks across the kitchen. He opens the cabinet, grabs a paper plate, and sets it down on the counter. He then reaches over the toaster with his thumb and index finger and pinches a Pop-Tart up and out of the steaming appliance. The pastry is still hot, and he works fast to drop it over the paper plate before it burns his fingertips. He repeats the process with the other Pop-Tart, grabs a paper towel, and carries his breakfast to the kitchen table.

He sits down in the wobbly wooden chair then pulls his phone out of his pocket as he waits for the pink frosted pastries with red sprinkles to cool down. A few minutes pass before he sets his phone to the side and picks up one of the Pop-Tarts off the paper plate. He grasps it with both hands and slowly splits it in half. Steam emanates from its red gooey inside, and a smell of cherry flows up and through his nostrils. He waits for the steam to diminish a little, then takes a bite and chews. He smiles as all of his taste buds awake, and a feeling of warmth and goodness momentarily takes control of his body. The memories of last night arise in his mind.

"*How could I think that dream was actually real?*"

The silliness and absurdity of his dreams usually only become apparent after he awakes the next morning. He'll still have to verify with Victoria that the real her was there with him last night, but he's sure that everything else, including the "Naroshi" character and the singing orange, were just parts of their imaginations.

He swallows the chewed-up yet still warm pastry and looks to his left. The sun has just risen over the neighboring complex and is beginning to shine its rays onto Teddy's apartment. He narrows his eyes as he peers out the kitchen window which overlooks their small front yard patio. It's still too early to greet the sun. He picks up the same Pop-Tart and takes another bite, then walks toward the window. With his free hand, he grabs the plastic wand by the side of the window and starts to twist the white blinds shut until he sees something which causes him to stop.

"Uh, ok. That's kind of creepy," he says as he brings his head closer to the glass and tries to get a better look. It appears that some small animal is sitting in the wooden rocking chair that rests just in front of the kitchen window. Teddy lets go of the wand and walks toward the front door.

As he enters the patio, he makes sure that the screen door doesn't slam shut behind him. He takes the final bite of the piece of Pop-Tart in his hand then begins to inch closer toward the rocking chair. A few moments pass before he's close enough to see what sits atop it. He exhales and relaxes his shoulders.

The head of a stuffed toy bear is on the ground by Teddy's feet while its brown and fuzzy body sits on the rocking chair. He picks them both up and walks toward the large dumpster in the parking lot. Never in his life has he seen this stuffed animal before, but there are a lot of children in the neighborhood, so he assumes it's probably one of theirs. That still doesn't explain why the head is ripped off or why it was sitting in his rocking chair though.

"Yup, still creepy," Teddy says as he lifts the heavy lid to the metal dumpster up and tosses the bear inside.

He then lets go of the lid, and the dumpster slams shut. A swarm of flies rushes toward his face, and he works to swat them away as he heads back through the parking lot and toward his apartment.

The other Pop-Tart is cold by the time he returns inside, and he finishes what is left of it in under a minute. He then tosses the paper plate and towel in the trash and walks by the fridge to read the note his mother left him:

Good morning Teddy,

I have some errands to run after work today and won't be home in time to cook dinner. I left $20 on the counter for you to order us some pizza. We already have drinks in the fridge, so just use the money for food. I should be home around 6.

Have a nice day!

Love,
mom

Teddy looks toward the counter and verifies the twenty-dollar bill is there, then smiles. *"Pizza night."*

He scoops up his skateboard and walks through the living room and toward the front door. His backpack is hanging on the coat rack. He picks it up off the hook, straps it over his shoulder, then exits through the door and skates to class.

The start of his day at Cameron Creek goes just about the same as most others—with him not communicating with anybody until biology class.

"Why didn't you come sit with me at lunch today?" Kristi asks after Teddy walks in the room and sits down across from her at their table.

Teddy just stares at her.

"Ah, come on, Teddy. Sean is harmless. You can still sit with me."

Teddy shakes his head, then opens his backpack and pulls out pencil and paper.

"Ok, and I'm sorry for not sticking up for you when he took your cupcake. If it makes you feel any better, I got mad at him after school. He said he feels awful about it and that he was only trying to act tough in front of me."

Teddy laughs and is about to say something, but Kristi speaks up again first.

"And I brought you something." She stands up and pulls a brown paper bag out of her backpack and walks toward Teddy's side of the table. He tilts his head and looks at the bag, then back up at Kristi.

"WhAt is it?" He asks, his voice cracking toward the beginning.

Kristi giggles.

"Sorry," Teddy says. "I haven't really used my voice yet today."

"It's ok," she says, then pulls out a small plastic tray of four frosted vanilla cupcakes with rainbow sprinkles from the brown paper bag and sets it in front of Teddy. "I told my mom what happened and asked her to bake some more."

"Wow," Teddy says.

Kristi smiles then leans down and hugs him. "Ew, Teddy. Why are you so wet and sticky?"

Teddy swivels his head around and attempts to look at his back. "Oh yeah, I forgot about that. Jeremy gave me another Gatorade shower in the hall this morning."

"What?! Why did he do that?"

"Why does he ever do mean things?"

"Yeah, but," Kristi says. "You mean he just came up and poured Gatorade on you for no reason?"

"Well, not exactly," Teddy starts. "I saw him walking down the hall with that same miserable, angry expression on his face. You know the one I'm talking about?"

Kristi laughs. "Of course. The whole school knows that one."

"Yeah, so I was just watching him and envisioned how terrible it must be to live inside that head of his. I didn't even realize I was smiling until he shoved me into a locker and dumped the juice on me."

"Teddy..." Kristi says as her face falls into a frown.

"It's fine," he continues. "It really doesn't even bother me that much anymore. I mean, yeah, I may be sticky on the outside, but he's still suffering constantly on the inside and now has to buy a new Gatorade."

"But, Teddy..."

"Oh, and you should've seen the look on his face once he saw that no matter what he did to me physically, I wasn't bothered. I just kept smiling."

"Well, I hope he doesn't pick on you more now after this."

"I don't think he will. He's just a bully, and bullies are only looking for fear and a reaction, and I'm not going to give him either of those from here on out. Plus, I just honestly don't even really care that much anymore. He can't touch my soul, you know? He doesn't control how I feel inside my own body."

"Touch your... soul? Where are you even coming up with all these ideas?"

Teddy smiles then looks down at the cupcakes in front of him. He pauses for a few moments, thinking of the best way to reply. "Eh, heard it from a little fox."

"Uhh... Ok, Teddy," Kristi says as she turns around and walks back to her seat.

Teddy's smile fades as he watches her walk away. "*Yup, that sounded a lot cooler in my head.*"

Horsepower

Teddy releases his right hand from the reins and pats near the horse's rear to ensure the neutralizing sticker is still on. It had only fallen off once during a practice session, but that was enough to make him realize that he never wants to experience it again, especially during a race. He ducks his head to avoid a low-hanging branch then grabs hold of the reins with both hands again. Victoria and her horse Gemini are well in the lead, but Courtney and Sunny Days still seem within reach. Teddy veers his horse to the left as they exit out from underneath the shade of the forest and down into the sunlit open valley below.

The sudden change in light irritates Teddy's eyes and forces him to squint. He knows that the dark jungle to his right could offer his vision some relief, so he spares it a glance. The chimps screech and holler as he and his horse Miss B race past.

"*At least they still hate me,*" Teddy thinks to himself.

He prefers the predictability of rage rather than the stillness of the unknown he's been receiving from his other enemies. He hasn't seen Sean in nearly two months since their encounter by the picnic benches, and Jeremy and the other kids at Cameron Creek seem to have lost interest in teasing him after he stopped giving them a reaction. The peace is nice, but Teddy knows that they all still dislike him, and it will eventually come to an end. He just wishes they would be more open about it rather than making him constantly wonder what they're plotting next.

His thirteenth birthday passed yesterday with minimal fanfare. He chose not to mention it to his friends at Zarmore, so the only person who acknowledged it other than his mother was Kristi. The two of them are back to eating lunch together on the picnic benches, but it's never been quite the same since the Sean incident. He enjoys her company though, even if he can't talk with her about any of the real exciting parts of his life. It still feels good to laugh in a place other than inside his dreams.

In those sleepful states, his life carries on to a similar beat of calm. Ziruam has yet to come looking for him, and Caesar is still locked up in Frostlepeak, with Miss Butts's whereabouts continuing to remain unknown. He knows the day will arrive where he'll eventually have to deal with all that as well.

"Are you kidding me?!" A faint voice shouts from somewhere behind him. "Gooo!"

Teddy glances to the rear and sees that Calvin has just exited the woods. A few of the boy's dreadlocks have become untied and are dangling in front of his face while he yells at his horse Skull Crusher, who just stopped at the entrance of the valley to eat some grass.

Teddy smiles then returns his vision forward. Calvin will need to come in at least third to erase the last-place finish he earned the previous month and avoid more ridicule from his younger brother Ronnie. Teddy, on the other hand, feels satisfied with the second-place performance he had in October after beating Courtney Ackerly and her horse Sunny Days by a nose. However, he knows he'll have to work harder if he wants to beat her again today.

"Not going to happen!" The chubby girl with short and curly black hair shouts as she notices Teddy approaching from behind near the base of the mountain at the edge of the valley. "You got lucky last time, but weather is on my side today!"

A soft whistling sound blows from the noses of their horses as they race neck and neck up the face of the mountain. They remain even through the left-hand turn, then follow the track through another stretch of woods.

He hears a low roar erupting from near the castle. Victoria must've just entered back into the stadium. Another win here will make her undefeated, with already ten points accumulated in just two races.

Teddy and Courtney continue to jockey back and forth for second-place as they approach the final left turn leading back into the stadium.

"Come on, Sunnyyy!" Courtney shouts as she whips her horse's rear with a racing bat and looks back over her shoulder at Teddy.

The curve leading into the stadium is now only fifty yards away. Teddy remembers what Dickie told them during their first practice concerning this part of the race and decides to pull the reins of Miss B and slow her down.

Courtney and Sunny Days speed forward past Teddy. She looks back and smiles at the boy with her broad and dimple-faced grin. "I told you, Teddy! Not during sunny days!"

Teddy wonders if he played it too safe by slowing down so much. However, he feels reassured once he hears Courtney shouting a few moments later. Her horse ran straight past the final turn and into a densely green area of shrubbery. Teddy and Miss B approach the curve a few seconds later. He smiles as he watches Courtney screaming up into the fiery red sun while Dickie hops off his black horse that he parked nearby and runs over to help her. "I told y'all! I told y'all! I told y'all!"

The tall archway leading into the stadium is now within view. Goosebumps roll like waves from Teddy's toes up to the nape of his neck as he feels the roar from the students inside. Even though most of the arena's seats are unfilled, the way it's constructed with its marble surfaces and thick walls make the echoes from the shouting inside sound much more deep and profound.

He passes under the gleaming white marble archway and the raised gate that's attached to it. Once through and into the arena, he nearly loses his breath while taking in the scene that awaits him. A sea of cheering students in green plaid uniforms fill the lower rows of the stadium with all eyes fixed on the new entry from below. "Yay, Teddy!" He hears a familiar voice shout.

He glances to his left and sees Ava, Olivia, and Ronnie standing and cheering in one of the front rows by the archway. Teddy flashes a smile toward them, then looks back ahead and whips the rear of his horse with the racing bat. Miss B picks up speed as they move across the final wide right-hand turn of the track inside the arena. For the first time since the beginning of the race, he sees Victoria. Her horse Gemini is already parked and tied up in the stable underneath the west gate while she stands near its entrance. Her long strawberry blonde hair is tied up in a bun, and her light blue eyes stand out against the similar backdrop of the sky above. She sees Teddy then smiles and claps her hands as she waits for him to cross the finish line.

By the time he does, neither Courtney nor Calvin have even entered the stadium. He hops off his horse and rubs her nose. "Good job, Miss B... Even though I know that if it weren't for that neutralizing sticker, you probably would've tried to throw me off the mountain." The crowd continues to cheer as Teddy walks into the stable and ties his horse up next to Gemini. He then turns around and nearly falls backwards into Miss B when he notices Victoria standing directly behind him. "Whoa! Uh, hi there."

She smiles and gives him a hug. "Sorry, I didn't mean to scare you. Good race today, Teddy."

"Thanks, it was a little more luck than skill though, I think. You're the one who should be congratulated. Two first-place finishes in a row."

"Thanks, the credit goes to my horse Gemini though. He's really great."

"I don't know. You seem to have a pretty good knack at leading and controlling other animals."

Victoria laughs. "If you're referring to that silly orange of yours as an animal, please don't. None of that was real."

Teddy smiles. "Hey, come on, it still counts in there. And you got him to behave. You saw what happened when I tried to ask for help from a dream character."

"Yeah, that was pretty scary. What'd you even say to that horse to make him want to throw you off the hot air balloon like that?"

The crowd roars again as another rider enters through the archway. Teddy and Victoria turn around and walk back out from under the gate.

"Alright, Calvin!" Victoria cheers, then looks back toward Teddy and laughs.

It's hard to tell who's riding who as the brown horse jerks to the finish line with Calvin bouncing and screaming on its back.

They cross the finish a few moments later, and Calvin dives off his horse and rolls toward Teddy and Victoria.

Their eyes expand as they look at each other then back down toward Calvin on the ground. His sudden tuck and roll produced a cloud of dust and forces Teddy to close his eyes and cough. He swats the dirt out of the air, then reaches a hand down toward Calvin and helps him up. "You know, you don't have to do these races if you don't want to."

"What are you talking about?" Calvin says as he reties his dreadlocks behind his head. "I'm getting better. I got two points today."

Victoria walks over toward Calvin and brushes some dirt off his back. "This is true, Teddy. He did place third. What ever happened to Courtney anyway? She was pretty close to me in the beginning."

"I think she might have gotten disqualified after veering too far off the track," Teddy says.

"That explains some," Calvin adds. "I saw her arguing with Dickie outside the arena when I made the final turn."

Calvin's horse trots away from them and wanders around the grassy area in the middle of the arena.

"You planning on tying him up, Calvin?" Victoria asks.

"Nope. I'm clocked out for the day. He's Dickie's problem now."

A loud voice emerges from the speaker system inside the arena, and the group stops talking. "Ladies and gentlemen, goblins and creatures, I ask you to please direct your attention to the center of the arena for the commencement of the ribbon ceremony and the congratulating of our victors."

Calvin puts his arms around the shoulders of both Teddy and Victoria. "That's our cue, my fellow victors." He takes a deep breath inward, then exhales and smiles. "Ah, feels good to say that."

. . .

"But you're not a victor!" Teddy hears Ronnie shout at his brother as he exits the hall and into the castle foyer. "You got third and only because one horse was disqualified."

"Still got me a blue ribbon for the month, and two points is two points, little bro. Check the standings."

"You guys are still arguing about that race?" Teddy asks as he walks up and greets his friends. "It's December now; you gotta let it go."

"What's up, Teddy," Calvin says. "Check out these standings that Professor Jones just posted. I'm still pretty low in them but better than dead last and in the negative."

"You hear this guy?" Ronnie says.

Teddy laughs, then walks up to the bulletin board and examines the long sheet of paper that's pressed underneath a green thumbtack:

Zarmore Racing League Standings

Regular Season
First-Yearers

=====================================

Place	Points	Runner Info	Jockey
1st	10pts	Bonfire in the Rain	Giovanni Ginesi
2nd	10pts	Gemini	Victoria Addington
3rd	8pts	Von Schnickerlonger Jr.	Connor Graham
4th	8pts	Dark Mist	Michelle Price
5th	7pts	Rachel is Fast	Rachel Redburn
6th	6pts	Miss B	Theodore Lancaster
7th	6pts	Dream Machine	Alice Torbett

"I don't see you," Teddy says.

"You have to flip a few pages," Calvin replies as he reaches over and lifts up the first three sheets of paper.

Place	Points	Runner Info	Jockey
22nd	0pts	Skull Crusher	Calvin Whitaker
23rd	-4pts	First-Place Freddie	Fredrick Townsend
24th	-4pts	Jake	Jake Milbourne
25th	-4pts	Not Last	Asmita Lee

"Oh. Well, um," Teddy starts to say. "Uh, yeah, man, congrats! You're ahead of three people now and have some momentum heading into this month's races."

Calvin smiles, then looks over at his younger brother. "See, Teddy gets it."

Ronnie sighs. "He's just being nice. Now let's go eat. I'm starving."

The three boys make their way into the dining hall and load their trays up with food at the buffet table. Olivia and Ava are sitting in their regular seats and greet the trio when they walk up. "Nice job moving up in the standings, Calvin," Olivia says after they sit down.

"Oh, why *thank you*, Olivia," Calvin says as he looks at Ronnie. "It is a nice job, isn't it?"

Ronnie shakes his head then looks across the table at Ava. "Hey, I've been meaning to ask you something. How is it that this food here is so tasty and satisfying, but when I wake up in the middle of the night back on Earth, I'm hungry enough to eat my foot?"

"Why are you asking me?" Ava says.

Ronnie raises his hands in the air. "I don't know. I figured... You're a year ahead of us, so..." He looks toward the other second-yearer at the table. "Olivia?"

She takes a bite out of her bowl of macaroni and cheese and looks up. "Dude, I have no idea. I just know this stuff tastes great and doesn't cost me a pound."

Some sounds and commotion emerge from near the entrance of the dining hall. A sixth-year boy is holding a large red sign cut out into the shape of a heart with something written in permanent marker on it.

"Ugh, gross," Ava says as she turns her attention back toward her plate.

Teddy turns around in his seat. "What's going on over there?"

"Another boy asking out another girl to the Winter Ball," Olivia answers, then reaches over and grabs a biscuit from the center of the table.

Calvin perks up in his seat. "Wait, we're going to have a dance here?"

"We, as in Ava and I, will be going to a ball," Olivia says as she spreads butter over the biscuit. "But you first-yearers aren't invited. Dean Spear and the staff want all the new kids to stay focused on their studies."

Calvin relaxes back into his chair. "Lame."

"It is," Ava cuts in. "I don't even want to go. But unless I want to try and stay awake all night on Earth to avoid being transported here, I don't really have a choice."

"It's during a school day?" Teddy asks. "So what are the rest of us first-yearers supposed to do?"

"It takes place on the last Friday before winter break," Ava replies. "Last year, we just slept through it and into our regular dreams like any other day off."

"Why are you so against it?" Ronnie asks.

Ava looks like she's about to laugh, then shakes her head. "Because boys are jerks."

"Uh, what do you call us then?" Ronnie asks as he motions toward Calvin and Teddy.

"No, not you guys. Like *real* boys," Ava says. "Like *boy* boys. You three are different. But regardless, Olivia and I have both agreed to go to the Ball without dates this year."

Olivia raises a thumb in the air as she continues to chew her biscuit.

"Well, this all sounds super boring for us not *boy* boys," Calvin says as he looks toward Ronnie and Teddy. "You guys want to share a dream that night instead?"

Ronnie looks over at his brother. "But you suck, dude. We haven't been able to share one yet."

"That's because you're always trying to imagine frequencies too complicated!" Calvin says.

"That's the point!" Ronnie responds.

"Ugh," Ava says as she rolls her eyes and looks toward Olivia.

"Whatever, man," Calvin says. "Forgive me if I can't hold the thought of a Labrador retriever playing golf on the moon long enough for it to manifest."

"It's not that hard," Ronnie mutters.

"Listen," Calvin says. "We'll figure it out before the dance. I'm not floating around in my regular dreams while the rest of Zarmore is out having fun that night." He then looks at Teddy. "How does that sound to you? You up for a game of mini-golf on the moon later this month?"

Shadow Play

"Ugh," Teddy says as he adjusts his helmet. "I can't see anything, and this is killing my neck. I'm taking it off."

"Don't you dare, Teddy," Calvin says through the microphone system inside his helmet.

"Yeah, please don't," Ronnie adds through the same speaker. "This is the first time anyone has been able to share this dream with me, and I'd rather not be trapped in here with just Cal and this dog all night."

"Hilarious," Calvin mutters.

"I'm just taking the helmet off," Teddy says. "I'm not going anywhere. Even though I have no idea where I'd go anyway since all I can see in front of me is black and stars."

"And what do you think will happen if you take off your helmet in space, Teddy?" Ronnie asks.

"Yeah, come on, Teddy," Calvin says. "This place is awesome anyway. Stop being so dramatic, and come play some golf with us."

"Your friend sounds kind of depressing," a new rough and deep voice says through the helmet speaker system.

"Who was that?" Teddy asks.

"Who was who?" Ronnie replies.

"The guy who just called me depressing for being lost in the middle of space!"

"Oh, that's Sebastian," Ronnie says.

"You say that like he's my best friend, and I should know who he is or something."

"You'd be lucky if he was," Calvin says before lowering his tone of voice to something more soft and baby-like. "Because he's a good little boy. Aren't you, buddy? Yes, you are. Yes, you are."

"Uh, are you still talking to me or the dog now?" Teddy asks.

"Hey, Teddy," Ronnie says. "You know, I think I had your problem once during this dream before. You're probably just on the dark side of the moon. I'm going to shine a light up from our location. Let me know if you see it."

Teddy waits a few moments but doesn't see anything. "Nothing so far."

"Are you sure?" Ronnie asks. "I got this spotlight over here cranked up on full blast."

"Nope, nothing yet," Teddy says as he swivels his head to his left and right then turns around. "Oh crap, nevermind." A bright beam of light is now shining up into the black emptiness of space not too far away in the distance. "I see it, guys. I'm coming your way!"

"Hallelujah," Calvin says. "Because we can't see a thing over here now."

Teddy laughs. "Go ahead and turn it off. I know where to go now!"

The spotlight shuts off, and Teddy jogs toward the other side of the moon. He glides over rocky craters, and his body moves in a slow-motion sort of manner on the weakened gravity of the lunar surface. After a few minutes, the horizon around the curvature of the bright side of the moon starts coming into view, and he has a better sense of what's in front of him. His breaths are long and deep as he continues to jog toward the light.

"No rush, Teddy," Ronnie says. "You can take it down a notch if you want."

"Yeah," Calvin adds. "The way you're breathing right now sounds like Darth Vader is running toward us. Relax, dude"

Sebastian laughs. "That was a good one, Calvin."

"Thanks, buddy," Calvin says. "Want to play fetch with this golf ball while we wait for Uncle Teddy?"

"Yeah! Yeah!" The dog says. "I want to play!"

"Are you sure, buddy?"

"Yeah! Yeah! Give me the ball!"

Teddy finally escapes from the shadows and can now see the moon's bright gray surface below his white boots. He looks up. The icy north pole of the Earth, thousands of miles away in the background, comes more into view with each stride he takes. He glides for several more minutes and shakes his head in awe as his home planet rises into a view from which few have ever seen. The sun shines atop the continent of Africa, and he imagines the millions of people now just waking up to greet a brand new day. His thoughts then drift to how incredible it feels to be alive and a citizen of this planet. Formed out of nothing billions of years ago, and now here it is, staring back at him. So much life passed through here, from the dinosaurs to the ancient Egyptians to every human being who ever existed. It's all encapsulated right here. All the joy, all the sadness, all the glory, all the defeat, all the love, all the heartbreak—everything. It all took place right here in front of him, on this mysterious blue sphere floating in the middle of infinity. Even though it's just a dream, the truth and beauty of it all are still heavy to take in. He keeps jogging, and a few minutes later, he sees his friends.

It almost feels as if he's stepped back onto Earth and walked into a carnival. If it weren't for his home planet floating in the background, he probably would believe it too. A miniature golf course equipped with twisting and looping holes has been constructed on several green strips of artificial grass. There's a scaled-down steaming volcano oozing red lava and several life-size dinosaur skeletons standing erect throughout different areas of the course. He finds his friends hanging out near a fake Tyrannosaurus rex skeleton holding a black and white sign that reads "Hole 1".

Ronnie looks up and sees Teddy. "There he is."

Ronnie is attired in a white astronaut uniform similar to Teddy's and is sitting on a blue metal bench. His older brother Calvin and the brown-furred Labrador retriever both wear similar spacesuits and are just a little further to the right of

Ronnie. Calvin is laughing as he holds a golf ball high above his head while the dog jumps in slow motion toward it.

"About time," Calvin says as he finally throws the ball and watches it slowly drift away. "I was about ready to call the fire department."

"You sound like an idiot," Ronnie says as he sits up off the bench and walks toward the two boys.

"It's my dream, man. I can make anything I want happen here," Calvin says.

"Eh, actually doesn't really work that way in shared dreams," Teddy cuts in. "I've found that it's a lot harder to create in here individually."

"Hear that, Cal?" Ronnie asks. "No amount of dream power is going to make you smarter."

"And neither will it help you in capturing a horse, little bro. Actually, how dumb can I be if I'm the one in the races and you're just a fan sitting in the stadium?"

"I am not your fan, dude."

Teddy hears a crash coming from the speaker inside his helmet, but the brothers continue to argue.

"I don't know," Calvin says. "I'm pretty sure I saw you smiling when I entered the arena during last month's race."

"That's because you were bouncing all over your horse like a rodeo clown."

Teddy hears another crash and looks over toward the boys. "Are you guys not hearing this?"

"Been putting up with it my whole life," Ronnie says.

"No, the crashing sound," Teddy replies.

"I don't hear any of that," Calvin says.

"Me neither," Ronnie adds. "Maybe there's something wrong with your headset."

"Where's Sebastian?" Calvin asks.

"I almost got it!" The dog shouts. "That was a good throw, Calvin. You're really strong!"

"I love that dog," Calvin mumbles.

Something resembling the sound of papers falling makes its way into Teddy's headset. He narrows his eyes as he tries to listen more carefully.

"Dammit," a new voice mutters.

Teddy stumbles a step backwards. "You guys didn't hear that?"

"Nothing," Calvin says.

Ronnie looks a little concerned, then shakes his head no.

"I gotta go," Teddy says. "I think something's going on in the real world. He then closes his eyes and focuses all his intention on waking up.

. . .

"Uh, do you want to talk about it?" Teddy asks as he sticks a fork into the last cold and crunchy chicken nugget then brings it up to his mouth.

Kristi continues to sit still with her eyes fixed on the surface of the picnic table.

270

"Well, um, I'm here if you need me," Teddy says.

His father used to tell him that when he was upset and uncommunicative. Teddy feels mature for saying it then finishes eating his lunch. He pushes his tray forward, then reaches down and unzips his backpack and pulls out a yellow folder labeled "Algebra". He has a quiz next class and figures he might as well study, being that Kristi is a mute now. It was basically calling his name in his sleep anyway. He awoke from his shared dream last night with his math homework scattered across the floor next to the armoire mirror and a few pencils and pens. That didn't explain the voice he heard inside his space helmet, but it all did happen during a dream, and he decided that part was most likely just his imagination.

He pulls out a few wrinkled pieces of paper, sets them on the table, then begins using the side of his hand to smooth out the creases.

"I'm sorry, Teddy," Kristi finally speaks up.

He looks over at her.

"It's just that," she continues. "Sean and I have been arguing a lot lately."

"Oh," Teddy says. "Um... sorry to hear that."

"He's just like, I don't know. Like, really protective."

"That's one way to put it," Teddy says as he looks back down at his math homework and works out some more wrinkles.

"It's more than the cupcake thing, Teddy. He doesn't like me having other friends that are boys, *especially you.*"

Teddy looks up. "Me? I haven't seen that guy in like three months. Why *especially* me?"

Kristi sighs and looks back down toward the surface of the picnic table. Her long black hair drapes over her round, thick glasses, and Teddy can no longer see her face. "He told me not to talk or hang out with you anymore. But... I told him that we're friends, and I'm not going to do that." She pauses for another moment, then raises her head and looks Teddy in the eyes. "He said he's going to hurt you."

Teddy leans back and furrows his brow. "Hurt me?"

"I told him I'd be really upset with him if I ever saw you injured. Then he said he knows how to make you suffer in ways that no one can see."

"Uhh..."

Kristi's eyes turn glassy. "I don't know what to do."

Teddy exhales and shakes his head. "I knew things were going too well for me lately.... But seriously, Kristi, why do you even continue to date this kid?"

She looks back down and smiles. "I don't know. He's sweet, funny, nice, and obviously good-looking."

Teddy lifts an eyebrow while Kristi continues to stare at the picnic table and smile.

"I just really really like him, Teddy. I don't know. We were great together until... well, until you showed up."

"Until I showed up?"

Kristi stops smiling and looks over at Teddy. "Yeah, Seanie and I were actually really just about perfect before you."

"Did you just call him... nevermind. Um, well, I don't know. I guess I'm sorry for my existence? Even though I'm pretty sure you were the one who came and sat down across from me in biology class and suggested eating lunch together."

"That was because I felt sorry for you."

Teddy looks back down at the table. "Well, ok then."

"Yeah," Kristi says as she starts packing her backpack. "You know, maybe we should just stop eating lunch together now that the first half of the school year is over. We choose new lab partners after winter break as well, so we don't have to hang out in there either."

"Whoa, hang on," Teddy says. "What's gotten into you? I thought we were... I thought we were friends."

"Ugh," Kristi says as she tosses her backpack over her shoulder. "We still are, Teddy. It's just that, I really don't want to lose Sean over you."

"Ouch."

"I didn't mean it like that."

"I don't think there's another way to interpret it."

The bell rings, and students make their way across the black pavement of the basketball courts and toward the classrooms.

"We're not doing anything in biology today, so I'm going to ditch," Kristi says as she follows the crowd. "I'll see you around, Teddy."

Teddy shakes his head and looks back down. He waits until she's long gone before grabbing his math homework off the table and placing the sheets back into their yellow folder.

Something written in red ink on the upper right-hand corner of one of the papers grabs his attention and causes him to stop packing up. He furrows his brow and brings the sheet closer to his eyes. "*What the...?*"

He sits still and looks to his left and then his right. All the kids are almost back to class now. His heart pounds against his chest as he tries to think who possibly could have written it and what it's supposed to mean:

Quiz Review # 4. **Last Warning...**

Name: Teddy Lancaster

Instructions: Solve the following problems. Show your work.

Part I. Multiple Choice

1: __A.__ Solve the inequality: $x + 5 > 8$

A) $x > 3$

B) $x < 13$

C) $x > -13$

D) $x > -3$

$$\begin{array}{r} -5 \quad -5 \\ \hline x > 3 \end{array}$$

2: __A.__ Solve the equation: $5|x + 4| - 8 = -3$

A) $x = -5, x = -3$

B) $x = 3, x = 5$

C) infinite solutions

D) no solution

$$+8 \quad +8$$
$$(1/5)\,5|x+4| = 5\,(1/5)$$
$$x + 4 = 1 \qquad x + 4 = -1$$
$$-4 \quad -4 \qquad -4 \quad -4$$
$$x = -3 \qquad x = -5$$

3: __B.__ Solve the inequality: $\tfrac{1}{2}x - 8 \leq 14$

A) $x \leq -44$

B) $x \leq 44$

C) $x \leq -4$

D) $x \leq 4$

$$+8 \quad +8$$
$$(2)\,\tfrac{1}{2}x \leq 22\,(2)$$
$$x \leq 44$$

Lucky Charms

The cold New York City air creeps through the thin crevices which separate Teddy's bedroom window from the wall. He rolls onto his side and pulls his heavy white comforter over his head, letting the soft patter of snowfall outside lull him back to sleep. The spell of drowsiness nearly overtakes him completely before his conscious mind remembers something and forces his eyes open. He slides his head out from underneath the comforter then reaches over for his cellphone atop the nightstand.

Today 4:14 AM

Ava
> Merry Christmas, everybody!!!

Ronnie
> Aye, Merry Christmas guys

Ronnie

Well, everyone except for Teddy lol

Ava

Aww, poor Teddy :'(

Calvin

Hey, come on. It's not my man's fault we live in the UK and he lives in the states!

Another cold wave of air blows in, causing his teeth to chatter. He throws the comforter back over his head and continues to read the texts from earlier this morning.

Calvin

I'll still wish you a happy xmas, Tedster.

Olivia

You guys do realize that it's already like 4 in the morning where Teddy lives and Christmas as well, right?

Calvin

Is it really Christmas without all of us there with him though?

Olivia

Shut up dude! Lol

Ava

Merry Christmas, Olivia!! <3 <3 <3

Teddy hears his mom's bedroom door open from across the hall. The floor squeaks as she makes her way toward his room, then gets silent right before she knocks. He removes the comforter from over his head and looks to his right. His mom has the door cracked open and is peeking inside. She's wearing a white robe, and her dark brown hair looks frazzled. Although Teddy knows she went to bed early last night and had a restful sleep, the heavy dark bags under her eyes would fool anyone else.

"Merry Christmas, honey," she says with a tone that warms the room.

Teddy smiles. "Merry Christmas, mom."

She yawns and rubs her eyes. "I'm going to turn the heater on downstairs and make some French toast. Come on down when you're ready."

Teddy nods then throws the comforter back over his head.

His mom laughs a little as she shuts the door. He then grabs his phone and scrolls down to the bottom of the chat.

Today 8:40 AM

Ava

Your mom really bought you guys matching sweaters? That's so cute!

Olivia

> Omg please find a way to bring those into Zarmore and wear them to class.

Calvin

> Yes she did, and no we will not.

Ronnie

> Yeah, not gonna happen.

Ronnie

> Hey so is Teddy really still sleeping or does he just not like us? Lol

Teddy laughs.

Today 8:52 AM

Me

> Lol merry christmas! I just woke up. About to go eat some french toast then I'll catch up with the chat!

Teddy places his phone back on the nightstand then braces himself for the cold. After a count of three, he throws the comforter off from over his head and to the side. He then springs himself out of bed, walks out into the hall, and down the creaky staircase. The warmth from the heater and his mom cooking breakfast in the kitchen makes him smile. "Smells good," he says as he steps into the living room and looks at the presents underneath the short yet well-lit Christmas tree. There are only a few with his name on them and one other poorly wrapped gift destined for his mom.

"It'll be ready soon!" She shouts from the kitchen. "Why don't you bring our stockings in here, and we can see what Santa brought us?"

Teddy shakes his head then walks over toward the heater where the red and white cotton stockings are hanging above on a shelf. His smile falls into a frown as he grabs the two socks labeled "Mom" and "Teddy".

He walks into the kitchen, lays them on the table, and takes a seat.

His mom flips over a piece of wet and golden-colored bread in the pan with a plastic spatula, then turns around and looks at her son. "I'm sorry I haven't cooked us breakfast in a while. I get so exhausted on my days off and just don't have the energy for it anymore... Maybe I'm just getting old."

Teddy gives a weak smile then looks back down at the candy-filled stockings on the table. "It's fine, mom."

There's a long pause. Teddy listens as the cold snow pads outside while the hot butter sizzles above the stove in the kitchen.

"I know this feels different without your father here," his mom says as she flips the toast again. "But he would want us to be happy. You know that."

"I know, mom," Teddy says as he fiddles with his stocking for a moment before pulling out a plastic toothbrush and letting out a sigh. "Do we still not know what happened to him?"

The grease in the pan crackles louder, and his mom turns down the heat. "No, honey, they don't know for sure, but these things unfortunately just happen sometimes."

"People just die in their sleep?"

"Yes, Teddy. It's quite common."

"Yeah, for older or unhealthy people. But he was only forty-four and in great shape. Heck, mom, the guy ran a marathon every year for the past decade."

He hears his mom sniffle as she turns the stove off and stacks the French toast onto a large white plate. "Teddy, I don't know, and neither do the doctors. Can we please not have this conversation again today?" She picks the plate up, turns around, and walks toward the table. Teddy slides the stockings to the side, and his mom sets the tower of golden and soggy French toast down in front of him. "And there's nothing we can do about it now anyway."

Teddy doesn't say anything.

His mom turns around, walks toward the cupboard above the stove and fumbles around for something. A few moments later, she returns with a jar of honey in one hand and two white plates with silverware resting on top in the other. She sits down next to Teddy and puts her hand on his shoulder. "Now let's enjoy our breakfast and go open some presents, ok?"

. . .

The gray cat with black stripes paces back and forth atop the large professor desk in the front of the class. His paws rest inside his trouser pockets while the buttons on his black collared shirt bulge out against his big belly underneath. It's a sunny day in Zarmore, and the light blue sky matches the professor's eyes. The cat takes his left paw out of his pocket and scratches the white fur underneath his chin as he looks toward the class. "Now controlling and creating luck isn't just a skill that can be employed within your whimsical and pointless dreams," Professor Mun says. "Depending on where you are in this reality, the methods in which you call upon luck and chance into your life are quite different."

The professor stops pacing and furrows his brow toward two boys laughing in the front corner of the class. "You think I have no idea what you mice are squeaking about?" Mun asks.

The boys silence and straighten up in their seats.

The professor shakes his head. "Those timid thoughts are still leaking, children. See now; if you two would've paid more attention this year, you might have actually learned how to lock your minds like the rest of your fellow classmates have. But instead, you're too busy gossiping about how fat your professor looks today."

A few other students join the laughter. Mun stops staring at the boys, then turns and fixes his attention on the class as a whole. "But I suppose that's just the nature of you human beings on Earth, isn't it? You're always too busy documenting, criticizing, and trying to categorize the lives of others instead of creating and leading your own."

His whiskers twitch then he continues to speak. "Yet here we all are, and what else can I do but try and get this information through your fledgling minds." He returns to his pacing atop the desk. "As I was saying, luck is an energy which is always flowing and readily available to whoever knows how to summon it. On Earth and in Egaria, one can be trained to command this energy and live a fairly fortunate existence. However, not all beings have the ability, dedication, and *focus* to do so," he says while glancing toward the two boys in the corner.

"Also, there are situations which you may come across later in life which will require more luck than is readily available for one being to possess. For these instances, we have lucky charms."

Teddy smiles from his seat in the back of the class and slowly raises his hand.

"No, not like the cereal, Mr. Lancaster," the professor says before Teddy's hand is even all the way up. "I don't need to read your mind to know that was your question."

Teddy sinks down in his seat and lowers his hand at the same speed in which he raised it. He sees Olivia cover her mouth in an attempt to contain laughter from her tutor desk in the front of the class.

The professor continues to speak. "These charms will be formed by each of you, and once created, chance and good fortune will *always* find you while it is worn."

The volume in the class picks up as the students chat amongst themselves.

"Now I know this may sound like all your stupid little dreams have come true. I can see it on all your stupid little faces right now that you're already thinking of all the stupid little possibilities of what these charms could bring you. However, I must burst your bubbles and let you know that *if* you succeed in creating a lucky charm, you most likely will never see it again in your life."

The room gets quiet.

"You see, this universe we live in is always fair and is always balanced. No action happens without a reaction, and if you call upon a lifetime's worth of luck unto you in one go, there will be a price to pay. Each of these charms is intertwined with your DNA, and the amount of luck which is experienced while they are worn, that much misfortune or bad luck will be had unto someone in that same DNA tree. The vast majority of the time, it will be to the user themself. However, it could also be their father, mother, brother, sister, or any other family member with similar DNA. The closer the DNA match, the higher the probability. And the longer the charm is worn, the greater the misfortune will be."

Professor Mun twitches his whiskers again. "Now, learning to form a charm isn't as simple as directing a thought or emotion. It typically takes several years to master, and for that reason, we're beginning now during your first year. After creating these charms, you will learn how to lock them into a far corner of your mind, and if ever needed, you will also have the key to physically retrieve them, no matter where you are in the existence. Earth. Egaria. Wherever."

The cat closes his eyes then claps his paws together. Darkness falls upon the room as the lights turn off and the heavy drapes clamp shut over the windows. A girl near the front of the class lets out a squeal.

"Oh, would you shut up," Mun says.

The class laughs as the professor continues to speak. "Where there is light, there is life. From the deepest depths of the oceans to the highest areas of the galaxies, there are animals and stars which reveal this truth to you. Inside your own body, you can find electricity and light. However, light is not something that you, the stars, or the other animals are creating. That which will eventually die cannot create that which is eternal. You see, because it's the light which is the mother to life, and not the other way around. This is true throughout all the existence. Behind this physical shell which you call your body, you are light. You are an eternal being passing momentarily through life, and when you connect to the true nature of who you are, you can do amazing things. Now I want everyone to close their eyes and tell me what they see."

There's a long pause, and no one says anything.

"Mr. Lancaster," the professor says. "What do you see right now?"

"Uh, a lot of black."

"There is something more there though, is this not so? Look closer."

There's another pause before Teddy speaks up again. "Well, I guess it's not all black."

"What do you see, Mr. Lancaster?"

"There looks like there's uh, like a layer or grid of tiny stars flashing or something scattered above the black, maybe. I don't know. I don't really have great eyes."

"Very good," Professor Mun says.

"But still a ton of black going on here," Teddy adds.

"That's more than enough, Teddy. You can be quiet now."

He hears the professor's paws clap together, and light returns to the room.

"What you saw there, Mr. Lancaster, and what I hope at least some of the rest of you saw as well, was a peek behind the curtain of the true nature of your being. It's easier to notice in the dark, but do know that those lights you saw exist at all times whether your eyes are closed or not."

A student near the front of the class raises her hand, but the professor continues to speak. "Now I know many of you did not see the lights, and that's quite the norm for a first-year class. In time you will not only learn to see them, but you will also learn how to collaborate and work with them. You see, if you stare at these lights long enough, you will find that they are simply not just specks of brightness but rather thousands of complex interconnected geometric shapes. And if you stare even longer, you will realize that all these shapes are exactly the same and that they can only be formed into larger sizes of that which they currently are. And if you stare even further beyond that, you will begin to understand much more of the true nature of your being. Now in terms of creating your lucky charms though, you will have to fold the lines of the geometric shapes you see and carry them out of the vision of your mind and infuse them into the physical charm itself. Olivia will be passing these out now."

He motions to a brown box sitting on his desk, and Olivia stands up and grabs it.

Professor Mun looks pleased while observing the confused faces of his students. "As I said, there's a reason we're beginning this in year one."

Olivia walks past Teddy in the back of the class and sets a small golden hourglass with a matching chain on his desk. "Cereal," she says with a grin.

"For the last fifteen minutes of our remaining classes this year, we will turn the lights off and give you an opportunity to try different methods to first, find your light and learn to understand it, and second, to infuse your charm. At the end of each class, you will return all the charms to the box. In the event that one of you hairless monkeys actually manages to achieve in wrapping your essence around one of these necklaces, you will see the charm move from the physical realm in front of you to the nonphysical inside you."

"Then how do we get it out after that?" A girl near the front of the class asks. "You said we'd also be getting keys."

The cat pauses and glares at the student. "Would it kill you to raise your hand, or is that too much of a complicated thought for you as well?"

There's another pause then the professor proceeds to speak. "If you learn how to create a lucky charm, you will also understand how to lock it into your mind and call it forth into the physical reality at will. I know it may not make sense right now, but if you get to that point, you'll understand."

The same girl raises her hand, and the professor nods for her to speak. "So are you going to guide us or give us any recommendations on how to infuse it or...?"

"This is one of the tasks at Zarmore which cannot be taught. Just as if you were a dog and I tried to describe to you what long division was, there's no way for you to understand something as complex as attaching your essence to a physical object and then bringing it into the nonphysical. The only advice I can give you is not to waste your time trying to infuse objects back on Earth, as this skill can only be initiated inside the Kingdom of Egaria. However, *if* you are successful, your charms will then be able to be retrieved no matter where you are in the existence. Also, do know that this is one of the more difficult tasks you will encounter here at Zarmore, and although it isn't a graduation requirement, it is a skill that may just save your life once off this campus and potentially as a citizen of Egaria."

Teddy furrows his brow. *"A citizen of Egaria?"*

Before he can raise his hand and ask a question, the professor claps his paws together, and the lights shut off again. "You have the remainder of class to work on your charms. If you have any questions, direct them toward my aide, Olivia."

The professor then moves onto all fours and hops from the desk he was pacing on and over to a cushioned office chair in the corner of the classroom. He sniffs the velvet seat, then walks three tight circles atop it and plops himself down. Within a few seconds, Teddy hears light snoring.

"You figure it out yet?' A voice whispers from behind Teddy.

He flinches then turns around. "Jeez, what's with everyone sneaking up on me lately?"

Olivia laughs then pulls up an empty seat next to him.

"And no," Teddy says. "Half the stuff this cat says is in riddles."

Olivia laughs again. "Well, at least you're killing it in the horse department. I saw that win last month shot you up to fourth-place in the standings."

Teddy tilts his head. "I didn't know Professor Jones posted those yet."

"Yeah, dude! It's looking pretty good for you, especially since you're matched up against *Skull Crusher* again this month."

They both laugh this time, and Teddy notices the neon glow from Olivia's finger key pulse a little faster.

"That is unless your farmer friend doesn't find you first," she adds. "What's going on with all that anyway? Wasn't he supposed to come kill you if you didn't find his horse you stole or whatever?"

"Well, first off, I was only borrowing that horse. And second off... I don't know. The last I heard about him, or Caesar or Miss Butts for that matter, was four months ago back in Slaybethor, like I already told you guys. And as for

Naroshi... Well, I know she's wandering around somewhere in these forests, but I've yet to see her."

"Tough luck," Olivia says. "Better get to working on that charm."

Teddy sighs, then leans back in his chair. "Yeah, I could probably put it to good use back on Earth as well. I think someone left me a threat atop my math homework before I headed into winter break."

Olivia laughs. "Wait, what?"

Teddy goes on to explain what he heard during his shared dream with Calvin and Ronnie and the condition he found his room in after he woke up.

"Dude, Teddy. Uhh, that's not good."

"It's fine," he says. "It's an old crappy *armoire* my mom and I found on the side of the road. The mirror falls off all the time."

"Yeah, no, I'm not really talking about the mirror. I'm more concerned about the voice you heard and your room being trashed part. Oh, and the note saying 'Last warning' written across your math homework? That's a *littleee* weird, don't you think? I mean, what the heck is that even supposed to mean? Last warning? What was your first one?"

"Beats me," Teddy says as he fiddles with the hourglass charm on his desk. "There was a teddy bear with its head ripped off on my front porch awhile back too, but I don't think..."

"Dude!"

"What?"

"Your name is freaking Teddy Lancaster!"

The bell rings, and the lights flash on. Olivia's eyes are wide open as she shakes her head.

Teddy smiles, then stands up and grabs his backpack. "I'll be fine, Olivia. If my biggest problems on Earth are people threatening me with stuffed animals, I think I'm in good shape."

"Still," she says. "Just be careful, alright? You're my best entertainment for this class, and I can't afford to let you get yourself killed."

Teddy laughs, then throws his backpack over his shoulder. "I'll be fine. Seriously, I really don't think it's anything."

Strangers in the Dark

"Screw that," Calvin says as they walk through the forest and toward the arena. "If they're giving us first-yearers the night off tomorrow while the rest of the school goes and has the times of their lives at another dance, then we're doing something cool too."

A surge of cheers erupts in the distance.

"Well," Ronnie says. "I guess we'll be missing the second one of the day as well." He looks over at Teddy on his right and smiles. "Not like any of these early morning races are important anyway."

"Exactly!" Calvin says. "The only races that matter today are Teddy's at 11:00 and mine at 2:00."

Ronnie furrows his brow. "Wait. What makes you think your race is significant at all? You and *First-Place Freddie* going to battle it out to see who finishes in the eighteenth spot on the year?"

"Actually, *little bro*, if all plays out correctly, a win here would put me into the top fourteen. Check the standings."

Calvin reaches into his pocket and pulls out a few folded pieces of paper.

"Are those the standings from the foyer?" Teddy asks. "Are you even allowed to...?"

Calvin raises a hand in the air. "Yeah, it's fine. The last races of the season are today, so who cares."

Ronnie shakes his head. "What I would pay to see you get caught one of these days."

Calvin glares at Ronnie, then unfolds the papers and points to the one on top. "Look here. So, obviously, Victoria is pretty much guaranteed a spot in the Cup right now. But if Teddy wins today and Victoria places ahead of Giovanni, then Teddy should qualify for the second spot. However, if we look at page number three, where Skull Crusher and I are, we can see that..."

Ronnie rips the first page out of his brother's hands. "Yup, not interested in page three. Thanks, though." He then brings the first sheet closer to where he and Teddy can both see it:

Zarmore Racing League Standings

Regular Season — First-Yearers

Place	Points	Runner Info	Jockey
1st	31pts	Gemini	Victoria Addington
2nd	29pts	Bonfire in the Rain	Giovanni Ginesi
3rd	27pts	Miss B	Theodore Lancaster
4th	26pts	Von Schnickerlonger Jr.	Connor Graham
5th	24pts	Dream Machine	Alice Torbett
6th	24pts	Bum Bum Bum Blam!	Joshua Holstead
7th	24pts	Sleepy Sami	Alejandra Gonzalez

"Yeah, you actually kind of almost control your fate with this race, Teddy," Ronnie says. "Do you have your schedule on you? I forget who else you're going against besides Giovanni and Victoria."

"Yeah, I got it," Teddy says as he reaches into his pocket and locates today's race on the schedule. "I don't think it's anyone to worry about though."

May 13th:

11:00 a.m.

Runner Info	Jockey
Bonfire in the Rain	Giovanni Ginesi
Gemini	Victoria Addington
Not Last	Asmita Lee
Miss B	Theodore Lancaster

"Oh, at least you have that going for ya," Ronnie laughs. "I think Lee has something like negative fourteen points in the standings."

"Well, actually," Calvin says. "If you guys want to come back over here and look at the rest of these papers, I think her exact points are..."

There's another roar from inside the stadium.

"Crap, I gotta go," Teddy says as he sticks his hand out toward the boys. "My race is next."

"Do your thing, man," Ronnie says as he slaps Teddy's hand then pounds it with a fist. "I'll be rooting for ya."

"Likewise," Calvin says as he imitates the gesture. "So what kind of shared dream we doing tonight?"

"I'm good with whatever," Teddy says as he adjusts the straps on his backpack and prepares to jog toward the arena. "We can go to the moon again if you want since I had to leave early last time."

"Yes!" Calvin says as he pumps his right hand downwards into a fist. "I've been missing that pup, Sebastian."

Ronnie sighs and shakes his head while Teddy jogs ahead of them.

When he arrives at the arena, the horses are already in their starting positions. Teddy hops on Miss B, and the two exit from underneath the west gate and join the other racers.

"Cutting it a little close today, aren't ya?" Victoria asks atop her horse Gemini in the stall next to him.

"I'm here," he says in between ragged breaths while slicking his brown hair backwards and behind his ears.

Before Teddy can gather himself completely, a goblin standing on a block of wood in the grassy area of the arena begins to count down. He holds a microphone up to his jagged teeth with one paw and a pistol in his other. "Three... Two... One..." There's a loud bang, and the horses shoot off and race toward an open archway in the arena leading to the outdoor portion of the track. Teddy, Victoria, and Giovanni remain close as they exit out from the roaring stadium into the calm and shaded forest. The short Asmita Lee and her equally short brown horse trail behind.

After several miles into the forest, the three leaders remain neck and neck, with Victoria just slightly in the lead. The steady drum roll of the horse's hooves patting against the dirt path beneath them is all Teddy can hear as he lowers his head and keeps his vision focused. He holds this pace for a few more minutes until, like a hypnotist snapping his fingers, the trance is broken, and sounds flood his ears.

"Look out!" Victoria shouts as she veers her horse left and narrowly past a giant gray boulder that's rolled onto the track.

Teddy's eyes expand, and he thinks of following her to the left but then chooses to go right. His horse crashes into the side of Giovanni's and sends the brown-haired boy and his black stallion tumbling. Teddy's horse stutters from side to side but eventually catches her balance and proceeds forward on the track. He looks back at Giovanni on the ground and notices the boy isn't moving. Teddy pulls the reins of Miss B in an attempt to slow her down, but she doesn't listen. The horse snorts, then jerks her head to the left and picks up more speed. Teddy furrows his brow then yanks the reins even harder, but the horse continues to disobey. She then cuts down the side of the mountain, carrying Teddy off the track and toward the valley. As they sprint down the tree-laden slope, she briefly swings her head back toward the boy, and the two lock eyes.

"Crap," Teddy mutters before releasing his right hand from the reins and patting around the horse's rear. The neutralizing sticker is gone. He scours through his pockets in search of the silk pouch which contains the replacements. After a few frantic moments, he clenches his eyes shut then grabs back hold of the reins with both hands. The pouch is gone too. "*Probably fell off during the crash,*" he thinks while reopening his eyes.

He begins running through ideas in his head of what he should do as he bounces atop the horse and descends further down the mountain. Once near ground level with the valley, he catches a glimpse of his horse's neon orange eyes again; and although he knows she couldn't have, he would swear that she just smiled.

Not even a second later, they're out of the forest and in the center of the valley. The horse stops running and begins writhing and shaking her body before popping out of existence and appearing in a new, slightly darker area. Teddy grips the reins as tight as he can while trying to locate where he's at. Nothing looks familiar. His only hope is that he's still close to the track. Miss B tries some more to throw the boy off her, and then a second later, they're gone and in a much darker place.

The air is warm and moist, and Teddy instantly knows they aren't in the forest anymore. The horse once again works to rid herself of the boy while he bounces atop her back. His hands feel weak, and he isn't sure how much longer he can hold onto the reins. A whooshing sound then rushes toward them from deep within the shadows, and Miss B's jerky movements suddenly stop. She takes a few steps forward then crashes hard onto all four of her knees. Teddy hops off her back and freezes as he tries to figure out what just happened, but it's too dark to see. There's a loud thud and a strangled neigh. He walks closer to his horse and reaches his hand down toward her. She's now lying on her side. He slowly traces his hand up toward her chest area then stops when he feels something warm and wet. Adrenaline pumps through his veins as his hands start to shake. He then resumes feeling around her ribs but stops again once he feels what he feared. There's an arrow sticking out near her heart.

Teddy backpedals and stumbles away from the horse. He looks around to his left and right, trying to find any sort of light that can lead him out of the dark, but no matter where he looks, all he can see is black. His own heart drops to his stomach as panic sets in. A few more seconds pass, then he feels a leathery and warm hand grip tight around his left shoulder from behind. Teddy flinches and tries to run away, but the grip only tightens and holds him further in place. He clenches his eyes shut as a heavy and clear voice whispers just inches behind his ear. "What are you doing in my jungle, human?"

Chimps and monkeys screech from high above, and Teddy instantly knows where his horse has taken him.

"I said. What are you doing in...?"

There's a crash then an explosion of purple light in the distance.

"What was that?!" The voice shouts as he grips tighter into Teddy's bony shoulder. "How many more of you are here?!"

"It's just... me," Teddy mutters while clenching his teeth and trying to free himself from the painful grip.

Another purple boom sets off closer to them. Teddy clenches his eyes shut as the bright neon light floods toward him.

"WHAT WAS THAT?!" The voice bellows as he whips Teddy around and shakes him firmly with both hands.

The chimps in the trees above screech louder while Teddy tries to remain calm. The glow from the purple blast still lingers in the air, and he can now see the outline of the dark and muscular gorilla that grips him by the shoulders.

Another boom sets off even closer, dislodging Teddy from the clutches of the ape. The boy lands on his back then quickly moves his hands around his body to ensure that he's still in one piece. A high pitch ringing sound consumes his eardrums, but besides that, he's fine. He looks over toward the ape. The gorilla is lying face down toward the dirt with his massive black hands covering his head. The chimps and monkeys from above screech as they swing and jump from tree to tree in the bright purple light. Two of them then hop down to help the gorilla while the others throw rocks and twigs at the boy.

As the light from the explosion fades back into darkness, he sees three glowing balls of neon purple in the form of a triangle rushing toward him from deep within the shadows of the jungle. He closes his eyes and raises his arms over his head in preparation for another explosion. But one never comes. A few more seconds pass, and as he slowly reopens his eyes, a cold and soft hand slaps hard against his right forearm, gripping then yanking him up off the ground. He lands atop the back of some sort of moving animal, and before he can figure out what's happening, the darkness dissipates, and the light from the valley comes into view.

"Hold on," a soft female voice says.

It takes a moment before Teddy realizes that the person who just yanked him off the ground is sitting in front of him atop what looks to be a black horse. He debates the idea of jumping off and making a run for the valley, but at the last moment, decides against it and wraps his arms around the stranger's waist.

The bright light from the valley in front of him disappears, and he finds himself near the dirt racetrack again. The air is brisk, and he recognizes the wide and tall trees casting shadows above him.

"Really?! Another shifte..." He starts to shout before they shift to a different location.

The scenery looks similar to other areas of the forest he's seen before, but he's confident that he's never actually been here. The black horse shifts again, and he finds himself in a grassy location surrounded by more of the tall redwood trees he's accustomed to around the castle. The girl who sits in front of him pulls the reins, and the horse eases into a trot before eventually stopping completely. Teddy hops off then watches as the girl does the same. She then turns around and smiles. "Well, that was fun."

In the open grassy area underneath the sun, Teddy can now see her clearly. The girl wears a delicate black and purple dress with black shoes, black stockings, and a tall black and pointy hat with a purple buckle. Her long hair matches her outfit, and she looks no older than the age of seventeen.

"What just... Who are you?" Teddy asks, his heart still pounding.

"I'm Radella," she says as she sticks her hand out toward Teddy. "Pleasure to meet you."

His ears are still ringing from the explosions, and he's having trouble hearing her. "I didn't catch that. Did you say Radella?"

She smiles and puts her hand on Teddy's back while pointing toward a wooden cottage surrounded by yellow, white, and purple daisies. She then takes the lead, and Teddy follows her down a winding cobblestone path and into the home. The girl takes her tall hat off and hangs it on a hook by the entrance, then walks into a cramped kitchen. She points to a wooden table that rests near a large window, and Teddy takes a seat. She then opens the fridge and pulls out a small black pot from inside. The ringing in Teddy's ears finally calms down a little, and he asks her again. "Ok, so who are you? Rachelle?"

"You had it right the first time," she says as she places the pot on a counter next to an old stovetop. "I'm Radella."

"Ok, uh, Radella. So, what's going on? Are you some type of benevolent witch or something, or are you planning on cooking me inside that pot?"

She laughs, then sticks a wooden spoon into the pot and pulls it back out. A yellow and thick batter drips from its bottom. "Of course I'm not going to eat you! I'm making pancakes."

"Um... Ok, and are you like...?"

"A witch?" She laughs. "You kids always say that. Well, I'm not *not* that. I just wear these dark clothes whenever I have to travel into the shadow jungle. They help conceal me a little better from those crazy apes."

"Crap! The black hole! How long was I under for?" Teddy asks as he squints his eyes and looks up toward the wooden beams on the ceiling. "Had to be at least ten minutes. So what's that equate to back on Earth? Like, eight months? Nine? More?!"

"Relax, kid. I'm making pancakes," Radella says as she lights a flame underneath a large pan on the stovetop.

"I don't care about your pancakes!" He shouts. "I'm probably dead back on Earth!" He sinks his head toward the surface of the wooden table and covers his eyes. "Just like Miss B is here...."

Radella shakes her head then pours the batter into the pan. "You know, you remind me a lot of a boy that used to come and visit me many years ago."

Teddy remains with his head down and in the palms of his hands.

"Can't remember the name of him for the life of me though," she says as she flips some of the batter inside the pan.

"Cool," Teddy mutters. "Not too interested in stories right now though. And what are you, like sixteen years old? How long is *many years ago* for you, anyway? Like one?"

She laughs. "Same stubborn attitude as well. And thank you for the compliment, but I'm actually more like three hundred and... something? Perhaps, four hundred? I don't know. I stopped counting a while ago."

Teddy lifts his head out of his hands. "Huh?"

The pancakes finish cooking, and Radella stacks three onto a plate then sets them down on the table in front of Teddy. "Yeah, I grew up in this house with my mom back before Zarmore was even a school, and any of you kids were down here yet. Then around the time of my seventeenth birthday, the Council trotted in and told us that they would be placing a time enchantment spell upon the colony, and we had to decide to either get out and find a new home in the Kingdom of Egaria or choose to never leave Zarmore again. And yeah, we love this little house, and Wondorsyth Woods is our home, so it was a pretty easy decision."

"Oh, um, ok," Teddy says as he sits a little straighter in his seat. "So, where's your mom now?"

Radella sighs as she walks back toward the fridge and pulls out a six-pack of red aluminum cans. "She died trying to protect the castle a while back ago during the chimp uprise."

"I'm sorry," Teddy says.

"Part of life," Radella replies as she sets the cans down on the table and takes a seat across from Teddy. "She lived a good life, and it's not like it's over for her. Just this part on this plane, you know."

She cracks open a can then pours the sticky and brown liquid over the pancakes. "Have you ever had Mapsy's before?"

"Uh, I don't think I'm old enough."

Radella laughs. "You really do remind me of that boy in so many ways. He used to race with a shifter as well, you know. Although his was much faster and not nearly as clumsy. Matter of fact, he and his horse were so fast that I believe he was the only student ever to win five Cups in a row. And it would've been six, I'm sure, had they not kicked him out and banished him to the island."

Teddy furrows his brow. "What'd they banish him for?"

"Could have been a number of reasons, but initiating the whole chimp uprise thing was probably the one that did him in."

Teddy sighs, then looks back down toward the table as he considers the possibilities of what his own life on Earth might look like now after spending time underneath the jungle's black hole.

"Yes, I sure do miss that boy," she says. "At least Naroshi still comes by and plays with Ariouk every now and then."

Teddy freezes then looks up at Radella. "Did you say... Naroshi?"

The girl smiles as she looks out the window into the open grassy area where her black horse Ariouk is trotting around. "Yup, one of the only few shifters left with all three eyes intact. The boy used to ride her every year through these woods and stop by to say hello to my mother and me. Now besides her and my Ariouk, I'm not sure if there is another non-mutilated shifter in these woods left."

Teddy looks out the window toward the black horse and catches a glimpse of his eyes. Instantly he understands what the glowing purple triangle was that he saw back in the jungle.

"Wait. Why does he have three eyes?" Teddy asks as he continues to watch the horse through the window.

"All shifters are born with three eyes," she says as she looks back toward Teddy. "Do you not know this?"

He shakes his head.

Radella releases a sigh, then runs a couple of fingers through some of her hair and tucks it behind her ear. "These woods used to glow from all the eyes of the shifters. But many years ago, poachers discovered the power that lay hidden in their third eyes and began to hunt them down one by one, extracting their top eyes and taking them on as their own. That's why you see so many shifters today with scars in the middle of their foreheads. And that's also why some of these same horses conceal their neon glow with a dark jet-black color, in fear of being hunted again."

Teddy rubs his head. "What do you mean that the poachers *take the eye on as their own?* What does it do?"

"They really don't teach you kids anything in that school, do they?" Radella asks as she shakes her head. "The third eye sees above all. It's a gateway to the nonphysical realm and allows one to understand everything as it truly is without the memory or misconceptions of the two eyes below. When these shifters have all three of their eyes intact, they can live forever as powerful beings. And if a poacher can extract the eye and take it on as his own, he inherits that power."

Teddy sits with his brow furrowed and eyes fixed on the girl as she continues to speak.

"And as for the horses, they still can continue to live indefinitely as long as their stolen eye is unharmed, but their power and sense of peace will be greatly reduced as they now have to live with and listen to all the thoughts of their robbers."

Teddy clenches his fists under the table as he thinks of Ziruam. "Do these poachers sometimes hide these eyes with a patch?"

"I suppose that's a good idea if they want to keep it. But the Council is pretty on top of this type of black market, and I think most of the offenders in Egaria were caught many years ago." She pauses, then looks down and grumbles. "But of course the Council still keeps all the eyes they stole."

There's another pause before Teddy speaks up. "Slaybethor isn't a part of Egaria, right?"

Radella looks up and leans forward. "Yeah, it's not. Why do you ask?"

"And what kind of other powers besides immortality can these third eyes give?"

"Lots," she says as she narrows her eyes toward the boy. "How do you think Ariouk and I were shooting off those purple explosions earlier? Now, what are you getting at with all these questions?"

"I'm just trying to put some things together," he says. "When was the last time you saw Naorshi, and do you know where I can find her?"

"I actually haven't seen her in several years." She says as she continues to stare into Teddy's eyes. "Are you thinking of hunting her down and stealing that beautiful green eye of hers? I swear, I'll take these pancakes off the table and let you die in these woods if that's the case!"

Teddy calms Radella down then goes on to explain all that happened with Naroshi and Ziruam in his past.

Radella scratches her head. "Well, that's strange."

"In what way?" Teddy asks.

"If he does have that kind of power and is wearing a patch over his eye, then it makes sense that he stole it."

"But?" Teddy asks.

"But, that doesn't explain why she would be so obedient toward him and remain at his side for all these years. Horses in Egaria have better memories than most humans and usually become quite aggressive after their eyes are stolen, especially toward their attackers. Plus, I saw Naroshi no more than four years ago, and she had all three eyes intact. If this guy is as old as he says he is, it can't be due to her eye."

"Well, when I saw Naroshi, she only had two eyes," Teddy says. "And I didn't see a scar either, but at the same time, I wasn't really looking."

Radella raises a hand to her chin. "Well, come to think of it, I also live outside of time here in Zarmore. So even though

I feel like I just saw Naroshi three or so years ago, for her, it could've been a lot more."

"Thousands more?"

"Depends on where she likes to roam when she's not here in Zarmore."

There's a faint roar in the distance, and Teddy looks back out the window. "Is that...?"

"Yeah, my little cottage isn't too far from the arena."

Teddy sighs. "Well, at least Victoria gets to go to the Cup. I guess I should just start getting used to the thought that I'm probably dead back on Earth and never going home. You think I should even try to exit through the oak today or probably just pointless now, huh?"

"Oh, would you just relax and eat your pancakes?" Radella says. "You know it takes me nearly fifty years to gather enough ingredients to make just one batch, and you're letting them get cold and go to waste."

"Fifty years? For... pancakes?"

"Yes," she says. "And I was planning on using them for something much more fun and profitable before your situation this morning threw me into a moral dilemma. Now hurry up and eat. I have to go see a toad about my water bill soon."

Teddy furrows his brow, then slides a fork through the stack of pancakes and takes a bite.

"Good," Radella says as she sits up and begins to walk toward the front door. "Now, I have to get going, but you just stay here and enjoy your breakfast, ok? We'll continue our talk about Naroshi another time."

Teddy's starting to feel dizzy, and his vision gets blurry. "Wait..."

He sets the fork down and watches as a fuzzy image places a pointed hat on its head and opens a door.

"Good luck, and try not to make the same mistakes again!" The image shouts. "That's all I have left. Oh, and don't go telling Dean Spear or any of your friends that you came and saw me today. That'll just create more problems for the both of us."

The door slams, and his vision gets blurrier. A few moments later, he's asleep.

. . .

The steady drum roll of the horse's hooves patting against the dirt path beneath them is all Teddy can hear as he lowers his head and keeps his vision focused.

He feels a headache coming on, and the track in front of him looks blurry. He glances to his right and sees Giovanni and his black horse sprinting along the side of him. *"What the...?"*

He then looks forward to his left and sees Victoria and her horse Gemini.

"Look out!" Victoria shouts as she veers her horse left and narrowly past a giant gray boulder that's rolled onto the track.

Teddy's eyes expand as his vision returns to clear. He hesitates for a moment, then finally veers his horse left and behind Victoria. Once safely past the boulder, he glances to his right to see how Giovanni fared. The boy narrowly avoided the boulder as well and is now working to gain ground on Teddy and Victoria.

Teddy relaxes his shoulders, then turns his head back forward and smiles. "Pancakes."

Victoria's horse has slowed down for some reason, and Teddy is now only a few feet behind. His jaw clenches as he yanks the reins of Miss B and tries to avoid the crash, but it's too late. One of his horse's front legs entangles with one of the rears of Gemini's, and both stumble. Teddy watches as Victoria bounces atop Gemini while he does the same with Miss B. After a few long seconds, both horses recover, and Teddy guides his toward the right. Giovanni looks over his shoulder as he passes them both. "You guys ok?" He shouts.

Teddy gives a thumbs up then watches as the boy proceeds down the track. The forest gets quiet again, and Teddy spares a final glance over his left shoulder to ensure Victoria is ok before continuing with the race.

"Crap," he says as he yanks the reins of Miss B and moves back toward the girl. "You ok?!"

Victoria grimaces. "I'm fine, but I think Gemini might have a broken leg."

Teddy looks down and sees that her horse is limping.

"Yes!" A squeaky voice shouts from behind them.

Teddy turns around and sees a small girl with a short horse slowly galloping past them.

"Well, at least Asmita will finally finish better than fourth for once," Victoria says, rolling her eyes. "I swear that horse is actually a donkey."

"I'm really sorry," Teddy says. "I thought that if I veered left that..."

Victoria raises a hand in the air. "Stop. It's not your fault. No one could have seen this coming."

Teddy looks away.

"Go finish the race," she says. "At least one of us should get to participate in the Cup this year."

Teddy exhales as he watches Victoria hop off Gemini.

"Go!" She shouts as she begins to examine the horse's leg. "And tell Dickie that Gemini needs help."

Teddy shakes his head, then whips the reins of Miss B and races down the dusty dirt track.

He passes Asmita a few moments later and enters under the archway into the stadium well after that. The crowd cheers as Teddy crosses the finish line, and he hears the announcer mention something about him and Giovanni racing in the Zarmore Cup next month. He grits his teeth then continues to ride until he finds Dickie and tells him what happened with Gemini. The young man thanks Teddy, then hops onto his black horse and races out of the stadium. Teddy shakes his head again, then rides Miss B under the west gate and ties her up in the stable. He then walks out toward the center of the arena for the ribbon ceremony but stops when a large snail with a brown and white swirled shell blocks his path just before the exit. He looks around for a second, then approaches the snail and taps twice on the back of its shell. There's a folded up white piece of paper wrapped in plastic inside. He removes the wrapping then brings the paper up closer to read:

Teddy,

I gotta write quick before one of these goons catch me. Ziruam knows where you are and is coming for you. I can't explain how he got this info, but he has it, alright. They still got me caged up here in Frostlepeak like a dog with diarrhea, but believe me, man, I'M INNOCENT! I just said all that stuff about working with that freak so that I could have some protection in here from him, but now I can't get out! And I don't know what happened to Miss Butts. I know you're wondering, but he took her after she saved you. That's all I know, kid.

- caesar

P.S. Don't write back. It's not secure.

P.S.S. But if you do write back, might as well drop a can of Mapy's inside the shell. I feel like it's been years since I tasted one.

The Zarmore Cup

"Because he's a good little man," Calvin says in a soft baby-like voice as he crouches down in front of a brown-furred Labrador retriever in a spacesuit. "Aren't you, buddy? Yes, you are. Yes, you are."

"Yes, I am," Sebastian says as he wags his tail and tries to lick through the glass of his space helmet toward Calvin.

Ronnie shakes his head then looks over at Teddy near the seventh hole of the miniature golf course. "Is this really how you wanted to spend your night off?"

Teddy laughs, then swings the golf club, watching as the small blue ball travels upside down through a loop and into a tunnel. "I'm having a good time."

"Right?" Calvin says as he pats the top of Sebastian's helmet, then stands back up and carries his club over to where Teddy and Ronnie are standing. "This is great. It's always just baby Ron Ron with the complaints." Calvin drops a red golf ball onto the turf and swings his club, then turns back around. "Your turn, Ron Ron."

Ronnie rolls his eyes, then grabs his club off the blue metal bench that rests behind them and walks up to the turf.

"Hey, guys," Teddy says from behind the two. "I think I'm going to take a little timeout and use the bathroom."

"What? You serious?!" Calvin shouts.

"Yeah, come on, Teddy," Sebastian says. "Even I can hold it up here."

"Well, first off, Sebastian, you're not even real."

"How dare you," Calvin says.

"And second off," Teddy continues. "I just have to go. Do I really need a reason?"

Ronnie laughs. "Alright, we'll be waiting for ya."

"But if you don't show back up within the next fifteen minutes, Sebastian is taking your place," Calvin adds.

"About time," the dog says.

Teddy shakes his head then focuses on waking up.

He feels as if his body is being sucked up further into space for a moment and maintains his eyes shut until the feeling goes away. When he opens his eyes, the urge to use the bathroom feels even stronger. He starts to sit up in his bed, but his motion is stopped when he feels two cold fingers press upon the area in between his eyebrows. "You're not supposed to be awake yet," a deep voice says.

Teddy falls backwards, and his head crashes into the pillow beneath him. He tries to keep his eyes open, but they feel heavy, and it's a struggle. His body is numb, and no matter how hard he tries, he can't get it moving. The lights then flicker on, and his heart races.

"*Sean,*" he thinks to himself.

Teddy then lets his eyelids fall shut and tries to summon all the energy inside himself to wake his body up and out of bed.

"Yeah, a little trick my parents taught me when I was younger," Sean says as he walks over to Teddy's desk by the bedroom window and thumbs through some of his homework. "It doesn't work too well on trained people, but dummies like you, it's not very difficult."

"*Get out!*" Teddy screams inside his own mind, his eyes now back open but body and mouth still paralyzed.

"I would," Sean says. "But, I have to teach you a lesson first."

"*You can read my mind?*" Teddy thinks as he watches the strong boy with a blonde buzz cut toss the papers onto the floor.

"It's not that hard when you're in this kind of state," Sean says as he walks over to a poster on the wall and smirks. "You're such a loser. You know that, right?"

Teddy tries not to think as he watches Sean tear down his poster of the four turtles skateboarding.

"You know, if your mommy wasn't so poor, she might've been able to try and help you out in a situation like this. But no, she's hard at work, isn't she?"

Teddy tries again to get his body moving as he watches Sean pace around the room.

"And then, of course, there's your daddy," he continues. "Now, where is he tonight?"

"*Shut up.*" Teddy thinks.

"Oh yeah, that's right. He's dead."

There's a loud thud, and Sean flinches backwards.

Teddy laughs inside his own head.

Sean gathers himself, then looks at the heavy mirror on the ground and smashes the top left corner of the glass with the heel of his shoe. He then turns around and walks toward Teddy. "Oh, you think that was funny, huh?"

Teddy's heart thumps faster as he watches Sean grit his teeth and pull his fist back. Teddy then lets his heavy eyelids clamp shut as he awaits the punch.

"You know I can kill you right now, right?" Sean asks.

Teddy opens his eyes again.

"But Kristi would hate me if I did that, so I won't."

"*Kristi?*" Teddy thinks.

"Yeah, you idiot," Sean says as he clenches his fists, looking down upon Teddy's inert body. "Kristi Johnson. Don't act like you don't know who I'm talking about!"

"*No, I know who she is,*" Teddy thinks. "*It's just that I don't know why she would care. I haven't talked to her in months. She won't even look at me anymore.*"

Sean relaxes his grip. "Good. Make sure it stays that way."

Teddy doesn't think anything as he watches Sean turn around and walk toward the open bedroom window.

"Don't make me return here or come find you in Egaria," Sean says as he turns his head back toward Teddy and begins to climb out the second-story window. "Kristi is mine."

. . .

"What kind of freaky crap you been doing that would get you sent down there?" Olivia asks as Teddy walks out from the cave of Dr. Borut's office and into the hallway.

Teddy rubs the back of his head as he approaches the girl with dark wavy hair and her blonde friend who await him near the sliding stone door. "I have no clue. Last thing I remember is cleaning some Gatorade out of another t-shirt, then verifying my bedroom window was locked and going to bed. Next thing I know after that, I have some yeti sticking his blue pinky in my ear."

Olivia laughs as the three walk toward the elevator at the end of the hall.

"It's not funny," Ava says. "Teddy, you walked out of the oak this morning and collapsed face down on the bridge."

Teddy raises an eyebrow. "I did what?"

"Yeah," Ava continues. "Are you sure Sean didn't cast any sort of time spells on you when he broke into your room last month?"

"Um, no, I don't think so," Teddy says. "Like I told you guys, he just kind of stood over my body and vented his insecurities to me."

"Was that before or after you wet the bed?" Olivia asks as she presses the call-button to the elevator at the end of the hall.

Teddy turns around and locks eyes with the girl. "What do you think?"

Olivia giggles then Ava speaks up again. "I don't know, Teddy. I overheard Dean Spear and Professor Mun talking, and they said it sounds like you must've been playing with some sort of time magic."

The elevator arrives, and they step inside and begin to ride it up toward the foyer.

"Well," Teddy says as he questions if he should tell them about the witch.

The elevator stops, and the doors creak open. "Teddy!" Calvin shouts. "Happy Zarmore Cup Day!"

Teddy smiles. "Yes, sir."

"Hello to you too, Calvin," Olivia says.

"Oh, yeah hey, what's up."

"Well," Ava says. "Olivia and I are going to go grab a snack before heading to the arena. We'll see you in there later. Alright, Calvin?"

"Yeah, for sure!" He says. "Ronnie is already up there saving us some seats. I'm going to walk here with the champ for a little while before it all gets started though."

Olivia shakes her head, and Ava smiles. The two girls then walk into the dining hall while Calvin and Teddy head toward the courtyard.

"So, what were you guys doing down in the lower halls?" Calvin asks.

Teddy rubs his head and exhales. "I don't know. I guess I passed out or something when I stepped out of the oak this morning, so they brought me to see the doctor."

Calvin laughs. "Finishing out the school year just like you started it."

"Like what? Unconscious?"

Calvin laughs again. "I was going to say unpredictable, but yeah, I guess you did sort of finish the day unconscious that first one as well, huh? Anyway, check this out. I snagged the final standings for you."

He hands the paper to Teddy as they finish walking through the courtyard and back into another section of the castle.

"I would show you how I ended up fifteenth on the year, but Ronnie tore that paper up. You got the final top seven in your hands though."

Zarmore Racing League Standings

Regular Season — First-Yearers

Place	Points	Runner Info	Jockey
1st	34pts	Bonfire in the Rain	Giovanni Ginesi
2nd	30pts	Miss B	Theodore Lancaster
3rd	29pts	Gemini	Victoria Addington
4th	29pts	Bum Bum Bum Blam!	Joshua Holstead
5th	28pts	Von Schnickerlonger Jr.	Connor Graham
6th	27pts	Sleepy Sami	Alejandra Gonzalez
7th	26pts	Dream Machine	Alice Torbett

Teddy hands the paper back to Calvin.

"I still can't believe you actually beat Victoria in that final race," Calvin says as he shakes his head. "I mean, seriously, she was in first for almost the entire season and then just blew it at the end."

"She didn't blow it," Teddy says. "My horse crashed into the back of hers. It could easily have been me not racing today."

"I hear ya. I hear ya. No need to get all tense before the Cup, champ. Let's just be glad that fate was rooting more for you that day than it was for her."

Teddy doesn't reply.

They arrive just outside the arena several minutes later, shouting and screaming are already well heard from inside.

"I thought the Cup was just one race," Teddy says as he looks back toward Calvin.

"It is."

"Then why is it already so crazy in there? The race doesn't start for another hour."

"Beats me," Calvin says as he walks behind Teddy underneath an archway and into the stadium. "It is the last day of school though. Most people are just excited in general."

Two hands plant into Teddy's chest and send the boy flying backwards into Calvin. They both backpedal a few steps and nearly fall into the dirt before catching their footing.

"What gives, man?!" Calvin shouts as they watch the older boy continue to sprint past them and into the woods toward the castle.

The shouting and screaming from inside the stadium grows louder, and Teddy sees a mob of students rushing toward them under the archway.

"Move!" A girl in front of the pack shouts as she elbows past Teddy and into the forest.

Teddy furrows his brow and looks at Calvin. "What's going on?"

A siren then sounds off from inside the stadium and back by the castle:

"WARNING: Time and healing enchantments disabled. All students, please evacuate through the oak immediately. All faculty, seek refuge. Goblins, to your posts. THIS IS NOT A DRILL."

The Eye of Naroshi

The stampede of students running out of the stadium reaches a near standstill by the time it arrives at the tall set of stairs near the back of the castle. Teddy cringes as his face gets pinned up against the rear of a fatter student a few steps above him while the throng of students behind him continues to shove.

"Move, Tommy!" Calvin shouts.

Teddy knows the other boy can't hear him over all the screaming.

An explosion sets off at the bottom of the staircase, and suddenly the crowd starts moving again.

Once at the top of the stairs, Teddy and Calvin continue to run along with their classmates to the left down a hall then to the right down another. They pass through a corridor where only portraits hang, then sprint up a short set of stairs. The stained glass double doors leading into the courtyard come into sight shortly after that. Teddy looks over at Calvin. "What the hell is going on?!"

One look at his friend's face tells him everything that he doesn't want to hear. Teddy continues to run.

Another boom hits, and this time they can see the walls shaking.

Calvin slows his pace and glances backwards. "Ronnie!"

"He's smart!" Teddy says as he grabs hold of Calvin by the sleeve and pulls him forward. "I'm sure he's safe! We gotta keep moving though!"

Calvin's speed continues to decrease as he looks over his shoulder and shouts his brother's name. More and more students then start to pass them in the hall, and a large fifth-yearer with panic in his eyes shoves Teddy to the floor then darts into the courtyard.

"Calvin!" Teddy shouts as he tries to find an opening in the stampede where he can stand back up. "We gotta go!"

Calvin cringes, then turns back around and sees Teddy struggling to get up off the floor as a sea of students run past and over him like a beggar in the city.

"Move!" Calvin shouts as he pushes a few students to the side, then reaches a hand down and helps Teddy to his feet.

The two resume running and get back up to pace with the mob as they pass through the open doors leading into the courtyard.

There's more space and room to breathe out here. The two pick up their speed and are able to pass several more students by the time they arrive at the giant rose petal covered knight statue in the center of the courtyard. The fountain's soft and steady drip of water resonates into Teddy's left ear while the siren attached to the ivy wall blares into his right.

The courtyard's opposite set of double doors leading into the foyer are already pushed open. Teddy runs through them first and proceeds into the red-carpeted foyer where the castle entrance and drawbridge are now visible. Something then feels off, and he stops. Calvin is no longer with him.

"Keep going!" He hears a voice shout back from the courtyard doors. "I have to wait for Ronnie!"

Teddy raises his hands in the air. "He might have already made it back through the oak for all we know! Calvin, we have to leave!"

The boy shakes his head. "I can't! Not without Ronnie! Five minutes! After that, I promise, I'm out!"

A cool and welcomed gust of wind blows past Teddy's face as a couple more students run by. He then nods his head. "Alright! But I'm not leaving here without you today!"

Calvin gives him a thumbs up. Teddy exhales, then turns back toward the castle entrance and sprints through alone. The sturdy wooden drawbridge thuds and reverberates as he and several other students make their way across. A large crowd of people is already huddled around the broad trunk of the oak and waiting to enter, the song of the flute now competing against the siren.

"There's no way we're all getting out of here," Teddy says as he continues across the drawbridge.

He feels something warm and furry brush across the nape of his neck, then an immediate tug downward on the rear collar of his shirt. Teddy slams straight onto his back and hits his head hard against the wooden surface of the bridge below.

"They'll all get out just fine," a rough yet high-pitched voice says as Teddy curls onto his side and rubs the back of his head. "It's just you that won't be leaving today."

Teddy rolls over again onto his back and opens his eyes. Everything in his vision is a blur, but he can still recognize the outline and feel the hot breath of what can be nothing other than a short goblin standing just a few inches above his face.

"I got him, sir!" The creature shouts.

The flute continues to sing on the oak's side of the bridge as murmurs and a crowd gather by the castle's. Teddy glances around and realizes that it's now just the goblin and him who remain on the bridge, precisely in its center, one on top of the other.

"I told you not to injure anyone, Michael," a deep voice says from across the bridge and near the forest.

"But he was getting away, sir."

The remaining students by the oak scream and run into another section of the forest as a man on horseback approaches the bridge.

Teddy raises his head and sees a blurred vision of what looks like a tall, bearded man climbing off a black horse with two glowing red eyes. "*Crap.*"

"Ride my horse back to Slaybethor," the man says. "I can take it from here."

"Pleasure to serve, Ziruam," the goblin says as he pushes himself off from Teddy and shuffles across the bridge toward the black horse.

A voice then calls out from somewhere above the castle. "Michael!"

Teddy rolls his head upwards and can make out the blurry image of another goblin atop one of the watchtowers.

"How could you?!" Gobo shouts.

The goblin on the ground grits his short and spiky teeth, then hops onto the back of the black horse and turns to face the castle. "How could I?!" He shouts up to the watchtower. "No, father! How could you?! Submitting your life to one of slavery for these humans as your own people struggle!"

"You know that is not true!" Gobo shouts as he grips his spear. "And you know that I can't let you leave here."

"I know," Michael mutters as he reaches into his pocket and flings a small, pointed silver object up toward the watchtower.

Teddy can't tell where it hits, but he hears Gobo scream in agony. Michael then reaches into a pouch tied at his waist and pulls out another similar-looking object.

"No!" Ziruam shouts. "That is not what we came here for!"

The goblin growls, then overhand throws what's in his paw downward at an angle toward the drawbridge. Teddy hears the object connect to the wood just a few feet from his head, then looks over and counts five pointed razor tips on a small silver star. Michael flashes his barbed teeth toward the boy, then whips the reins of the black horse and rides past the oak and down the mountain.

More students continue to mount near the entrance of the castle, but none dare exit outside. Ziruam takes his first step onto the drawbridge.

"Teddy," he says, taking another step toward the boy on his back.

The siren remains sounding off at full alert from inside the castle as Teddy tries to fight the pain and clear his vision. He finally manages to sit up enough to where he can scoot backwards on his rear while he attempts to rise to his feet. The pain won't allow him to stand though.

"Stop!" Teddy shouts, raising an arm in the air.

Ziruam continues to walk closer, and the boy scoots further away.

"STOP!" he shouts again.

Teddy is once again at the front of the castle entrance. The crowd of students have retreated further inside toward the middle of the foyer but continue to watch the scene playing out on the drawbridge. Ziruam smiles down at Teddy as he takes another step forward. "Do you think I'm going to hurt you? Teddy, look at me."

"I know who you are!" Teddy shouts. "I know what you've done! To the goblins, to Miss Butts, and now to all those students!"

"Teddy," Ziruam says as he continues to step closer to the boy.

Teddy scoots further away on his rear and hears the castle door slam shut behind him. He keeps sliding backwards until his own back presses against the door. The siren inside the castle is now a dull roar, and he heard the last whistle of the oak's flute go off a few moments before. The only sounds which remain are the ragged breaths of his own and the creaking of wood underneath Ziruam's each advancing step.

"I never hurt anyone, Teddy. The goblins are safe. Your classmates are safe. Miss Butts is safe. I only threatened them all to get closer to you. If you would just look at me, you would understand that I'm incapable of the things you accuse me of."

Teddy feels a fist banging on the opposite side of the castle door as someone shouts. "Teddy! Are you ok?! Teddy! Someone open back up this door! Teddy!"

Teddy rubs his eyes and tries to use the door against his back to prop himself up to his feet, but the stabbing pain along his spine sends him sliding back down. He can feel his body starting to tremble, then grits his teeth and stares back up at the man. "And what about Naroshi?! You stole her eye so that you could live forever, didn't you?!

Ziruam smiles. "I would never."

"And don't tell me to look at you when I can't see a thing right now *because* of you!" How can you order someone to slam my head into the ground then claim to be my friend?!"

"I am not Michael, Teddy. I don't believe in the things he and his people do, nor did I instruct him to harm you. The only reason he is here today is because of his knowledge of the jungle portal."

"You deactivated the enchantments!" Teddy shouts. "People can die here now...."

Ziruam laughs. "That's just a safeguard of the Council's. They have to deactivate them in order to open up certain portals so *their own* members that live inside the colony of Zarmore can escape. Their interests will always lie within themselves before any of you."

Teddy cringes as he tries to gather himself back up to his feet again.

"How about I end that pain of yours so we can quit all this nonsense?" The old man says as he grips his wooden staff and points it at the boy.

Teddy's eyes expand as the pain in his back increases, and his body slips back down to the ground. Ziruam then starts whispering something, and Teddy feels the energy in the air being pulled toward the man's wooden stick. Teddy raises his arms over his head and clenches his eyes shut.

"AKASHATAKAH!" Something screams from above the castle.

Teddy opens his eyes and sees the blurred vision of a goblin in knight's armor falling from the sky. Then there's a loud thud, and Ziruam drops his staff.

"Son of a..." Gobo mutters as he rises back to his feet and tries to locate his spear. "I missed him!"

Teddy blinks a few times as his vision finally starts to clear up somewhat, then hears a thud and looks forward.

The old man has fallen to his knees, and there's a long bloody gash running from the top of his forehead all the way down through the leather patch covering his left eye.

Teddy's jaw drops. "No, Gobo... I think... I think you got him."

Ziruam lets out a strained grunt as he reaches his left hand up toward the patch, then flings it off and into the blue moat of water that flows beneath the bridge. A cyan, twinkling green mist of light then escapes from the man's large and gashed eye up and into the air.

Gobo and Teddy watch in silence as the man writhes in pain and desperately tries to cover his damaged eye with his hand. He struggles for several more moments before a screeching sound erupts from somewhere deep in the valley below. At first, Teddy can't tell what the noise is, but as the sound jumps closer every few seconds, it becomes much more apparent.

Naroshi gallops out from underneath the shade of the redwood forest and runs across the wooden bridge toward the three of them. After spending time with the horses of Zarmore for so long, Teddy forgot how big and strong Naroshi truly is. The sun reflects brightly off her white coat, and she looks as if she's just ridden down from the clouds of heaven. She then eases up toward the side of Ziruam and whimpers as he rests his arm across her back and falls onto her side.

"It's ok, girl," he says as he strokes her nose and lets out a flurry of coughs.

"Why is she sad?" Teddy asks. "You stole her eye. You ruined her life."

Ziruam coughs again, and Teddy sees red blood spot over the man's white beard. "No, Teddy. We saved each other's lives, and then we shared one together for many years."

Naroshi continues to whimper as the man rubs her nose and smiles.

"I don't get it," the boy says.

"Would you just come here, Teddy? Please."

Teddy furrows his brow and shakes his head no.

Ziruam coughs again, and more blood dots his beard. "I found Naroshi in these woods several years ago when I was a young student just like you. During this time, there were many poachers out in search of eyes like Naorshi's. I found her, and we took her in. She was kept safe on campus, and together we raced and won every Zarmore Cup all the way until my senior year."

"And then you were banished... Weren't you?" Teddy asks.

"I was only trying to bring everyone together," the man says before coughing some more. "I spent a few weeks on the island before I managed to escape with the help of a friend. After that, I went to Slaybethor, woke myself up, and returned to my life on Earth."

The man holds a prolonged gaze at Teddy then continues to speak. "I vowed to myself to never return to Egaria again, but the years passed, and the longing for the magic of this place became insurmountable. I returned every night in my dreams for many years, Teddy. I climbed to the pinnacle of Frostlepeak. I bathed on the beaches of Caislia and visited all the ancient temples of Bioni. There isn't a spot of Egaria I left untouched and unexplored. And then the day arrived where I was recognized by an off-duty goblin. I was captured and banished once again. They sentenced me back to the island, and this time, made sure that I wouldn't escape. I grew into the old man you see today and was just nearly about dead before she found her way to me."

He rubs the white horse's nose and lets out another flurry of raspy coughs. "Naroshi gave the truest part of herself away and brought me back to life. But in doing so, her own power as a shifter was diminished, and we couldn't escape the island. I had a family back on Earth and wanted to return and see them, but as far as I searched and as hard as I tried, I couldn't find a way off that wretched shadow of a rock. The millenniums then began to pass, and I knew that although only months had gone by on Earth, my time there was over. I eventually found a secret underwater river that led me back to Slaybethor, but it was two thousand years too late. Naroshi's eye had altered my soul, and my physical body back on Earth was dead. I would never see my wife or son again and would be cursed to this world forever. I then resolved just to live my life here. I flipped my mind around and started from the back with everything, even up to my name. I made sure to never think of my life back on Earth again and chose to live a humble existence in Slaybethor."

Ziruam pauses and looks back at the horse as he continues to pet her nose. "And that's exactly what Naroshi and I did for many years until a shadow of my past crept back into my life."

He coughs more violently, and Naroshi whimpers louder. He looks up toward the boy, who has now managed to rise to his feet. "Naroshi will just be a regular shifter now that the eye is destroyed, Teddy. She'll grow old and eventually will die, just as I. Take care of her. She's yours now."

Teddy's vision is finally clear, although his body is still enveloped in pain. He starts inching closer toward the old and wrinkled man lying on the bridge but then stops as his heart drops to the bottom of his stomach.

"This isn't the end for us, my boy. Don't separate this life from the next."

Teddy takes another step forward and furrows his brow before dropping to his knees. He pauses for a moment, then picks the old man's shaky and leathery hand off Naroshi's side and places it in between his palms. Tears well up in his eyes as he looks down at the man's wrinkled and weathered face.

"Go with the light, son... I love you."

Teddy clenches his eyes shut, and tears slip down his cheeks as he squeezes the limp hand in between his palms. "No... Dad, no!"

There's a bang, and the castle door flings open. Many of the students gasp while a few others run out onto the drawbridge.

"NO!" Teddy screams even louder. "Dad, PLEASE!" Teddy begins to hyperventilate uncontrollably before clenching his eyes shut again and resting his head on his father's chest. He wraps his arms around the old man and begs one last time. "Please, dad... don't... don't go... I need you..."

A few moments pass before Teddy feels a soft hand rest atop his shoulder. "He's gone, Teddy. I'm so sorry."

The girl crouches down to her knees beside him and his father. Teddy sniffles, then turns around and hugs her.

"I'm so sorry, Teddy," Ava says again.

. . .

The summer is well underway in New York City, but it seems like most of Teddy's friends are already eager to get back to their classes at Zarmore.

Today 8:39 PM

Ronnie
> You need to chill. Look, you weren't even in the race and Spear already said it's canceled.

Calvin
> You never know, man. Maybe the 6th yearers will come back in the fall to finish it.

Olivia
> Do you guys not live together or what? Stop clogging up the chat!

Calvin

> Hold up. Aren't you supposed to be flying in a plane rn, Olivia?

Teddy doesn't feel like talking. He slides his phone back into the front pouch of his white hoodie and continues to wander through some unexplored neighborhoods further out in the city. His mom doesn't like him arriving home late at night, but she also doesn't know what's going on inside his head. He sees two spotlights shining up into the sky and decides to meander in that direction.

After climbing up a small mountain of dirt and hopping a chain link fence, he finds himself close to the lights and behind a large red and white striped tent big enough to fit a football field under. The sounds of children laughing and arcade games being played emanate from inside.

Someone bumps into him from behind, and Teddy swings his head around.

"Oh, sorry, kid," an older man wearing a clown costume says. "Didn't see ya there. This area is actually just for staff only though. You'll need to enter back in on the other side."

Teddy nods then continues to walk along the side of the tent. The sound of people talking increases louder and louder as he moves toward the front. When he finally arrives at the tent entrance, he notices a good hundred people or so waiting in line.

"Do you see it, daddy?" A little boy near the front says as he points up toward the sky. "It's aliens."

The father looks up. "What the hell?"

"Jason!" His wife shouts as she slaps the man's arm. "Watch your language in front of our son."

"I'm sorry, honey," the father says. "But I think he might be right. Look!"

Teddy looks up and sees a large bright light hovering in the sky for a brief second before it shoots out of sight behind a cloud.

The wife sighs. "Have you never seen a shooting star before, Jason?" She then looks down and smiles toward her son. "Make a wish, sweetie; it's good luck."

Teddy continues looking to where the man was pointing. He doesn't have any wishes that he thinks a star can grant him, but it does remind him of someone. Teddy closes his eyes and smiles. "I love you, dad."

"And I love you too, Teddy," a deep voice says from several feet behind him.

Teddy's heart races as he jolts his head around and flings open his eyes. He looks to his left, then his right trying to locate where the voice came from but then lowers his shoulders and sighs when he sees a father and young daughter walking out from underneath the tent. The girl is pressing a brown teddy bear against her father's leg. "But no, daddy. Teddy reallyyy loves you."

The father laughs. "And I love him too, dear... but not as much as I love you!" He then tickles the little girl. "Now, let's hurry and get to the car so we can go home and show mommy your new friend that you won."

Teddy exhales, then throws the hood of his sweatshirt over his head and walks back past the side of the tent, over the fence again, and down the mound of dirt. He feels his phone vibrating nearly nonstop throughout his walk back home but chooses not to look at it.

The streetlights are shining bright, and a cool breeze has joined the evening when he finally arrives in his neighborhood. He turns the final corner on the sidewalk and notices several flashing red and blue lights in his apartment complex parking lot. It isn't the first time he's seen ambulances and police cars around his home at this hour, but it is the first time he's seen this many.

"Watch it, kid!" A woman dressed in a suit and holding a microphone says as she runs past Teddy. A few seconds later, he sees a camera crew following her.

Teddy continues to walk through the parking lot and toward his apartment door but stops when he sees yellow tape blocking the entrance. He furrows his brow, then lowers the hood of his sweatshirt back down and lifts up the tape.

"Hey! Hey! No one in or out!" A police officer shouts as he runs up to Teddy and pulls him back by the shoulder.

"But I live here," Teddy says.

A loud commotion erupts from inside the apartment. The same police officer pushes Teddy to the side and lifts up the yellow tape. A stretcher carrying a middle-aged woman with brown hair is being rolled out the front door.

"Mom?" Teddy mutters as he walks toward her.

The police officer lowers the yellow tape again after the stretcher passes through then pushes Teddy back once more. "Take a seat on the curb and wait."

"But that's my..."

"Sit!" The officer shouts.

Teddy's heart races as he walks over to the curb and sits down. Nearly all the lights from the neighboring apartments around him are dimmed a dull yellow as the residents peek out their windows and watch the scene. Teddy rests his elbows atop his legs then sinks his head down into his hands as he begins to think.

A few seconds pass before two medics walk out from behind an ambulance and start chatting. "So, what's the story again?" The first medic asks the other, not noticing the boy sitting on the curb behind them. "Mom is snooping under kid's bed and burns herself on something?"

"Weirder than that," the other medic replies. "She goes into her son's room and begins to vacuum underneath his bed but hits something. So she slides the bed back and finds this old dusty book titled *Zarmore Poison Garden: Keys and Cures*, or something like that, lying underneath."

"Wait. What'd you call the book?" The first medic asks.

The other medic smiles. "Just wait. This is where it gets strange. So she goes to pick up the book, but it burns her hands, and she drops it. This happens several times before she calls us. She then tells the operator what's going on and that also her son hasn't returned home, nor is he picking up her calls. So while she's on the phone with us, she decides to kick the book open and then starts screaming. She's saying something about a bright black light and then drops the phone."

"Whoa," the first medic says.

"Right? And then we get here and find her lying unconscious in the boy's bedroom with the book by her side."

"Is she going to live?"

"We think she'll make it. All her vitals are good, but it looks like she fell into a pretty deep coma. The real problem for us now though is that not even the bomb squad can pick the damn book up. Plus, the media just got wind of the story, so you know they'll be on our backs about this until we can find an answer for them."

Teddy sits frozen as he listens to the conversation, thinking about his first time in Dean Spear's office. "*Stupid... book?*"

When the medics finish talking and walk away, Teddy digs into the front pouch of his hoodie and pulls out his cell phone.

MESSAGES	4h ago

Ava Bailey
Hahah it's ok. Enjoy your wandering.

MESSAGES	3h ago

Mom
What is this book I found underneath your bed?

PHONE	2h ago
Mom	
Missed Call (12)	

MESSAGES	2h ago
Mom	
WHERE ARE YOU???	

PHONE	2h ago
Mom	
Missed Call (3)	

MESSAGES	4m ago
Olivia Tilly	
Hey Teddy, my family and I just landed in NYC, and idk, but I think they might be talking about you on the news. What's going on, dude?	

Teddy's phone slips out of his hands, and he hears it crack as it bounces onto the black pavement below. The officer by the yellow tape points at Teddy as he walks toward him. "Get up off the curb, and move slowly toward me, young man. And keep your hands where I can see them!"

Teddy stands up and follows the officer's orders. His hands are shaking, and when the officer spits out his next sentence, Teddy feels like he's about to have a heart attack.

"We need to have a talk about Zarmore...."

Johnny Rapp was born and raised in California. He is a U.S. Air Force veteran, has been traveling off and on nomadically since 2015, and is fluent in Spanish.

instagram.com/johnbrapp

Made in the USA
Middletown, DE
07 March 2022